ROBERT EDGINGTON
Where next, Annette?

A TALE OF VAGABONDING SENIORS

Foreword by
Sir Wallace Rowling

*Best Wishes
Bob Edgington*

Published by
Gai-Garet Design & Publication Ltd.
Box 424
Carp, Ontario, Canada K0A 1L0
(613) 839-2915

ISBN 0-921165-06-4
Printed and bound in Canada
©1989 by Robert Edgington

All rights reserved. No part of this book may be reproduced, stored in a retrieval system or transmitted in any form or by any means electronic, mechanical, photocopying, recording or otherwise, except for purposes of review, without the prior permission of the publisher.

Book design by Wendelina O'Keefe
Cover design by Mary Mayhew and Wendelina O'Keefe
Editors: Gail Pike, Joy Parks, Paul Legault
Text formatting by Mayhew and Associates, Kanata, Ontario
Photography by Robert Edgington
Colour separations and film work by Chromascan, Ottawa, Ontario
Printed by Runge Press Limited, Ottawa, Ontario

Canadian Cataloguing in Publication Data

Edgington, Robert 1917–
    Where Next Annette?

ISBN 0-921165-06-4

    1. Voyages around the world — 1981–   . 2. Aged — Travel.   3. Edgington, Robert, 1917–   — Journeys. 4. Edgington, Annette — Journeys. I. Title.

G440.E33E33 1989   910.4'1'0240565   C89-090062-0

Cover photograph Mt. Cook and Mt. Tasman reflected in Lake Matheson, New Zealand. Photograph by Robert Edgington. Inset photograph of Robert and Annette Edgington taken by Dave Andrews, Andrews-Newton Photographers Ltd., Ottawa, Ontario.

Dedication

To Barry, Betty, Brent, Rob, Kristy, Scott and Cléo. May my children and grandchildren achieve happiness through the attainment of knowledge and bask in the sunshine of life's enriching journeys.

Acknowledgements

I am grateful to many people whose identities appear in the text, but particularly:

- to my wife, Annette, without whom the tale would have no meaning.

In addition, I owe a debt of gratitude:

- to Mary Cook and Charles Long for literary suggestions,
- to Nesta Cowlishaw, Rebecca Holt, Stephanie Holt and Arnold Stinson for critical analysis
- to Sir Wallace Rowling and Marjorie Lutterman for their support and advice on New Zealand
- to Ruth Argue and Mollie Woodard for typing duties
- to Laurel Hall for the title suggestion
- and to my enthusiastic publishers for their assistance in the various aspects of publication.

Foreword

Not for Bob and Annette Edgington the kind of retirement where you simply wither up and blow away.

For them retirement has meant time and opportunity to open new doors in every corner of the world.

In this book they not only share their experiences in a very personal way but encourage others to seek adventures of a similar kind.

I know I found the section on New Zealand not only a source of information but an open invitation to action.

Sir Wallace Rowling,
former prime minister of New Zealand
retired ambassador to the United States

Sir Wallace & Lady Rowling

Sir Wallace Rowling with the author in New Zealand

Table of Contents

PART I

    Introduction 11

    New Zealand 13
       (The Land which Prompted our World Travels)

    Around the World in 180 Days 26

    Great Britain and Europe 63

    Madeira, Portugal, Spain and Morocco 74

    On A Slow Boat to the Persian Gulf ...and Beyond 87

    Australia 115

    Italy and Greece 132

    South Pacific 144

PART II

    Preparing for the Vagabonding Experience 175

    Epilogue 191

Part I

Introduction

My story starts on a dismal note and ends on a happy one. The dismal aspect of the tale is brief in duration and brief in description. The happy period covers many years and is the subject of this book.

My wife, Annette, was in the hospital being treated for a stomach ulcer when I was admitted to the same institution with my second heart attack. These occurrences, in 1969, made it simple for our children to visit both of us and also made it easy to agree with my doctor's recommendation for an early retirement. In the first paragraph, I promised a brief description of the dismal aspect of the tale. That's it. I have given it. My retirement relieved the tension which apparently caused my troubles and it presumably cured Annette's ulcer, for all such symptoms gradually faded away. The rest of my story is indeed a happy one as it relates to many of our adventures in travel after my retirement.

While the first two years of my retirement were spent in a steady recovery program, it did not preclude travel. During that time, however, we confined our travels to the North American continent. It was here, in North America, that we learned the basics of vagabonding: travelling about without advance reservations and roving here and there as fancy or inspiration dictated. My story, though, does not concern our North American travels. This book is the tale of our vagabonding experiences in many exotic lands around the world.

Annette and I have participated in a few organized tours, but have found them both expensive and tiring. We have proven to ourselves that the vagabonding method of travel is not only considerably cheaper but much more enjoyable.

The greatest advantage that seniors have over people

still in the work force, as it applies to travel, is time. People tied to their jobs have little choice but to take organized tours if they wish to fill their holiday time with travel. While these provide the means for people in a hurry to see a great deal of the world in short periods of time, the atmosphere of a foreign land can only be absorbed through an extended stay.

Without the advantage of plenty of time and no fixed schedule, we would not have dined with a king in Karachi or talked casually with the Governor-General of the Cook Islands as we watched and listened to the pounding surf on the north shore of Rarotonga. I would not have been asked if I needed a wife by a Polynesian woman as I strolled leisurely on a Samoan beach or seen rats for sale at a food market on a back street of Kowloon. Without having time to stop when unscheduled events occurred, we would not have witnessed the festivities associated with the cremation of a high-ranking person on the island of Bali or the birth of a calf in rural Holland.

Having planned an area of the world to visit, you may find that you get to a certain place and hear of yet another spot that piques your interest. It is often the little side trips which prove to be the highlights and taking one, whether it be in Belgium, New Zealand or at home in North America, can be a delightful experience and conditions the mind to a carefree existence. If you enjoy the place you have come upon by design or by chance, stay there and absorb some of the customs and viewpoints of its inhabitants. If you tire of a place, move on in a true vagabonding spirit.

Time and maturity give the senior citizen the opportunity to converse with people of other lands and to develop a tolerance of diverse philosophical and religious persuasions. Every age group has its advantages, but seniors who travel, especially those who go it on their own, have the advantage of truly observing and appreciating a wealth of different cultures.

I am convinced that the 'itchy foot' syndrome is incurable, and when I get beyond the physical capabilities of vagabonding, I will still have many dreams to dream.

Now come with Annette and me on some of our vagabonding trips abroad...

1

New Zealand

(The Land which Prompted our World Travels)

The three hour crossing of Cook Strait was bracing in a stiff wind. As we stood at the rail of the ferry watching the waves, we thought back to Rideau Ferry and the events leading up to our being here.

Our first visit to New Zealand was prompted by the move of Annette's youngest sister, Marj, and her husband, after his retirement from the Strategic Air Command of the United States Armed Forces. They had come to visit us, ostensibly for the last time, as they had decided to move halfway around the world. We were eating what we thought would be our last meal together while looking out over the lake at our home in Rideau Ferry when Marj jokingly said, "Instead of going to Arizona or Florida this winter, why not come to see us in New Zealand?" We all laughed at this nearly impossible dream, but before my laugh was finished I started to wonder if the dream really was impossible. Before we finished our meal, I was formulating plans in my mind on the best way of convincing Annette to consider going, and of how I would go about finding prices and obtaining passports. We had never before left the North American continent! Before our relatives left that day, they and Annette knew of my tentative plans.

That was in June, when the sunshine was warm and sparkling on Lower Rideau Lake. Now it was December, and we knew that the lake would be frozen over and our cottage would be cold and uninviting while we were standing at the rail of the ferry watching the bright sunshine turn the salt spray to silver.

Our relatives were at the dock in Picton to greet us and drive us to Nelson. If they had not been there, we could have taken a bus or hired a car, both means of transportation being readily available. They took the minor road from Picton to Havelock instead of the main road through Blenheim, and immediately we were enchanted with the South Island.

We were introduced to gold-panning a short distance from Havelock, at Canvastown, and experienced the excitement of seeing 'colour'. On we went through the beautiful Rai Valley and the twisting road through the mountains to Nelson, a town of rare beauty built on the many hills overlooking Tasman Bay.

When formal colonization by Europeans commenced after the 1840 Treaty of Waitangi, shiploads of immigrants from England arrived, some at Nelson, but very soon small parties spread out into the fertile valleys. Although Nelson is one of the older settlements, it and the whole Nelson province was, and continues to be, an area apart from the rest of the country inasmuch as it has never had a railway connecting it to other centres. Further, it is not on the main roads even of South Island. Golden Bay, in the northwest sector of Nelson County, is even more isolated since the road into Golden Bay is also the road out from Golden Bay. No road connects Golden Bay with the west coast communities of Wesport, Greymouth and the Glaciers. Western Nelson Province, consequently, is seldom included in the itinerary of overseas tourists, but it is immensely popular with New Zealand residents. During the prime holiday season, from Christmas to the end of January, motels, hotels and campgrounds are filled to capacity.

Our first visit to Nelson was part of our first trip around the world. We fell in love with the area, so much so that we almost cancelled the remainder of the trip. At Motueka, just fifty kilometres from the city of Nelson, we looked at a house for sale. It was a showplace of flowers, and on its three acres were one hundred trees, all native varieties. A small stream ran through the property and emptied into the Motueka River which, in turn, emptied into Tasman Bay. We struggled with our emotions, and although the temptation to settle there was very great, the thoughts of being so far from our children and grandchildren, plus my urge to wander, resulted in rejecting any further ideas of making Nelson Province our home. We contented ourselves with driving to the beautiful little towns and communities of Stoke, Richmond, Wakefield, Takaka and Collingwood, and vowed we would return. And return we did, visiting the same communities again and again and finding them just as delightful as before.

We were fortunate to fly in a small airplane over the Marlborough Sounds to Blenheim and, on another occasion, over Takaka Hill or Marble Mountain as it is sometimes called. While the beauty of Marlborough Sounds is legendary, relatively few people have the opportunity to view the main source of Springs River near Takaka from a small plane. This is Waikoropupu Springs, commonly known as Pupu Springs. From the air they look like a huge paua shell with iridescent colours so vivid that it brought gasps of delight from all four of us in the air. We resolved to see the springs at close range by driving to them.

The drive over Takaka Hill is somewhat of a challenge. It is steep and winding, although not dangerous. The challenge is to the car, not to the nerves of the driver. To the occupants of the car, driving the Takaka Hill is a lovely experience. Much of the area is marble rock, and at the crest the marble can be seen as bare outcroppings. This marble rock is famous for its cave system, sinkholes and underground rivers. Overlying much of the marble is a thick layer of impervious sandstone which does not allow surface water to seep into the flooded chambers below. In the Waikoropupu Valley, however, these waters seep through the cap rock and then the underground water, with increased pressure, surges through to emerge as springs. Pupu Springs are the largest in New Zealand, and while the volume of their discharge is not always constant, they never fail to fascinate. They are in a reserve, and the Parks Branch have built trails through the area. Unfortunately, the original viewing platform which allowed visitors to look down into the springs has been replaced in recent years with a surface deck which does not afford good viewing of the main attraction. Apparently, steps are being taken to remedy this situation, partly as the result of suggestions by the author.

The Springs River is not the only river emanating from underground waters. On the southeast side of Takaka Hill, the Riwaka River emerges from a cave in a great rush of white water amid beautiful greenery. And even freshwater springs offshore in Golden Bay are so strong that their upwelling can be seen on the surface during calm sea conditions. Local fishermen, who bring in fine catches from this area, swear that the presence of these offshore springs can be felt as their vessels cross over them.

Golden Bay (at one time called Murderer's Bay after the 17th century Dutchman, Abel Tasman, lost some of his men at the hands of hostile Maoris) is generally tranquil and peaceful. In one area, a group of people from Europe and North America are trying out theories of holistic living in what are often called alternative lifestyle communes. Within the communes are many people of superior intellect who shun the conventional standards of living. One commune has a great number of elderly residents, and there is some concern as to its future due to the shortage of suitable new and younger members. We had the good fortune to be invited to one of these communities where a better balance in age groups was evident, for there were children of all ages, as well as young and older adults. In past years, Golden Bay residents resented the presence of these people; however, with a few notable exceptions, they have been gaining acceptance and respect through their strict adherence to the laws of the land and through their high ideals and superb craftsmanship in many fields of endeavour. They are, indeed, different from the people one usually meets, but they are extremely interesting as are many inhabitants of the whole of Nelson Province.

The province seems to draw writers, weavers, potters (excellent pottery clay is found here) and artists. Annette's sister, Marj, belongs in this last category since she is an artist of considerable talent. While she has a conventional house, her lifestyle is quite different from ours. She travels around the South Island on a motorbike, taking her sketching pad to the most outlandish places. When she bought her first bike, she went to the police for a licence, and on being asked her occupation she replied, "bikie"! This "bikie" is now a grandmother and still rides hundreds of kilometres in the land she has adopted as her own. She took out New Zealand citizenship several years ago, and while she enjoys periodic trips to Canada and the United States, she is always anxious to return home.

Marj lives in Nelson City, but her bike has carried her to Golden Bay on many occasions, particularly when we rented a house in Takaka for three months while the owners lived in their yacht cruising the waters of Cook Strait and the Sounds. We had bought a used car in Nelson, finding it through an advertisement in the local newspaper. It proved its worth when we went back and forth across Marble Mountain several times. In addition, we drove to most points of interest in the Golden Bay area and often to Collingwood, a fascinating village considered by New Zealanders to be "off the beaten track".

Collingwood, thirty kilometres from Takaka, is the last place of any size before Farewell Spit, a long, high series of sandy dunes on the extreme northwest corner of the South Island. Private cars cannot make the trip all the way out, but rides in four- and six-wheeled drive vehicles are available at Collingwood Motors. Also available in Collingwood are rides with the rural mail service to areas so remote that children there do not attend school but study by correspondence courses delivered six days a week by post. These tours are available at the Collingwood Post Office.

A nice walk, within the capability of all but the infirm, is the half-hour tramp to Wharariki Beach. It is a beach so seldom used by anyone that you are almost startled to see another person a kilometre away. The reflections of monoliths in the wet sand at low tide create some of the best pictures in this land where at every turn a picture presents itself.

Very close to Takaka, just off Motupipi Road, is The Grove, a lovely little glade where dense forest and startling rock formations combine to delight the senses. If you have any tendency towards tension, this short hike will certainly relax you. It is peaceful, uncrowded and idyllic. Each time we went there we were enchanted with the tiny birds called fantails which will land on your shoulder if you stand perfectly still.

In Anatoki, another spot close to Takaka, a little, old lady feeds blanc-mange to giant, freshwater eels, some weighing over twenty kilograms and measuring nearly two metres in length. Apparently, the largest of these creatures are senile and fail to obey the breeding and migrating urges. Staying in one place and feeding continuously, they gain weight. How does this little, old lady feed blanc-mange to the eels? With a teaspoon! They come to a certain spot in the river at the same time every day and open their large mouths while she daintily spoon-feeds them. Believe it or not!

At 9:30 p.m. on a New Year's Eve, Annette answered the telephone in the house we were renting in Takaka. The voice said, "You were supposed to look us up. I'm Pat Timings". It was true. Mutual friends had asked us to contact Pat and Fran Timings and we had every intention of doing so, but since our arrival in Takaka two weeks before we had simply enjoyed driving around the countryside in our little car and had not done any visiting. The voice went on to say, "Come and see the New Year in with us. We're having a beach party." Annette replied, "Oh dear, we haven't been to a New Year's Eve party for years". The voice commented,

"It's time you did. Let me talk to your husband."

After a brief chat, I readily agreed we should go to the beach party, and Pat gave me directions on how to find their place in Paton's Rock, just ten kilometres away. What a happy event! Pat had set fire to a huge pile of driftwood which sent flames seven or eight metres into the air, and all around the pile were big logs on which several people sat. When we arrived, Pat put down his guitar to come and greet us. He was very tall and very slim with a shock of wavy gray hair, a prominent pointed nose and the friendly and sincere manner of most New Zealanders. He introduced us to his lovely wife Fran, a former Canadian. Also present were local people, several people from Christchurch and Auckland, and two Canadian university professors from Carleton University in Ottawa.

Everyone talked for some time until Pat resumed his guitar playing. Then we listened or sang along with him. But when he started to whistle, no one spoke, sang or even hummed the tune. While Pat was not of the calibre of Robert MacGimsey or other famous whistlers of the world, he was superior to most people in this seldom-heard art form, and we listened with rapt attention. It was so enjoyable that I was startled when someone announced that it was midnight. As we all sang "Auld Lang Syne", a nearly full moon broke the horizon over Golden Bay to further enhance the beauty and charm of that New Year's Eve.

On another visit to New Zealand we did not rent a house. Instead, we travelled about the country and stayed at campsites which provide a great variety of accommodation, including tenting, basic and deluxe cabins, on-site caravans, lodges and tourist flats. Campsites are considerably cheaper than motels, and discounts are generally available for extended stays. In addition, you meet some of the nicest people in the world. During such a visit, we saw much of the South Island's west coast. The Buller Gorge and Pancake Rocks impressed us greatly as did the greenstone, or jade, available for reasonable prices at Hokitika. And for sheer beauty, the National Parks of the South Island's west coast are almost without parallel.

The Westland National Park, established in 1960, is comprised of over eighty thousand hectares of mountains, lakes, rivers and glaciers. The glaciers, Franz Josef and Fox, extend almost to the sea. There are so many superior scenic areas that we could have stayed a full month within the park to fully appreciate its beauty. There are many places of interest within easy driving distance from Franz Josef Glacier. At Fox Glacier, farther south along the main highway, the same criteria applies. Plan to spend, at the very least, a day and a night at each community even though they are less than twenty-five kilometres apart. From Franz Josef, leave at dawn to go the eight kilometres to Lake Mapourika; from Fox, leave at the same time to go to Lake Matheson, aptly named "The Mirror of the Alps". The smart traveller packs a lunch the night before, hopes for clear weather and takes off as day is breaking. The surface of the lake is calm at that time and excellent reflection pictures are possible.

The glaciers, Franz Josef and Fox, are very sensitive indicators of climatic change as are other glaciers around the world, but these New Zealand glaciers are so accessible. You can drive very close to the ice itself, and you can walk on it, fly to it and feel the numbing cold of the rivers formed by them. The Cook, Fox and Waiho rivers are loaded with rock flour, giving them a gray, soupy appearance.

We saw the Southern Alps from several outstanding viewpoints, including a reflection in the chancel window of St. James Church at Franz Joseph. From inside the church, the view through that same window provides a backdrop which surely must hold the attention of the parishioners more effectively than the sermons.

On the main road between the glaciers, there are several places where it is steep and winding. At one spot there is a mirror strategically placed so that drivers can see around the hairpin bend in the road. On this same road, it is amazing to see tropic-like growth so close to the ice and snow of the glaciers.

Farther south, as we crossed over the mountain ranges at Haas Pass, we were greatly impressed with the abundant waterfalls as the rain teemed down. Later, when the clouds gave way to brilliant sunshine, we were equally impressed with the dramatic scene. The road was quite dramatic at times too, being reduced to one narrow lane due to land slides and without guard rails.

As we came down towards Lakes Hawea and Wanaka, we thought that surely these were the crowning glories of Mother Nature's handiwork, but as we continued our travels through New Zealand we debated their merits with ever increasingly beautiful vistas. We turned onto Highway 89 and made a gradual climb to 1127 metres. After that, we made a dramatic descent over what we agreed was the most perilous road we had driven anywhere. Annette drove it while I handled the camera duties! We eventually came out to Highway 6 and ended up at Arrowtown, a picturesque community which has been preserved in its original state and where the residents are determined to keep it that way.

We travelled on from there to Queenstown. Queenstown is probably visited by more tourists than any other town on the South Island. Although it has fallen into the trap of touristic ugliness to some extent, the natural beauty of its setting dispels any aversions one may have. Return visits have confirmed that Queenstown is still a very special place to visit. In Queenstown, as well, there are attractions of breathtaking excitement such as the chairlift which takes you to the Skyline Restaurant, the jet boats in the Shotover River, the hang-gliders off Coronet Peak and the ride through Skippers Canyon. Of course, we didn't try hang-gliding, but I'm sure it can't surpass the fright you feel when sitting in a front seat of a bus giving rides through Skippers Canyon. The wheels of the buses are close together so that the corners of the vehicles are often well out over the precipice when navigating the extremely sharp bends. At one point, between the Gates of Paradise and the Gates of Hell, we narrowly missed hitting a similar bus coming in the opposite direction. The Skippers Canyon road remains in our memory as one of our most frightening experiences.

Foveaux Strait has a reputation for very rough seas, but the waters were calm on the day we crossed from Bluff, the point farthest south on the South Island, to Half Moon Bay on Stewart Island. The beauty of this island close to the bottom of our planet was so intriguing that we took several days to explore the fourteen kilometres of roads that make up the entire road system. We took small boats to little adjoining islands and to bays and inlets where it would seem that no human had been before. The weather was perfect for the entire time we were on Stewart Island. The only clouds to be seen were white and billowy, making ideal backdrops for pictures of unsurpassed beauty.

The re-crossing of Foveaux Strait was as calm as before. As we came ashore at Bluff we noticed black clouds rising in the sky, and shortly after we got on the road again, the rain came down in sheets. It had settled into a continuous, moderate rain by the time we arrived in Gore where we stopped to have a lovely meal of mussels, blue cod, and plum duff with a liberal helping of brandy sauce.

We lingered over our meal since we did not want to arrive too early at the home of a friend near Tapanui. When we came out of the restaurant we were greeted by a glorious rainbow as the storm abated. The roads were dry well before we arrived at our friend's sheep station.

We had no trouble finding the station as a large Canadian flag was flying atop a tall pole at the entrance to a beautiful home. Doug and Yvonne, our hosts, were at the door before we could ring the bell. We had met and hosted them in Canada a few years before, and we were now fulfilling our promise that we would come to see them on our next visit to New Zealand.

So here we were on a four thousand hectare sheep station in a lovely house that we would call home for the next week. For part of that time, we would act as housesitters while our friends would go to Milford Sound to attempt walking the famous Milford Track. The evening before they left, Doug showed me how to feed the hens and gather their eggs, and how to feed and care for his sheep dogs. At no time did I have any trouble with the dogs. They obeyed my commands instantly, and although they jumped all over me at feeding time, they were never a threat. Annette, however, was always fearful of their great exuberance and would go back to the house when I opened their pens.

When our hosts returned after their successful tramping expedition, Doug put the dogs through tests with mobs of sheep, and my admiration of these working animals grew even more. The dogs were Border Collies, a breed specially trained for the job they had to do.

Later on, Doug drove his Land Rover to the top of his portion of the Blue Mountains from where we had a panoramic view of the countryside. It looked like the Big Country area of Montana, and I reflected that here, in this small community, almost every scenic variety of big North America could be seen within a relatively short distance.

Some scenic areas which can be seen in New Zealand and not in North America, however, are the great Sounds on the southwest coast of the South Island. Of very special beauty is a trip to Doubtful Sound. We boarded a launch to cross Lake Manapouri where we disembarked to get on a bus which would take us down a corkscrew road blasted through solid rock two hundred metres under the mountain at West Arm. At the bottom was a hydro-electric station built to supply power for an aluminum smelter. From here, the bus took us across Wilmot Pass to Deep Cove, an arm of Doubtful Sound. It is at this point that the water from Lake Manapouri and the hydro-electric station is discharged into the sea, having travelled ten kilometres through a tailrace tunnel under the mountains. From Deep Cove, another launch took us well out into Doubtful Sound where mountains and sea are dramatically close together.

Many noted writers and artists have attempted to describe the beauty of Doubtful Sound, Milford Sound and the roads and tunnels of the area, but even the most famous of these have failed to express the extravagance of beauty which unfolds at every turn. Few seniors are capable of walking the Milford Track, possibly the most renowned in the world for tramping enthusiasts, but there is plenty of beauty to behold without such exertion.[1]

Of considerable interest, too, are the glow-worm caves at nearby Te Anau, but even these are surpassed in beauty by those of Waitopo on the North Island. The sheer numbers of glow-worms astound you, and this sight, combined with the boat ride on the underground river, leaves you with the impression of unlimited peace.

Another place to find a relaxing atmosphere is in the baths of Rotorua, a town famous both for its thermal activity and as a centre of Maori culture. The Maoris are not natives of New Zealand, but they were discoverers in much the same sense as the Dutchman Abel Tasman and the Englishman James Cook. The difference is that these Polynesians arrived in New Zealand some eight hundred years before the Europeans. As time went by, wars between factions developed and competitive tribalism became the basis of their way of life. Warfare became an integral part of their lifestyle to the point where some factions were completely annihilated. Such extremes were not the norm, however. Most wars were little more than displays of grandeur or pursued in the manner of a sporting activity.

With the exception of the Maori cultural centre of Rotorua, Maoris were mainly domiciled in remote rural settlements until recently. In recent years, Maoris have been moving to the urban areas, and the fusion of Polynesian and Pakeha (European) culture is an interesting development. Today there are virtually no full-blooded Maoris, yet there are an increasing

---

[1] My assertion that few senior citizens would be capable of walking the Milford Track was questioned by Sir Wallace Rowling KCMG, who so kindly did an editing job on this chapter. It was his contention that even seniors could conquer the Track if they were physically and mentally prepared. He and Lady Rowling had done it just one week before our conversation. Scarcely a year before that, while Sir Wallace was still New Zealand's ambassador to the United States, they had rafted the Colorado River!

number of New Zealanders who elect to be known as Maoris.

Many Maoris have achieved greatness in business and in the professions, as well as in music and other forms of entertainment, but they seem determined to preserve much of their heritage and, fortunately, the governments of New Zealand no longer try to impose European values and customs on these proud people. The Maori and Pakeha have been learning to live together peacefully, perhaps better than in most countries where racial discord has existed.

Taupo, in the centre of the North Island, is a lovely, well-planned town on the shores of a lake of the same name. The lake is considered to be the best in the world for trout fishing. We would like to have stayed there for a period of time to digest the flavour of the town, but time was beginning to be a factor and so we went on to Napier on the east coast.

A lady on the bus told us we might encounter difficulty in finding accommodation, but her friend told us not to worry. She said, "If you have trouble, just come around to my place and I'll put you up". She then searched through her purse for pen and paper to scribble her name and address. She was quite sincere. It was people of this calibre who volunteered their services in rebuilding Napier after a devastating earthquake in 1932. The whole waterfront, now called the Marine Parade, was rebuilt by volunteer labour. In some cases materials were donated so that the finished product cost only $40,000. It is a monument to the unselfish efforts of their residents.

It was in Napier that we saw our first Kiwi bird. Although we had been in many rural areas and on nature walks throughout the South Island, we had not previously spotted one, mainly because Kiwis are nocturnal creatures. Here in Napier, a naturalist brought one out of a cage to a lighted, grassy enclosure. His careful handling of the bird and his talk on its habits were ample proof of the love he had for this symbol of New Zealand.

Napier's citizens seemed to express their gratitude in being spared from the ravages of the earthquake in so many artistic ways. The floral clock and the lovely fountain are prime examples, not to mention the exquisite statuary.

It was a Sunday morning when we decided to return to Wellington by bus. At the depot we learned that no seats were available; all had been reserved. We booked seats on the next bus which would leave Napier in the early afternoon and, after checking our luggage, strolled leisurely through the nearby Civic Square, a delightful little park in the centre of the city. We were admiring the landscaping and the flowers when the sunshine gave way to huge black clouds. Soon a soaking rain forced us to seek refuge in the entranceway of a large church, the only building available to provide shelter from the downpour.

The big door opened at the moment we arrived. We saw no one at first, only some fingers near the bottom of the door. Then a large head emerged, followed by a small body whose spine was badly bent. The straggly hair was brushed from the face with calloused hands. The long, pock-marked nose and the watery, pale blue eyes did nothing to enhance the appearance of this little man, but when he spoke his smile was almost angelic and his voice rang clear in a deep baritone. We confessed that we were simply seeking shelter from the rain and were not dressed for church. He responded, "There is plenty of room here and no one will be offended with your attire". So we entered St. John's Anglican Cathedral.

The little man informed us that he was the sexton and handed us a pamphlet listing details about this imposing structure, including its seating capacity, the costs involved in its construction and upkeep and, of course, mentioning that donations would be appreciated. The sexton (whom I couldn't help comparing to Victor Hugo's famous resident of Notre Dame Cathedral in Paris) spoke again in his marvelously resonant voice. "The service starts in fifteen minutes". I asked if there would be many people in the balcony and he replied, "There's never anyone up there". As he shuffled away, we made our way upstairs, comforted by the fact that we would be unobserved in our everyday travelling clothes.

Looking over the railing from our vantage point in the front row of the balcony, we could see the entire congregation as they arrived...just a few elderly ladies and gentlemen taking their seats in cushioned pews close to the choir stalls. The clergyman entered from a small door opposite the one through which we and the congregation had entered. He climbed the steps to a pulpit just above the little group of people and sat in a throne-like chair with a luxurious looking cushion. The clergyman did not look up into the balcony at any time during the service, confirming that the balcony was seldom occupied, and there was neither a choir nor an organist to provide music. As the clergyman opened the service with a reading from the Scriptures, I counted heads. In that lofty edifice which could hold 1,060, there were only 47 souls!

We left St. John's Cathedral hoping that it and all the other fine monuments in Napier would not be sacrificed in any future manifestation of power by Mother Nature. Earthquakes and thermal activity are fairly common on the North Island, but, amazingly, there has been relatively little loss of life as a result. The most tragic loss due to earthquake activity was the destruction, in 1886, of the pink and white terraces of Mount Tarawera. These marble terraces were unparalled in their beauty, and nowhere else in the world could such a sight be seen. The very rich, the only people who could travel extensively in the nineteenth century, came from all parts of the world to view the sight and to take their black and white photographs. The destruction of these terraces is one of the great disappointments for modern travellers, but the area is still one of exceptional beauty.

It had not taken much persuasion to have some Rideau Ferry friends join us in Auckland during one of our stays in New Zealand. We met them at the airport in our rented car and drove north of Auckland towards the Bay of Islands. As we approached Whangarei we stopped to admire the view, and when we attempted to resume our trip, the car would not go into any gear other than third. Help came along in the form of a road repair gang who pushed the car until it was up to speed sufficiently for me to let out the clutch. We found the car rental agency in Wangarei and exchanged the car for a new one.

We made our next stop at Pahia, on the beautiful Bay of Islands, where we found accommodation high on a hill overlooking the bay. The next day, we took a ferry to Russell, a lovely little town across the bay. We also took a short cruise to the "Hole in the Rock" where the boat goes through the hole at high speed when the tide is deemed to be favourable by the operator. Along the way the boat delivers mail to homes in small communities where accessibility by land is limited.

In Pahia, we visited the Treaty House, where the Maoris and Pakehas signed a peace treaty in 1840, and the Shipwreck Museum, a museum in an old sailing ship anchored at a dock. It was here that we talked for some time with a man and his wife who had sailed around the world in a ten metre boat. It had taken them almost six years, but they had been in no hurry. It was their one and only trip outside New Zealand and it was enough to last them a lifetime. We were so fascinated by their stories that we agreed to meet them again the following evening.

The next day, we kept to our plans and drove to Cape Reinga, the point furthest north in New Zealand. We parked in the area allotted and commenced the short walk to the lighthouse where a pole shows the distances and directions to the equator, the south pole and some major cities around the world. Tommy and I had arrived there first and were studying the pole when we heard a scream. Marion, Tommy's wife, had fallen, slipping on the little pebbles strewn on the steepest part of the path. We hurried back and helped her to the car.

Three of us thought that her leg was broken, but Marion thought it was sprained and insisted that we carry on with our plans to drive the length of 90 Mile Beach.

On the journey up, we had enquired as to the feasibility of an ordinary car accomplishing this trip without dire results. We were assured that it could be done, so off we went to drive down to the river bed which would be the start of the adventure. I had been told to go immediately after the tour buses started, which is at low tide. There were two buses there when we arrived and they appeared to be waiting for the right moment to move. After a delay of about fifteen minutes, the first bus went into the river bed which was now devoid of water. The second bus followed and we, in turn, followed it. On both sides were great sand dunes. It was a pretty picture, but I had been warned not to stop; others had and they had lost their cars. The buses soon disappeared from sight, travelling at a much greater speed. At one point where it appeared to be hard-packed sand instead of the gravel rock, Tommy urged me to take it out of first gear and make more speed in second, but I doggedly heeded the warning I had been given to keep in low gear with the gas pedal to the floor throughout the three kilometre ride to where the river emptied into the sea. Although portions of the ride were rather rough, we arrived there without incident. Only then did I look back to see the pain reflected on Marion's face, and I knew that she should see a doctor.

If you look at a map of this extreme northern part of New Zealand, you will see that the fastest way to get to a town is straight down 90 Mile Beach which is, in fact, fifty miles or ninety kilometres long. We could see the buses far ahead, and when we came to the midway point at The Bluff we stopped to let Marion soak her ankle in the sea water. The buses had stopped too, along with two other buses coming from the other direction, so that the passengers could climb The Bluff which becomes an island at high tide. From the top, I took a picture of the four buses and our little car. I asked one of the bus drivers if many people drove their cars here and he replied, "Only blokes like you who rent cars".

We drove to Kaitaia and found a doctor who examined Marion's leg and ordered an x-ray at the hospital. As time went by, we realized that it could be very late before we got back to Pahia and our date with the sailors, so we found accommodation in Kaitaia. Marion left the hospital with a cast and crutches on this her third day in New Zealand, the country she had dreamed of seeing for so many years.

The next day, back in Pahia, we went to the motel where our sailor friends had stayed. They had checked out an hour before, so we knew we would never hear the stories of the two retirees who had travelled the world in a ten metre boat.

When we left Pahia we drove to scenic Omapere where we went into a manufacturing plant to see beautiful furniture crafted from native woods. We spent some time there and talked to an intelligent chap about the rare trees of New Zealand. In the forests nearby, we saw the massive Kauri trees, so many of which were felled indiscriminately in the early forestry days of the country. Fortunately, laws have been passed to protect them so that now these giants of the forest can still be seen. A walk was required to view some of these huge trees and, of course, Marion couldn't accompany us to all of them, but she was good natured and insisted that we go along and not miss these beautiful sights.

As we drove out of the forests we came to a large dairy area where hundreds of cows formed one herd. We were forced to stop while a particularly large herd of Jerseys crossed the road. Coming from the opposite direction was a bus loaded with people, many of whom had their heads stuck out the windows. We noticed that most of the cows had short, stubby tails, and Annette called out to the farmer asking why the tails were cut off. He replied, but she couldn't hear and so asked again in a louder voice. He replied in a very loud voice, "To keep their arses clean!" Everyone in the bus and in our car roared with laughter. The exceptions were Annette and the farmer. Annette was stunned and the farmer stifled his mirth. As we travelled on, Annette's disbelief gave way to grins. However, she maintains to this day that cutting tails off is a cruel thing to do. In actual fact, the tails are not cut off. They are bound tightly and, due to lack of circulation, drop off!

The area around Mt. Egmont is another excellent dairy district. We spent a whole day taking pictures from many angles of this beautifully symmetric mountain. You could easily spend a lifetime there.

We spent some time in Wellington, New Zealand's capital city, before taking the ferry across Cook Strait to the South Island, and Newman's Bus to Nelson. Marion rested comfortably for a week in Nelson and had a new cast, a walking cast, put on her leg at the hospital. She would keep this cast until her return to

North America. Now, instead of crutches, she could use a cane which was given to her at no cost. The only expense she had was the $2 fee for the first doctor she visited in Kaitaia! New Zealand's policy is to treat everyone, resident and visitor alike, without charge for any accident that occurs in their country.

Shortly after getting the new cast, our friends rented another car to tour the South Island on their own. Two weeks later, they returned to Nelson full of enthusiasm for the beauty of the scenery and the friendliness of New Zealanders. They turned in their car and flew to Auckland to catch their International flight home. We stayed on for the balance of our five month stay, and when we finally did return to Canada, it was with some reluctance. Now when we return to New Zealand it feels like home almost as much as our place in Ontario.

The feeling of 'coming home' when we go to New Zealand is often the result of having been in other countries before arriving in Auckland. And mostly, the places that precede our arrival are the exotic islands of the South Pacific. New Zealand is so far away that taking connecting flights without stopovers makes for an exhausting trip. We have done it only once and found that once is enough! It is much better to arrange stopovers in Hawaii, Samoa, Fiji, Tahiti, the Cooks or other enchanting islands. Being fully rested on arrival is well worth the added cost.

The move of Annette's sister to New Zealand certainly was a factor in our first trip to that country and, therefore, in our first trip around the world. However, another event which had a bearing on our decision to go there occured many years ago. In 1909, my parents intended emigrating to New Zealand from England and would have done so except for the advice of their physician who felt my mother was too frail to survive such a long voyage. (She lived to the ripe old age of one hundred years!) The following year, in 1910, my father was restless again, and this time they sailed for Canada, a much shorter journey. This compromising action by my father resulted in my being born a "Canuck" instead of a "Kiwi". Like my father, New Zealand has always held a fascination for me, and like him I have a compulsion to see as much of the world as time and resources permit. It's a strange thing, though, that no matter how much you travel or how much you admire another country, the land of your birth always has a special place in your heart.

2

Around the World in 180 Days

We could hear the "clang, clang" of the cable cars on Mason Street just a short distance from the Gates Hotel. Looking out the window of our fifth floor room, we could see a neon sign blazing with the words "Professional and Amateur Photographers Welcome—Nude Models". To the left of that sign was another in very large letters which read "Bar—Nude Girls" and a little farther down the street yet another sign: "Bar—Strippers". What was a respectable retired couple doing in such a neighbourhood in San Francisco?

We had taken the bus from the airport and were standing with our luggage outside the main depot in the heart of the city, contemplating our next move, when several young men of questionable character approached us with suggestions of where to stay. An older man, a big muscular fellow who said he was a retired railroader, dispersed the ruffians with a wave of his hand and directed us to the Gates, an older hotel, which he described as clean and inexpensive. He told us about the risque establishments across the street but pointed out that the prestigious and expensive Hilton was less than a half-block away.

The signs didn't bother us, nor did the performers or their patrons. And although automobiles honked and the cable cars continued to clang well into the night, the discordant notes somehow melded into an orchestra of muted tones to carry us along into peaceful sleep. Tired from our long flights and the excitement of commencing our first round-the-world trip, the sounds and the pulse of the city were a balm to our weary minds.

The next three days were spent riding the cable cars and walking the streets. The vagrants asleep in doorways of vacant buildings and the large number of panhandlers seemed so out of place in this lovely and outwardly affluent city. Chinatown, of course, was fascinating, but most enjoyable were the musicians playing for coins at Fisherman's Wharf. One young man, a student flautist, was especially talented. He would practise his scales and arpeggios before launching into various pieces of classical music. Even his exercises were delightful to listen to. Later I regretted not having asked his name, for I felt sure that he was destined for fame.

Somewhat reluctantly, we kept to schedule and took our flight to Hilo, the capital of Hawaii's "Big Island". We landed in the rain, a common occurrence there. We had expected to be draped with flower leis on our arrival but came to realize that was something you pay for when you arrive as a member of a tour group. Our checked baggage was delayed because the handlers had trouble unlocking the compartment in which it was stored. At that time we had not learned how to travel with only carry-on bags so accepted the delay as a natural part of flying from place to place.

We took a taxi to the closest, reasonably priced hotel which was the Hilo Hukilau. The rain stopped just in time for us to unpack and walk through the luxurious gardens. This was our first taste of the tropics and it brought a feeling of elation. Our first taste of Japanese food, in a nearby restaurant, brought a feeling of satisfaction! When we returned to the hotel, the rain came down in buckets, but it was a soothing sound which, like the noises in San Francisco, aided in sending us off to sleep.

The next morning, we rented an older car and spent the next week touring the Big Island. We were intrigued by the sugar plantations, the native villages, Lava State Park, Isaac Hale Park and, of course, the lava flows. We walked over rough lava to the rim of the eruption. Words cannot describe our feelings at the sight of the molten, mercury-like sea of fury moving relentlessly to the side of the crater, there to split into red hot fingers of boiling lava. Staying there for just a few minutes, with only a thin rope to hold you back, results in a burning sensation on your face. The heat inside the crater is 1093°C. I'm sure that anyone who has ever looked down into that inferno will never forget it. To add to the awesome feelings we had experienced, we read in the next day's newspaper about the collapse at midnight of the viewing area at the rim of the crater. Everything went into that inferno...earth, lava, rope and all. We had been there just seven hours before! Fortunately, no one was at the viewing area at the time, but we heard later that the engineer in charge had been dismissed on the grounds that he should have anticipated the situation and closed the viewing area days before. In that case, I would have missed some superb pictures!

What was bothering me now, though, was my head. I am bald, but I enjoy the sun. At home I seldom wear a hat in the summertime, and I thought that here in Hawaii I would regain the tan I had lost. The walk to the eruption site took much longer than expected, the sun was very hot, and the heat from the volcano was intense. Before we got back to the car, my head was stinging. The day after, my head was a mass of blisters which made me very uncomfortable.

We stayed at an interesting place at Waiohinu, the Hotel Shirakawa. It was a lovely Hawaiian setting with hundreds of myna birds singing in the dense jungle surrounding the place.

The host's father, who was eighty-five years old, picked all the coffee beans on their small holding. He then spread the beans on the flat roof of the rear portion of the hotel and covered them at night and when it rained by sliding huge panels over them. These panels, mounted on castors, slid easily so that this old gentleman could complete his tasks without help.

From Waiohinu, we drove to Naalehu, the most southerly town in the U.S.A., and to Milolou, a little fishing village reached by a winding road which descends from nine hundred metres above sea level. This little village was, in 1972, a truly pure Hawaiian community seemingly untouched by the hordes of tourists and the commercialism of great highrise hotels. Perhaps the rough and somewhat treacherous road to the village shielded it from the pursuit of the Pakehas (Europeans). Not one car happened along while we struggled to replace a flat tire that was the result of hitting a sharp boulder. Hitting the boulder was a better choice than going over the precipice!

At the bottom, we watched Hawaiians casting their fishing nets from outrigger canoes. There were tidal pools as clear as crystal. Soaking our tired feet in them, we watched as colourful, little tropical fish scurried away.

We were completely enchanted with the peaceful setting and were sure that we were the only foreigners in the area when a young white lady and blond child came into view. They were from California. The little girl announced, "I'm Joy. I'm five. Mummy is twenty-five". Annette gave Joy a hug while the young mother, Dania, explained why they were there. "I couldn't stand the pace of Los Angeles. I left everything. My husband is forty-eight and very successful, but I had to get away." Little Joy said, "I'm hungry". We offered to get food for them, but Dania refused saying, "I'll help the fishermen pull in their nets. Everyone who helps shares in the catch. It's a tradition." I asked Dania where she and the little girl slept, and she pointed to an old Volkswagen which had been abandoned some time ago after its abrupt descent over the precipice, perhaps at the same spot where we chose the boulder! Dania and Joy had made this old wreck their home for the past two weeks. We offered to take them to a larger community, but Dania was determined to forego any of the amenities of the modern world.

Annette and I left to visit the City of Refuge, an historic place of Hawaiian kings, and the Painted Church with its simplistic murals and frescos. We could not miss going to Kealakekua Bay to gaze across to the monument erected at the spot where Captain Cook met his end. The Kona Coast is the poshest but least interesting because of its commercialism. Beyond that, however, is the beautiful Pololu Valley. And even the Pololu Valley pales in comparison to the Waipio Valley on the other side. Its beauty is breathtaking...no wonder it is considered the most picturesque spot in Hawaii.

Then there are the falls, the Akaka and the Rainbow. I am so enthralled with waterfalls that I often debate what is, in fact, the most beautiful spot in Hawaii! Leaving this island tugged at our heartstrings, but we felt we had seen it in the best possible way. We had to move on, so we planned a short stay in Maui and an even shorter stay on Oahu, but it was in Oahu that we started to change our schedule.

Maui, like the Big Island, has limited transportation available, so we rented a car principally to drive up to the Haleakala Crater for some very spectacular views. Early morning is probably the best time to go on this jaunt which, although short in distance, takes half a day. Since it gets rather chilly as you gain altitude and drive through the clouds, it is best to have a jacket along with you. If high altitudes bother you, you may consider the three thousand metre high Haleakala volcano too risky an adventure, but our gradual ascent didn't affect us as we drank in the beauties of the rare plants, trees and birds. Rather than taking only a half day, it would be advisable to bring along a picnic lunch and spend the whole day on the mountain to witness the changing colours of the cones within the crater as the sunlight and shadows interchange for subtle yet awesome splendour.

As beautiful as Maui is, we left it after two days. We had found cheap accommodation near the airport and could easily have stayed a week or more, but we knew we had scarcely started our trip and would have to cut some places short if we were to get around the world in six months.

At Honolulu, we rented a car and drove downtown, bought a newspaper and looked for lodgings. We ended up at the Wakiki Surf where we rented a studio apartment for only $10 per night. We intended to stay only a day or two in Oahu because we had pictured it as an overly commercialized place. It is, in fact, but there is much of interest there as well. The International Market Place and the Ala Moana Shopping Centre, along with the small stores along Kalahanu Avenue, provide everything you could wish for in shopping. As for entertainment, the Kodak Hula Show and other free shows abound. The Polynesian Show, which features entertainment from all parts of Polynesia, is excellent although rather expensive. This show is staged at the Polynesian Cultural Centre on the north side of the island which can be reached by riding the island bus. While the bus ride is cheap, the best way to see all the island is by rental car. (Often you can get a better rate if you show your airline ticket.) The beaches are very nice and the scenery is lovely and, of course, most seniors are interested in seeing Pearl Harbour. The U.S. Navy gave free cruises at that time, and commercial cruises of the area were also available.

A week later, we went to Pan Am, the only airline flying to Samoa, to make arrangements to depart on the next flight. We agreed to make hotel reservations as they suggested but were told that all rooms were fully booked. Despite being told that there was only one hotel in American Samoa, we remained firm in our decision to go there anyway. We felt that there had to be some accommodations available other than the posh Intercontinental.

From ninety-one hundred metres, the island of Samoa looked so small in the middle of that big ocean that we began to wonder if the people at Pan Am were right. Perhaps there was just one hotel! Our taxi driver assured us that this was not the case, however. It was an exciting ride on the coastal road, much of which is crowded between abrupt mountains and the sea. The driver seemed to become more elated with every audible intake of breath we made as he narrowly missed a huge boulder or a plunge into the sea.

Darkness fell quickly as we approached the capital of Pago Pago (pronounced pango pango) and our driver turned sharply up toward the mountain. Over a very rough road, we passed shelters where people were preparing to retire for the night. The shelters had thatched roofs and were open-sided with rolled matting to lower in case of storms. Single light bulbs dangling from the ceilings created eerie shadows inside as the inhabitants rolled out mats in preparation for sleep.

It was very warm. There were sleazy-looking bars where young men were lounging in the doorways or could be seen through a smokey haze bent over pool tables. Our anxiety mounted as we left the lights and continued the drive up the dark mountainside. Suddenly in the glare of the headlights we saw a building with a single, dim light shining in the entranceway.

The taxi driver took our heavy luggage and lined it up at the small reception desk as I arranged for a room. This was the "Herb and Sias' Motel". It had bamboo walls and a thatched roof. The old-fashioned, wooden ceiling fans droning lazily in that very tropical setting took me back to the visions I had formulated as a boy reading tales of the South Seas. Our room had no air-conditioning, although they had some available at added cost, but it did have a big fan and an atmosphere like that of the lounge. The walls, the beds and even the ceiling were made of bamboo. As in the lounge, the large chairs in our room were constructed of bamboo but had thickly padded cushions from which air gushed with an embarrassing low-pitched sound every time we sat down in them. The beds were comfortable and we soon drifted off to sleep, the sounds of the jungle all around us.

We slept well, arising at 6 a.m. to the crowing of roosters. We ate a beautiful breakfast in the communal dining room. At the table was a huge man from "New Yawk and Miama" who complained about being unable to get into the Intercontinental. Another big man, an Australian, was talking to him, but since the man from New York had difficulty understanding him, the Australian directed his attention to me. Fortunately, I understood his accent sufficiently to gather that he was an engineer who had been commissioned to do something in regard to fresh water. It was evident that he was quite partial to Polynesian girls since he often interrupted his own discourse on engineering with references to the great beauty of female Polynesians. There was another man at the table, a quiet, mysterious sort of person with darkly handsome features, who said little other than to explain why he had no luggage. Apparently it had been lost on Western Samoa under bizarre circumstances, but he declined to elaborate. We ate mangoes, papayas, avocados, eggs, bacon and toast, and were offered fresh coconut milk, tea or coffee to drink.

After breakfast we went for a forty kilometre ride on a sampan bus to see and experience some of the ways and atmosphere of the island. Annette, who is a shelling enthusiast, walked a long way up the beach while I confined my exercise to a shorter distance. Polynesian women smiled and nodded assent when I asked if I could take their picture eating breadfruit and raw fish. One asked if I needed a wife! Since I didn't fancy a steady diet of pulpy, grey breadfruit or raw fish, I decided not to trade in my present wife! In any case, these Polynesian women were not in the same category as those described by the Australian gentleman at breakfast. They were old, decidedly unshapely, and their smiles showed many snaggy teeth!

The next day, we noticed quite a difference in Pago Pago's main street. Everyone seemed to be excited and somewhat dressed up. A large ship had come into port at dawn, and the Samoans were putting on a big show for the newly arrived tourists. Traffic cops, whom we had not previously seen, were making a great exhibition, waving their arms and frantically blowing their whistles. The women, dressed in all their finery, were selling their goods at prices much higher than the day before. The cable car which ran up the side of Rainmaker Mountain was in operation. Fortunately, there was no cloud near the mountain, for if a cloud approaches and touches the Rainmaker, Pago Pago is drenched with rain. We were approached by a young man who wanted us to adopt him and take him back to America. No doubt he mistook us for passengers on the beautiful cruise ship, the Himalaya.

Crossing the International Dateline on our short flight to Fiji marked the start of a new adventure. Again we sought the advice of a taxi driver who took us to the Fong Hing Motel at Nadi (pronounced Nandi). While we could see rats in the courtyard from our balcony, we were not repulsed since these were kangaroo rats which hopped around on their relatively large back feet while their small front legs were tucked into their chests. They were inspecting the contents of the garbage can put out by the restaurant attached to the motel.

The motel was run by East Indians and the restaurant by Chinese. While the cooks were Chinese, the waitresses were Fijians, as were the girls who cleaned the motel, changed the linen and did the washing. When a waitress came to our table in the restaurant, she sat down to write our order in minute detail and then checked the menu for the price and carefully inserted the figures on the bill. When our waitress continued to sit, we wondered if something was expected of us, but it seems that the native Fijians are not in a hurry to carry out their tasks.

The firewalking display at the Hibiscus Hotel was quite spectacular. It is an attraction that, together with a fantastic smorgasbord, provided us with one of our most enjoyable entertainments. We sat beside a medical doctor who worked for the U.S. military on a small island in the mid-Pacific. He told us he had very little to do and came to Fiji occasionally to relieve his boredom. He was very drunk.

We took a bus from Nadi to Suva, Fiji's capital, and to make our bus trip easier we arranged to leave three of our four suitcases at the motel. The airport at Suva doesn't have runways which are long enough for the big jets, so all international travel flows in and out of the airport at Nadi, hence the necessity to return there. From my high school days, I remembered a poem that had a line in it about the 'dusty road to Suva', so I inquired about the condition of the road. When advised of the dust, we chose to take the air-conditioned bus over the cheaper, open bus used by the residents. However, the tourist bus had broken down that day, so we had to take the open-sided one and brave the dust. We were comfortable with our East Indian driver who navigated the ups and downs and the bends, as they call the curves in the road, with caution.

We loved the little villages with their grass huts called burres. At Sigatoka, where the bus stops for forty-five minutes, we used what must always remain in our memories as the filthiest of toilet facilities. At the market place in Sigatoka, we were fascinated by the unique method of cutting deliciously ripe pineapple. A young man had a fairly large knife, and with a few dexterous strokes the fruit seemed to burst into a golden yellow flower of superb beauty. Annette wanted to stay for a repeat performance so she could learn his secret, but the bus sounded its horn calling the passengers to board.

On the road again, we noticed that there were no fences, that cows were tethered or led, and horses roamed free. About halfway in our three hundred kilometre ride, the weather changed from dry to wet, and the dusty road to Suva quickly became the muddy road to Suva! The mud flew in the open sides, whipped by a strong wind. We hurried to roll down the canvas flaps which only partly stopped the onslaught of mud. We put our sunglasses on and wiped the mud off them regularly to see ahead. To make matters worse, our formerly cautious driver turned into a maniac, driving with reckless abandon up mountains and down valleys and not even slowing for the very narrow bridges across swollen rivers. At one point, he met a truck on a bend and went into the ditch. He pulled out but overcorrected his steering, and we were stuck in the opposite ditch. No one was hurt. All the young men piled out of the bus and with much pushing and yelling, backing up and going forward, the bus landed back on the road.

At Navua, the bridge was washed out by a hurricane which had passed through the islands a week before. We could see buses across the river. Our bus stopped and we all got out to walk in the pouring rain down a ramp of slippery gumbo onto a raft which was winched across the river. Two husky, young men came on each side of me and almost carried me onto the raft and held me all the way across. No one offered to help Annette; she must have looked too capable!

The driver of the bus on the other side of the river gave us an uneventful trip along the rest of what is known as Queen's Road. In Suva, the bus stopped only a few metres from the Metropole Hotel. We didn't hurry in the pouring rain. We couldn't have been wetter or dirtier. We were happy for two things: the bus ride was over and we had only one small suitcase to carry.

The Metropole Hotel, across from Suva's Municipal Market and close to the docks, is old but gracious. It lacked modern facilities and air-conditioning, but nothing could surpass the service and attention we received. We stayed a week at the Metropole and

Mirror allows view of oncoming traffic on road between Franz Josef and Fox Glaciers, New Zealand.

Fox Glacier, Westland, New Zealand.

Sheep on the South Island, New Zealand.

Doug Morton and I on his sheep station in the Blue Mountains, New Zealand.

Punga trees in foreground, Lake Ohareka and Mt. Tarawera near Rotorua, New Zealand.

Pupu Springs, the source of Springs River near Takaka, New Zealand. From the air, Pupu Springs resembles a giant paua shell!

The Arches monolith reflected in the sand on Wharariki Beach near Collingwood, New Zealand.

Beach near Kaiteriteri, New Zealand. Seems like all beaches are deserted...

Spoon feeding the eels! Anatoki, near Takaka, New Zealand.

Blowhole at dusk in Kuwaii, Hawaii.

Sunset at Nadi, Fiji.

Policeman at Nadi, Fiji.

Samoans eating raw fish and breadfruit. My would-be wife on the left!

Harvest from the sea at Kuta Beach, Bali.

Temple offerings, Bali.

Rice paddies, Bali.

Ceremonial rites of cremation for royal person in Bali.

A meat market in Singapore.

Street sweeper, Singapore.

Sidewalk barbershop, Singapore.

Chinese Medium Parade, Singapore. Note length of spears through cheeks!

Famous Raffles Hotel in Singapore.

View of Hong Kong from Victoria Peak.

Kinkakiyi Temple, Kyoto. Most photographed subject in Japan.

Building a bridge with teak over a small canal north of Bangkok, Thailand.

Canal trip north of Bangkok, Thailand.

On the wall of the Old Town in Dubrovnik, Yugoslavia.

Windmill in Holland.

A Switzerland scene, Route N3, west of Muhlehorn.

The unique Minach Theatre, Porthcarno, Cornwall.

Clovelly, Cornwall, England.

Cornish Cross enhanced by early morning sun, Lands End.

enjoyed the atmosphere of the place. We regularly ate in the dining room and chatted with many interesting people. One old lady had left England as a young girl to live in Malaysia with her husband who had been manager of a rubber plantation. When her husband died, rather than return to England, she decided to stay in the tropics and moved to Fiji. She told us she had a home on the Queen's Road, fifty kilometres from Suva, but liked to come for a stay at the Metropole every few months. She told us she had taught young Fijian girls how to keep house and cook. We suspect that is how she obtained housemaids without paying them!

One very interesting person we met was a regal-looking Fijian man from the Latoka area of Fiji. He stayed at the Metropole when the House of Representatives was in session, for he was Latoka's member. This massive man had a deep resonant voice which rang with laughter when I suggested he would be prime minister some day. When he extended his hand on our departure, I felt small indeed, for I couldn't bend my fingers. His hand was simply too wide to clasp.

We walked a great deal and enjoyed the sights at the market and the docks. The smell of copra (dried kernels of coconut), while delightful from a distance, was overpowering at the docks where large piles of the stuff had been brought in by small ships. The piles would be loaded into larger ships bound for ports where the coconut would be processed into oil and many other by-products.

The arrival of the P & O liner, the Oriana, resulted in high prices for souvenirs at the market place, but after the ship departed we found real bargains and mailed the first of many parcels we would send home. The prices of colourful grass skirts and wood carvings of primitive yet artistic beauty were reduced so drastically we couldn't resist buying them. Of course, all kinds of foodstuffs, including pineapple, taro and sugar cane, were available at the market, but we sent those home only in the form of the many pictures I took.

It rained again on the day we left. This time we went by the King's Road on the north side of the island. The windshield wipers on the bus had failed and an old man supplied a remedy for the driver: he took a wad of chewing tobacco from his mouth and wiped the outside of the windshield with it. And for a time it worked. The rain ran off quickly, leaving the windshield clear!

While the road was no super highway, it was infinitely better than the Queen's Road. The bus stopped often to board or let passengers off and to allow vendors to sell bananas, pineapples and hot, cooked corn-on-the-cob to the passengers. The corn-on-the-cob was not eaten in North American fashion. The cob was held in one hand while the kernels were dug off with the thumb of the other hand. After several kernels were caught in the palm, they were eaten much like peanuts.

We stayed a night at the Hotel Latoka in the northwest corner of Fiji, and the next day took a sailing vessel from there to Vomo Island. This was a most enjoyable experience—sailing on waters through which the Bounty had sailed and then, by auxiliary motor, through the opening in the coral reef to the beautiful lagoon. There was one small village of seven burres on that delightful island. This was paradise indeed.

The four hours we spent there disappeared like magic, and we reluctantly left after a delightful barbecued meal prepared by the ship's crew.

A decided contrast to our sailing adventure was the very posh hotel, the Mocambo, where we were assigned by Air New Zealand when our flight to Auckland was delayed due to a refueller's strike. We gratefully accepted the lovely surroundings and the superb dinner. In Auckland, we came back to earth in a third class hotel, stayed only one night and flew to Wellington, New Zealand's capital city. It is well named as "Windy Wellington", for the wind over Cook Strait, combined with the downdrafts occasioned by the configuration of the mountains, creates strong and shifting winds which test the ability of pilots. But it was here, in Wellington, that we got our first real taste of the hospitality of New Zealanders.

At the small Hotel Panama, a knock came to our door shortly after we had checked in. It was the manager's wife asking if we would like to see the sights of Wellington at night. She and her twelve year old daughter took us for a car ride which lasted for more than two hours. The lights of Wellington were most attractive and our hostess and her daughter most delightful. What kind people!

We felt at home so quickly. We stayed in New Zealand for seven weeks and in Australia for two. Since our first trip there, we have returned several times to both of these countries.

The northwest part of New South Wales, which is called Heartbreak Corner, got its first rain in three years, so the start of our flight across Australia was barred from view by the clouds. It didn't last too long, however, as we travelled on across the Simpson Desert and eventually over Alice Springs and Ayers Rock. The pilot of our Quantas flight, Captain Brown, gave us a running commentary of the sights below. He had been the pilot of the airplane which had viewed, at high altitude, the re-entry of one of the Apollo flights into the earth's atmosphere. (He had mathematically timed his position during a flight from Fiji to Sydney.)

We talked with a lovely Filipino lady on the flight and went along with her to a hotel at which she had made a reservation, the Wisma Samudra (also called Kuta Beach Hotel). We shared the cost of a taxi and, in following days, shared the cost of a car and guide. Our accommodation was somewhat similar to that on Samoa with the bamboo walls and thatched roof, but we had a small cottage within a guarded compound on the beach. The reception area, lounge and dining room were separate. The compound was guarded all night because of the proximity of young people who slept on the beach in flimsy shelters. These were not young Balinese, but young white people from North America and Europe who were not trusted by the hotel proprietors. We had no trouble. In fact, I talked with some of these young people on the beach and found them both pleasant and polite. I wondered if I wouldn't have travelled the same way if such opportunities had been available when I was young!

Later, when our Filipino friend left Bali, we moved into Denpasar, the capital of Bali. Rather than the Intercontinental or any other tourist hotel, we settled on the Denpasar Hotel which is patronized by Indonesian government officials from Djakarta and businessmen from Indonesia and Australia. There was an Australian woman staying there who was lecturing for a year at the Denpasar University. She was treated with great respect and all the staff addressed her as Doctor, but she insisted we call her Joan. We accompanied her to some classical dance performances. The grace of the Balinese dancers is legendary and this is very evident in the Legong, the Barong and the Kris Dances, as well as in the Ramayana Ballet.[2] We also attended a class in the School of Music and Dance as observers only. Apparently, they welcome anyone who is interested in their teaching methods.

What will always remain in my memory is the performance of the Ketjak (Monkey) Dance. There were several solo Balinese classical dancers, both male and female, who must have graduated from the school with top honours. There were no musical instruments. Their accompaniment was a men's chorus of eighty voices. These voices were so versatile and elastic that they could sound like a full orchestra at times and like a single, female voice at others. The dancers acted out the parts but did not speak or sing. The men's chorus, who sat on the floor cross-legged throughout the performance, provided all the sound. While they never stood, their bodies moved in unison like waves crashing on the beach or were so still that they scarcely seemed to breathe. A most moving performance!

We visited the mother temple of all Balinese at Mount Agung. The multitudinous steps to view the inside might deter many seniors, but the view is worth the effort. On the way to Mount Agung, you can stop to watch the making of batik, a fabric processed for colouring by covering parts of the cloth with melted wax before dyeing. In addition, you can see excellent Balinese carvings fashioned from sawa, sandalwood and ebony, as well as the most unusual painting methods at Ubud. The oil paintings at Ubud are done by specialists. Each canvas may be the creation of as many as eight artists: one who paints skies, one who paints trees, one who paints faces, and others who paint bodies, flowers or grasses. As a result, the paintings, while intriguing, take on a form which somehow resembles a "paint by numbers" product.

Along the roadways, you might see bare-breasted women bathing in nearby streams, or be fortunate as we were to witness the cremation of a royal person! As we watched, the body was transferred from a miniature temple to a hollow, carved bull, both of which had been carried to the cremation site by approximately forty men. As the bull was put in place, some of the deceased's clothes and other possessions were placed beside the body. The previously prepared pyre was lit and an orchestra of bamboo reeds, drums and cymbals played a mournful dirge. After the body was burned, the white bones were crushed to powder, mixed with resin and sculptured to form a likeness of the royal

---

[2] *Legong, Barong, Kris and Ramayana Dances are classical expressions of religious and secular life in Bali.*

person. It was then taken to the river and placed on a pad and floated out to sea.

We also witnessed a procession and burial of an ordinary person which consisted of a graveside service with the same kind of orchestra. However, the deceased was wrapped only in a cloth and buried in a shallow grave, covered with stones so the wild dogs and pigs couldn't ravish it. A decided difference in funeral rites!

In one short week, we experienced and saw so much of Bali that we were still engrossed with the place even as we landed in Singapore, our next destination. We had left Bali on Quantas in the late afternoon, and our flight took us over the Java Sea where we saw the most beautiful sunset and cloud formations we have ever beheld. In Singapore, a taxi driver took us to a new hotel, the Grand Central. We enjoyed the shopping and the sights, the sounds and the smells of the city, and were fortunate to see the Chinese Medium Parade. Young men dressed in colourful costumes paraded with great spears, some as long as two metres, piercing through both cheeks and shorter ones through their arms. Not a drop of blood could be seen! They marched to the beat of drums and cymbals, and appeared to be in a trance.

We had to have lunch at the Raffles Hotel[3] on Beach Road just to experience the grandeur of a bygone age.

And, of course, we visited Tiger Balm Gardens, a gaudy display of Chinese art. The House of Jade was much more interesting. To get past the guard at the gate, all that is necessary is a handshake with a one dollar bill in it. This little trick, confided to me by the taxi driver we hired, enabled us to see the finest exhibits of its type that we have ever seen. We had not previously realized that jade came in so many colours.

In Singapore, I had my Ektachrome film developed into slides in only four hours. I returned to the hotel with my slides just as a heavy rain started and so took advantage of this time to date and title each slide, a practice I have maintained throughout our years of travel.

Singapore is almost on the equator and only slightly above sea level, yet we felt the heat less than we had on Samoa or, in fact, less than at home during the really hot days of summer. It seemed a shame to leave after only three days, but we had many other places to visit if we were to confine our trip to six months. So off we flew across the South China Sea to Hong Kong.

We flew directly over Vietnam, and in the clear atmosphere it was possible to see puffs of smoke which a fellow passenger described as artillery warfare. What a strange feeling to view such a conflict from such a peaceful position. At an altitude of over ten thousand

---

[3] Named after Sir Thomas Stamford Bingley Raffles, and English East Indian administrator who secured Singapore for England's East India Company in 1819. The hotel has hosted many famous persons over the years.

metres, the antagonisms of the opposing factions below seemed somehow absurd.

In Hong Kong, we managed to get a free ride from the airport to the King's Hotel on Nathan Road in Kowloon. We had talked with a travel agent from Singapore and Hong Kong, and one of his assistants was at the airport to meet him. We gratefully accepted both his invitation of a ride and his advice on accommodations and on how to get discounts by simply asking for them. In Hong Kong, hotels add a service charge to your bill, generally ten per cent, but if you ask for a discount they may reduce the bill by the rate of the service charge. I practised this in hotels in other parts of the Far East with considerable success and wished I had started in Bali or Singapore.

Most travellers to Hong Kong spend an average of three nights there. We stayed two weeks. You might ask: "What can occupy a couple of seniors for that length of time?" Simple... Hong Kong is utterly fascinating. While we stayed at the King's Hotel, we walked through the lobbies of many of the superior hotels and often ate lunch there. The Peninsula Hotel, near the Ocean Terminal and the Star Ferry dock, is an elegant place to dine. You can wallow in the lap of luxury for a reasonable interlude, then return to your budget hotel to sleep. We rode buses, ferries and trains to so many places: to Macao, Rantan Island, Kam Tui and Sheung-Shui, Hong Kong Island, up Ladder Street to Cat Street and Thieves Market, Stanley Village, Repulse Bay and Aberdeen where we took a sampan ride. Just walking the streets of Hong Kong makes you conscious of the great mass of humanity. So many people seem to be in constant motion.

We rationalized that it was impossible to get lost on a bus, so we would board one and ride it to the end of the line. On our return trip we would get off at any spot that seemed particularly interesting. Then there are the markets and shopping for which Hong Kong is renowned. However, we found the shopping in Taipei, Taiwan, considerably better than in Hong Kong; and for certain items Singapore surpassed Hong Kong.

We were favourably impressed with Taipei, both because of its cleanliness and the friendliness of the people. Here we opted for a guided tour of the city because even with a map we couldn't find our way around. (All the street names were written with Chinese characters only, making the map impossible to comprehend.) The most outstanding part of the tour was an amazing museum of priceless antiquities dating back over three thousand years. Chiang-Kai-Shek brought them from mainland China over a period of three years, from 1949 to 1952. Our tour guide spoke entirely in English, yet surprisingly we were the only English people in the group. There were people from Germany, Sweden, Thailand, Japan and Indonesia, all of whom understood English. It really *is* the international language.

As we flew over Japan, I took pictures of the volcanoes, which showed so prominently below, until my camera jammed with the film advance arm sticking out the side. When we arrived in the beautiful city of Kyoto, I went to a small camera shop to see if they could fix my camera. What a quaint, little shop it was! There were two ladies dressed in traditional Japanese style which I had thought was worn only by Geisha girls. These ladies were huddled by a pot-bellied stove for warmth from the winter chill. One took my camera and put it in a dark box and, in a very short time, brought it back out with the advance arm in place and the film back in the roll. She smiled and pointed to '36' on the camera and to '24' on the film casing. I smiled, too, and said, "I bought this as a 36 exposure in Hong Kong". Both ladies shook their heads and said, "Ah, Hong Kong". They declined any payment.

Early March can be very chilly, and you feel the damp chill especially if you have been in the tropics for some time. Besides that, Japan is very expensive in comparison to most other countries. Accordingly, we shortened our stay there, but again took tours of Kyoto, Osaka and Tokyo, all of which were fascinating. Perhaps the most exciting experience was riding the "Bullet Train" from Kyoto to Tokyo. Its speed is legendary and the ride very smooth. Several people were wearing face masks to guard against breathing germs in the confines of the train.

The most exotic of all our meals in the air were the 'pheasant under glass' served on the Thai International flight back to Hong Kong, and the lobster salad with a duck entree served on the continuation of that flight to Bangkok. At the airport in Bangkok, the "Traveller's Service" people obtained a room for us at the Grace Hotel for the equivalent of $9 per night. A guide book on Thailand had shown the rates for the Grace to be $20 to $24, but this was apparently a slow season. Some airports have these "Traveller's Service" or "Traveller's Aid" counters which can be of great help to the vagabonder.

A tour of the Floating Market is a fascinating experience. The colourful temples, the orchids, the teak houseboats and the people make up a delightful medley of memories. Also of interest are some of the sightseeing boats driven by young fellows who love the speed produced by powerful engines mounted on long, straight shafts at the end of which are giant propellers. These speedy craft can carry twenty or more passengers and are used by tour groups to whisk their patrons through the area in the shortest time possible.

We engaged a private operator to take us in his small boat at a leisurely pace. Other boats, similar in size to the one we were in, are used by merchants who load them with all kinds of produce, exotic fruits and vegetables. Other vendors, generally women, surround themselves with draperies and dressmaking materials. We were happy not to be whipping past this mosaic of colour and asked our boatman to stop so that we could buy a few small, sweet, tree-ripened bananas.

While we were making our selection, another small boat approached carrying three unmistakably English people, an adult and two children. Their nationality was evident, not only from their speech but from their appearance. The adult, a woman in her mid-forties, was garbed in a white, tailored dress which resembled a nurse's uniform of the Florence Nightingale era. On her head was a large, broad-brimmed hat of straw, and from it a wide, white band of ribbon wafted in the breeze. Her eyeglasses, the old-fashioned pince-nez, swung at the end of a velvet cord attached to her dress. When she looked at the bananas and other fruit, she constantly changed the position of the pince-nez on her long, pointed nose. Around her neck hung a vintage camera which swayed back and forth as she moved, vying with the dangling pince-nez as they both attacked her huge bosom.

The children, a girl of about ten years and a boy approximately eight, were dressed in clothes that would seem to suggest that this was 1927 instead of 1972. The little girl was dressed in a pleated skirt and the young lad in short pants. Like the woman, both wore broad-brimmed straw hats. Both were fair in complexion, almost strawberry blonds, and both were amply mottled with freckles.

The little girl said, "Parmie, get *those* bananas", pointing to some out of reach, then whispered to the boy who promptly attempted to rock the boat. 'Parmie', whom I guessed was their governess, threw up her arms and cried, "Lionel, stop that this instant!", then sighed and shook her head as she asked the girl, "Whatever can we do with your little brother?" It was a question to which she expected no answer, for she returned her attention to the bananas and looked at ours saying, "I cannot seem to find any as nice as yours". We pointed out that the kind we had could be found directly behind the vendor who had not uttered a word.

Just then a large boat came by and its wake created a wash that delighted Lionel. He tried to add to the rocking motion of their boat, much to the dismay of Parmie. We left them, amused at the antics of the little boy, the connivance of the girl and the torment of their governess.

Shortly afterwards, we saw this trio again at the beautiful Temple of the Dawn. Parmie (I wondered what the nickname stood for) was attempting to take a picture of the children in front of the temple. The girl was smiling ever so sweetly, Lionel was making ugly faces and both were in a state of constant movement. Parmie, harassed as before, was attempting to keep them still when she saw us. She waved and, before we were within hearing distance, started to talk to us. I offered to take a picture of the three of them, and Parmie gratefully accepted. I positioned the subjects and gave the children a stern look which quieted them just long enough to snap a picture. The old camera was the folding type, similar to the basic box camera, but it had a collapsible bellows to shrink its size when not in use. It also had a short cable for the shutter release, eliminating any movement of the camera. With that and the children being temporarily immobilized, Parmie probably got one good picture.

Annette wanted to ask Parmie many questions and started with "Are you travelling alone with these children?", since it seemed evident that they were not hers. Parmie replied, "Oh no, the master is with us". She reddened from her neck to her hairline and was, no doubt, grateful that Lionel chose that moment to dash off behind the temple. She mumbled something about the boy and hurried off to catch up with him. The little girl skipped along behind her. We thought that was the last that we would see of Parmie, but our paths were to cross again.

Thailand in Miniature (TIM) is an exhibit of classical music, folk songs and dances, silk processing and weaving, working elephants, beautiful wood carving and inlaid work, Thai boxing and stick fighting and snake charming. It was in the area of the working elephants that we saw Parmie and her charges again. The display of these great animals lifting and rolling the boles of large trees had just finished when we saw Parmie making another attempt to take a picture of the children with the elephants in the background. The children were stepping up their efforts to frustrate their governess by moving forward just as she was about to snap the picture. She was backing up to keep them in focus, but her last step had disastrous results. The children had steered her towards a hefty mound of fresh elephant dung. Miraculously, she missed it, but landed heavily on her backside just behind it. The pince-nez flew off and landed over her shoulder while the camera made perfect contact with the bosom. Her straw hat sailed off to the side, and her dark brown hair cascaded over her face. She shook her head, grunted and started to rise, but she slipped and fell again. This time she had a soft landing...squarely on top of the mound of dung.

A roar of laughter arose from the crowd, and Lionel ran around his governess, whooping with excitement. The little girl exclaimed, with a voice of irritating innocence, "Parmie, what a mess you are! Whatever will you do?" Although she was silent, Parmie's actions reflected a new resolve. She firmly grabbed the children by their upper arms and, ignoring their screams, marched out of the park.

On another day, we arranged a boat ride through swampy canals to see some of the residential areas. These canals are their 'roads', and while there are large patches of open water, there are many areas where a boat is obliged to divide the tall reeds to make any progress. You will see many people doing many things in the water: fishing, bathing, brushing their teeth...and urinating!

Then there is the Grand Palace. 'Grand' certainly is the adjective to use for such an exquisite compound of buildings.

After a week in Thailand, we took to the air again, this time by KLM, the Dutch airline. As we flew over the Gulf of Martaban and Rangoon, the deltas of the Irrawaddy River came into view and, eventually, the delta area of the mighty Ganges River. Just off the wing tip was the most majestic sight of Mount Everest and the Himalayas. We flew on to Tehran, Iran.

Why didn't we stop in India, you might ask. After the cold of Japan, the heat of Thailand had seemed oppressive. Perhaps, too, the length of our stay in the Orient may have contributed to our feeling of being saturated with great masses of people. The romance of the Far East is enticing, but the same problems exist there as in many other countries. Boredom is clearly evident in the faces of hotel employees, shopkeepers and others who serve the public. Their interminable hours of work are reminiscent of North American society many years ago. And there is a much more obvious gap between rich and poor. What a great contrast between the elegant homes of the rich and the hovels of the poor.

Tehran! At the airport there was considerable delay caused by the arrival of Kosygin, the premier of the Soviet Union. Two identical Soviet airplanes had landed, as had three American Air Force planes. And behind them all was the beautiful, snow-capped Elburz mountain range.

At that time, the Crown Jewels of the Shah of Iran were the main tourist attraction in Teheran, but now, of course, no one would recommend a stopover there. Even then we felt uneasy and stayed only one day.

We entered Europe through the back door, so to speak, but as we landed in Athens we were favourably impressed. Although immigration officials did stamp our passports (something we were to find did not happen in many countries of Europe), the formalities of entry were almost non-existent. A taxi driver took us to the El Greco Hotel near Omonia Square, a very central point in Athens. From here we could have walked to the Acropolis, but taxis are relatively cheap in Athens and so we hailed one to take us there and another to bring us back.

We spent the whole day in the area of the Acropolis. Surely no one could visit this area without a sense of awe and wonderment. On our walks around the city, we were impressed with museums, Byzantine churches, markets, Hadrian's Arch, the Stadium and the changing of the guards at the Palace.

We would have liked to have gone to some of the Greek Isles in the Aegean Sea, but there simply wasn't sufficient time and we resolved to return some day. We began to think of this around-the-world trip as an exploratory mission to have a taste of many countries and to determine which ones we would like to visit again.

While entry at the Athens airport had been so simple, departure formalities were very thorough, particularly the search and safety aspects. When we checked our luggage, we discovered that we were now carrying 110 kilograms!

Before we had lined up to be searched by airport officials, we talked with an older couple from Sydney, Australia, who were on their way to England. They seemed so delighted that we, too, were going to Yugoslavia, and we learned later of their extreme apprehension of being in a communist country. Their travel agent had booked them into the Kompas Hotel in Dubrovnik and they begged us to go along with them.

Upon arriving in Yugoslavia, a porter at the airport put all of our suitcases on a dolly, including a small, hard-covered one that Annette had bought in Hong Kong to protect the delicate china she had purchased. When she rushed to take that little case off the dolly, the customs inspector sternly indicated that he wanted to look at it. When he saw the china and the packing inside, he gave us a most delightful and understanding smile. Then I asked our taxi driver who owned the Mercedes he was driving, and he promptly told us that it was his and that all the taxis were independently owned. No one, not the state nor any individual, owned a fleet of taxis. Rather refreshing, we thought, and in a communist country!

We felt that we had hit the jackpot at the Kompas Hotel. It was a first-class hotel right on the coast of the Adriatic Sea where everything was new, spotlessly clean and beautiful. Our meals were excellent, and our lodging with three meals per day was the equivalent of only $6.50 each in Canadian funds. Of course, that was off season and over fifteen years ago, but the Australian couple who had prepaid for the same accommodation paid more than twice that amount.

Dubrovnik is such a charming, old, walled city that we soon became entranced with the place, so much so that we almost gave up our resolve to stay only three days. The walks on top of the wall around the Old City and on the delightful paths on the edge of the Adriatic will always remain special in our memories. So, too, will the fine folklore concert in Fort Revlin, part of the old fortifications. This was a very professional performance in a most impressive theatre. Acoustical engineers could learn a few lessons here. We wondered if the sound was enhanced by the walls and arched ceilings built entirely of brick.

One day we were roaming through the Old City with our newly found Australian friends when I heard the voice of a very talented contralto. It was coming from a Catholic church, and although I am not a Catholic I went in. Our Australian friends, who were Roman Catholics, stayed on while Annette and I left after the music finished. Still this couple clung to us and asked us to accompany them up the coast by bus to Split and Trieste. We did go as far as Split, and after two days there we saw them off on the bus to Trieste. They were still nervous about being in a communist country, so we did our best to assure them they would be alright. They had Eurorail tickets from Trieste and said that they would feel much safer once on the train. They were such timid souls that we have wondered at times what happened to them. We never heard from them again.

Like Dubrovnik, Split also has an old section of considerable interest, but it lacks the charm of Dubrovnik. From our hotel window, we were fortunate to see a whale in the harbour. We decided to drive through Europe and attempted to rent an international car in Split, but that wasn't possible. However, the rental agency arranged for us to get one in Zagreb, so we flew there and soon we were on the road in a Seat, the Spanish version of the Italian Fiat. Driving north past Ljubljana, we saw the Alps for the first time.

The Austrian border is at a high altitude, and both the Yogoslav and Austrian border authorities came out of their shelters into the snow to ask us the usual questions. The Austrians asked for a Green Card. Since I couldn't produce one, I had to purchase public liability insurance for the time I would be in Austria. As it turned out, the Green Card was in the glove compartment as it is in all rental cars in Europe. It is the document attesting to the fact that the car rental company is covered with adequate insurance. My ignorance cost us 40 Austrian schillings.

It was in Austria that we first discovered the luxury of floating off to sleep on huge, down pillows with our bodies covered in 'federbetts' which are eiderdown comforters encased in sheets. They were in all the Gasthofs (guesthouses) where we stayed in Austria.

The Alps were breathtakingly beautiful, and our car performed well even at elevations above three thousand metres in the Arlberg and Tyrol regions. On we went to the 'picture postcard' duchy of Liechtenstein where you can drive every kilometre of every road in a matter of hours. Even so, you feel so elated with the majesty of its mountains, castles and little towns that you leave this fairyland with great reluctance.

In Lucerne, Switzerland, we were amazed at the heavy traffic and wondered what it would be like in the summer months. Beside the lake, we ate a picnic of cold meats, cheeses and dark bread, and we continued to buy the foodstuffs for similar picnics during our journey through the rest of Europe to Amsterdam. We took two weeks to go from Zagreb, Yugoslavia, through Austria, Liechtenstein, Switzerland, Germany, France, Luxembourg and Belgium to Holland. In all these countries, we stayed at Gasthofs or Pensions. We had no troubles of any sort, and even crossing borders, or frontiers as they are called, posed no problem. In some countries, in fact, the customs officials simply waved us on so that we scarcely had to slow down. We had no trouble understanding people since so many Europeans speak English. Only in France was it necessary to buy our food and book our accommodation in the language of the country. Fortunately, our little bit of high school French was sufficient for that.

The cleanliness of Holland, its beautiful barges, the region of the Zeiderzee and the town of Zierikzee impressed us and took us back to the geography lessons of school. How can anyone forget such intriguing names?

We gave up the car at the airport in Amsterdam, flew to Heathrow in England and rented another car there. Driving on the continent is the same as driving in North America, but in England you drive on the left hand side of the road. With the exception of major motorways, the roads are narrow and winding. Fortunately, we had gained some experience driving on the left in quiet, rural New Zealand, but there were times that we felt a little more than frustrated, particularly on the 'roundabouts'. The roundabouts are situated at a point where several roads come together. In the centre is an area sometimes large, sometimes the size of a postage stamp. As you approach the roundabout, there is a sign that indicates where all the roads go. You must instantly memorize this and count the number of exits to the road you wish to take. Don't get caught in the middle, or you may go around in circles forever! It is not quite as bad as that, but it can get to you nevertheless.

We drove to Abingdon, the birthplace of my parents near Oxford, and met cousins and other relatives for the first time. We also collected mail sent there by our relatives and friends in Canada and the U.S.A. We had not been in touch with anyone since receiving mail at the Thomas Cook office in Hong Kong. No matter how avid a vagabonder you become, there is always joy in receiving mail from your family.

Our mail was sent in care of a first cousin of mine, a maiden lady who was the spitting image of old Queen Victoria with her hair parted in the centre and pulled back into a bun on the nape of her neck. We had rung the bell several times before the curtain was pulled aside slightly and one large, bulging eye appeared. The door opened and the great bulk of her enveloped me. She started to cry. In between her sobs, I gathered that I looked very much like her younger brother who had died the previous year. She bustled about and served tea. I got a mouthful of tea leaves and felt decidedly uncomfortable trying to gather them in one area of my mouth without Marsie seeing me. When she left the room to gather our letters from home, I hastily spit them out into a tissue. I also peeked into the teapot. It was half full of old tea leaves!

After Marsie returned with a handful of letters, she settled herself into her oversized chair and proceeded to give us our mail one letter at a time, formally announcing the exact date each letter had arrived. Annette, of course, wanted to sift through them quickly to pull out letters from our children, but she sensed that my cousin would be shocked by such rash behaviour. After reading our letters (in the proper order), I commented on the great stacks of music piled on top of the piano and on a side table. Marsie said that she had not played the piano since her brother died. The church where she had played the organ for many years had not called her back since "her illness".

I asked her to play. I guess she assented to do so because of my resemblance to her deceased brother, for as she sat down she made a comment about how Teddy had always asked her to play, too. We were amazed at the professionalism of her rendition of Beethoven's Sonata Pathetique. When I asked her to play Gilbert and Sullivan, she opened the score of the Mikado. When she was about halfway through Mia Sama, I started to wonder what was happening. Her eyes rolled to the ceiling as her fingers flew over the keys. Glorious music still came from the piano, but it was not Gilbert and Sullivan. She was aroused. She was inspired. She was mad!

Poor Marsie had lived alone for more than thirty years. Her father was a tailor, and when he died she had attempted to run the family clothing store by herself. She would hire no one, for she feared that they would steal from her. So it was providential that her shop and the land it stood on was expropriated for road widening. Instead of selling off all the clothing which remained in stock, she had brought it home where it had filled up two rooms upstairs for nearly thirty years! The house, basically the nicest on the street, had been neglected all that time. Although no windows were broken, the drapes on the front windows, upstairs and down, remained closed. Their tattered condition, together with the weedy front yard within the high, bricked wall, made the place appear almost haunted.

After looking up other relatives, all of whom appeared to be normal, and after taking pictures of the houses in which my parents were born, we left for Windsor Castle, Stonehenge and Salisbury. At that time, you could walk through Stonehenge and actually touch the stones, but today, sadly, visitors are confined to an enclosed walkway. Salisbury Cathedral was the first of many fine cathedrals we visited in Great Britain. It became somewhat of a compulsion. Even on subsequent visits, we found ourselves seeking out cathedrals we had not previously seen. These magnificent structures never cease to intrigue me with their beauty of form built into strength.

We delighted in the lanes and hedgerows and were fortunate to see a hedgerow being rebuilt. While they often appear to be simply vines over a fence, we discovered that they have a core of well laid stone. It is certainly prudent not to run into one.

We drove to Six Penny Handley, a small community where more relatives lived. After a nice lunch and pleasant chatter, we set off again and drove through Yeavil, Horton Cross and the Vale of Taunton Dean to Dunster, a quaint old village with a castle dating back to Cromwell's time. We were amused at the names of communities along the way to a town with the very ordinary name of Minehead on the Bristol Channel. It was here, however, that we found a most delightful place to stop for the night. It was Woodbridge Guest House which at that time charged only £1.60 for bed and breakfast and a mere 75 pence each for a wonderful evening meal. The meals were so good, the beds so comfortable and the price so right that we made immediate plans to make Woodbridge Guest House our base from which we would explore the countryside for miles around. After breakfast we advised our hosts of our plans, only to find that they were fully booked for several weeks to come.

Disappointed, we travelled on through little villages to Porlock Hill and Robber's Bridge in the Lorna Doone farm area. We eventually arrived at Clovelly, a beautiful, little town built on a steep hill that meets the sea. It is a lovely place to spend a day or two if you are not pressed for time, as is the area around Land's End in Cornwall.

We stayed three nights at the Parc an' Greet Guest House. Formerly this was the rectory for the parish church across the road, but it might have figured in the history of smugglers since a tunnel connected this house to another inn further down the road. These buildings were considered to be between three hundred and five hundred years old. If only the walls could have told of the escapades of men smuggling goods between France and Cornwall.

The Parc an' Greet Guest House furnished their guests with plenty of bed covers and hot water bottles for their unheated bedrooms. Even in that most southerly part of England, spring can be very chilly, so hot baths and warm beds are very comforting.

While in the area of Land's End, we drove to many towns and hamlets...to St. Ives, where the streets are so narrow you could touch the fronts of stores while seated in your car, to Cape Cornwall and St. Just, and to the unique Minach Theatre at Porthcarno. Near Boleigh, we discovered a miniature Stonehenge consisting of nineteen huge stones in a circle. We enquired about these stones, which appeared to be in a farmer's field, but didn't get a satisfactory answer. What did they mean? We never found out.

We went to Mousehole from Lamorna Cove, and on the way we took a lovely picture of a water wheel pumping water to a weir (dam). Such restful scenes are rare treasures to remember. Of course, we went to see St. Michaels Mount (near Penzance) to which it is possible to walk at low tide. It was high tide at the time we were there, and although we vowed to return, we have not done so yet. We also visited the sight of the old tin mines of Cornwall. Long, vertical shafts had been dug, and from them horizontal shafts ran out below the sea. No protective fences had been erected to keep people away. There was simply a small, partly overgrown sign warning of the danger of these shafts. They have been a significant factor in many of the gruesome tales of the area and in the stories of English novelists. We walked to "Public Pathway to Sennen Cove", as it was described on the sign at its entrance. Some landowners have attempted to take over these walkways, but the right to walk over these lands is jealously guarded by the walking clubs. Finally, we went into the old church across the road from the guest house and learned that it was founded by St. Sennen in 520 A.D.

When we left Lands End, we drove to Dartmoor where we stopped at the Dartmoor Inn for a nut-brown ale and lunch. As we sat there we watched the snow fall on the moor and were happy that the host had seated us next to the fireplace where a fire was burning merrily. We were slow to leave Dartmoor but continued on until we got to Nunney, the site of the old castle ruins. We stopped at another delightful, old stone place called Bridge House where we had a typical meal of roast beef and Yorkshire pudding with jam tart and custard for dessert.

We spent three days in Stratford and saturated ourselves in things Shakespearean. On the way back to Abingdon we stopped in Banbury and Oxford, but since we were nearing the six month limit that we had set for ourselves and since we intended to return to England sometime in the future, we gave those cities little more than a glance.

In Abingdon we stayed at the Blue Boar Inn since the Oxford Inn, where we had previously stayed, was fully booked. We were happy we had to stay at the Blue Boar, for never had we seen a more typical English pub of a bygone era. Our room was the best in the house. It was located directly over the pub itself and we could hear the sounds of the patrons below. Sharp at 10 p.m., time was called and the last of the imbibers departed, leaving us to reflect on our trip around the world.

I am only 173 centimetres tall and here we were in a room where I had to duck to get through the doorway. The oak beams and rafters were open to view. I knew that my parents had never seen the inside of this place since they were teetotalers and, in their Victorian way, thought of such places as evil. But when we returned to Canada, I visited my ninety year old mother. She chuckled at my description of the Blue Boar Inn and then recited a poem when I told her of going to St. Ives. Her poem was a riddle:

> As I was going to St. Ives
> I met a man with seven wives
> Seven wives had seven sacks,
> Seven sacks had seven cats,
> Kits, cats, sacks, wives,
> How many were there going to St. Ives?

3

Great Britain and Europe

We saw the sun coming up at 2:30 a.m. E.S.T., but it was 7:30 a.m. local time as we landed at London's Gatwick Airport. We had seen an advertisement in the newspaper about cheap fares to the United Kingdom with Freddie Laker, the pioneer in discounted air fares. On the spur of the moment, we had called to reserve seats. Every year there are special rates advertised by almost all the carriers. I certainly wouldn't think of paying full economy fare to Europe and it's not necessary. The one drawback is the night flight. There are a few lucky people who can sleep in a crowded airplane. I have to be at the point of exhaustion to sleep for even a short time while in a seat, and the economy seats in planes seem to be much closer together than they used to be. With the excitement of being back in England, however, we forgot our lack of sleep.

While waiting for our new luggage, we realized that we had neglected to put a distinctive mark of any kind on it. As the blue bags rolled along on the carousel, we wondered if everyone had bought their bags at the same discount store! We had brought an extra bag since we knew we would have a rental car for most of our four week stay and we had brought presents for our English relatives and friends.

We had previously arranged with the travel agent to rent a car at the airport since it is generally cheaper that way. Even so, the car rental company, Kenning's, asked for a refundable £95 deposit before we could take the car on the road. Although we had learned to drive on the left in New Zealand where the volume of traffic is fairly light, we were careful since many of England's roads are narrow and winding and there are many more cars on those roads. Also, having driven in England previously, we knew how hazardous the switch to driving on the left could be.

My sister had joined us for this trip. Just six months before, she and her husband had met us in California and that trip had given Nesta the desire to see more of the world. Accordingly, she needed no coaxing to visit the land of her ancestors. Nesta doesn't drive a car and doesn't wish to navigate, but she does have the facility for relaxing when others do such chores. While Annette and I took turns at the wheel and at map reading, Nesta happily took in the sights from her position in the back seat.

We had written to Marsie, our eccentric first cousin, and to other relatives to let them know we were coming to England, but we intended to find accommodation in Abingdon at the lovely Oxford Guest House, just around the corner from 'mad Marsie's'. As we drove to the guest house, we saw the huge bulk of Marsie huffing and puffing her way towards us. How had she recognized us driving by the corner? She had never seen this rental car before, she had never seen my sister, and she could not have seen Annette on the other side of the car. She must have kept vigil on that corner until she saw me drive past. Although we were very tired, we promised that we would come around to see her immediately after checking into the guest house, and we did.

My sister wanted to see Marsie's back garden. On the pretense of needing to use the toilet facilities, I did not accompany the ladies. I wanted to see if the clothing from my uncle's store was still in the bedrooms. Curiosity had gotten the better of me; I had to see those bedrooms. I tried the door to one. It opened and showed, with its unmade bed and litter-strewn dresser, that it was Marsie's room. I had half expected the other two rooms to be locked, but the doors opened to reveal stacks of coats, pants, caps and other apparel still there, apparently untouched, for well over thirty years.

I was downstairs before the ladies returned from the back garden and was glancing through some sheets of music as they came in. Marsie took this as a request for a concert. She played beautifully at first, but I could see the look of appreciation on my sister's face turn to disbelief as Marsie went into a trance and played with wild abandon!

We visited briefly with Marsie again the next day but were able to excuse ourselves quickly on the basis of having so many people and places to visit. Marsie cried when we left. I felt mean as I slowly let out the clutch pedal while she still held onto the car. We never saw Marsie again. The following year, she wrote to us in New Zealand. It was her last letter, written the day before she died. Neighbours had seen no sign of life for several days and had called the police. They found her slumped in the oversized chair with a cup of tea still perched on the arm, and the large pot half full of old tea leaves!

Our other relatives were lovely people who served fresh tea with well-prepared food. We enjoyed seeing them again and were thankful for the efforts they had made to obtain information about our common ancestry. Being lifelong residents of Abingdon, they were able to escort us to all the places of interest, some of which I had heard about as a child when my parents would reminisce about their younger years.

From Abingdon we drove to Bath which somehow reminded me of Athens, Greece. After a night there, we drove on into Wales which, in turn, reminded us of New Zealand. We stayed at a 'Bed and Breakfast' farmhouse at Powys. We had spotted the small 'B&B' sign on a post so drove up the laneway until we came to a set of gates on either side of a railway crossing. We opened and closed them, as we were requested by neat, little signs, and continued up the lane to Pickins Farm. The stone farmhouse was five hundred years old, very well preserved and nicely decorated. We slept well and in the morning had a full English breakfast of bacon, eggs, potatoes, mushrooms, tomatoes, toast and marmalade. The meal was served to us by Mrs. Pickins, a pleasant, ruddy-faced woman who told us that her next job for the day was to help her husband butcher some sheep! We declined her invitation to witness that sight and continued our journey, stopping to see the ruins of Harlech Castle and Carnavon Castle. Both places brought back memories, the first for the song "Men of Harlech" which we had sung so robustly in school, and the second as the place of the investiture of Charles as Prince of Wales.

We carried on to the Lake District where we found The Old Mill, another delightful little, stone cottage where we stayed the night. Our hosts were delightful people. It was apparent that they were not in the 'Bed and Breakfast' business to make money since the cost was only £3 per person. They expressed their delight in our finding the place, for we had driven down country lanes and even through barnyards to find it.

Our host, Mr. Kegg, had been a miller and had run what he described as "the last water-powered mill in these parts". Although he had ceased operations four years before, he still enjoyed walking through the mill and explaining its workings to his guests. He walked with a shooting stick, a cane whose handle divides to provide a seat, for he had a slight limp, the result of an accident in his mill which had prompted its closing.

From The Old Mill, we took side trips to the castle ruins of the Parr family where Catherine, the sixth wife of King Henry VIII, had lived as a child. Nearby was the Kendal parish church where the Parr family had worshipped. In the churchyard, the following epitaph caught my attention:

> "London bredd me, Westminster fedd me,
> Cambridge spedd me, my Sister wedd me,
> Study taught me, Living sought me,
> Learning brought me, Kendall caught me,
> Labour pressed me, Sickness distressed me,
> Death oppressed me, Grave possessed me,
> God first gave me, Christ did save me,
> Earth did crave me, Heaven would have me."

The epitaph was on the tombstone of "Mr. Ravlph Tirer, late rector of Kendall who dyed 4 June 1627". The cemeteries of England are filled with interesting epitaphs, some of which are melodramatic, some thought provoking and others unseemly and atrocious.

From The Old Mill, we also toured the Lake District. This must surely be the crowning glory of England for elegance of scenery. To choose the loveliest spot in the Lake District is almost impossible because you no sooner convince yourself that one area surpasses a previous sight when yet another superb view presents itself. This feeling took us back to thoughts of New Zealand where at every turn in the road you are tempted to stop and take a photograph. We resolved to return to this area to absorb more of the serenity it seemed to generate.

At Mungrisdale, near Greystoke Castle, I was told we were in John Peel country and thought of the folksong "Do Ye Ken John Peel", one of the first songs taught to me in the early grades by my English-born music teacher. And when we went to the Isle of Skye in Scotland, the haunting melody of "Over the Sea to Skye" came to mind. As we travelled throughout Britain, I found many place names that had been stamped indelibly in my memory through songs or poems learned in school.

In Scotland, as in England, the names of places like Bannochburn, Stirling Castle, Loch Katrine and Loch Ness brought back memories of my childhood education. Who, for instance, could ever completely forget the Battle of Culloden Moor, the site of one of the shortest yet bloodiest battles of all time? In 1746, one thousand of the five thousand tired and hungry Scots fighting for Bonnie Prince Charlie were slaughtered by the English Royalists under the leadership of the Duke of Cumberland who lost only fifty of his nine thousand well-fed men. The battle lasted a mere forty minutes!

Just south of Culloden Moor are the Clava Stones, cairns dating back to 1800 B.C. Such dates served to impress us with the antiquity of civilization in this small country and emphasized the comparative youth of Canada and the United States.

Cawdor Castle, represented by William Shakespeare as the scene of Duncan's murder by Macbeth, aptly provides the foreboding atmosphere for such a gruesome tale. Further on we travelled over bridges named Dulsie, Dry and Coffin which somehow added to the aura of trepidation. But at the Faskally Home Farm, near Pitlochry, such feelings were dispelled in the company of jovial people.

The house, attached barns and courtyard of Faskally Home Farm were all built of stone. Yet the warm atmosphere of the interior was a distinct contrast to the cold and rather forbidding appearance of the place. We were assigned rooms which contained very old furniture and old, brass bedsteads. All the beds had comfortable mattresses and lovely sheets and bedspreads. The cost at that time was only £3.20 per person for bed and breakfast.

A fire was blazing in the large, stone fireplace, complementing the warmth of those gathered around it. A tall, regal lady greeted us. She, of course, mistook us for Americans, and when we told her that we were Canadians, she tapped the shoulder of a short man, who was engaged in conversation with another gentleman, and announced, "John, here are some Canucks". John was a rotund individual with large jowls and a red, bulbous nose. With his pudgy hand outstretched, he said, "Welcome Canucks. Jolly nice to see you. Maud and I are Cockneys". We laughed in disbelief at this revelation, and he added, "No, really, we both were born within the sound of the Bow Bells so we are true Londoners, or Cockneys".

The 'Cockneys' were the embodiment of hospitality. They had come to this establishment so many times to relax in its lovely, rural setting that they had taken on the role of a welcoming committee and proceeded to introduce us to all those present. They led in the entertainment, too, with Maud leading a sing-song while John's chubby fingers found all the right keys of the old, cabinet grand piano. Here, in Scotland, we sang the songs of England: folksongs like "Blaydon Races" and "Do Ye Ken John Peel", and pub songs like "Nellie Dean" and "On Ilkley Moor Bar Tete". Later on, in Edinburgh, we would enjoy a night of Scottish music and the poetry of Robbie Burns, but this harmonious evening at Faskally Home Farm will remain in my memory as an event especially enjoyable and full of good companionship.

On the way to Newcastle, we stopped at Housesteads to walk on Hadrian's Wall, one of the largest reminders of Roman works built during their occupation of Britain. It had been constructed early in the second century A.D. to guard against the attacks of the "barbarians" from the north!

Nearby was a 'Bed and Breakfast' which, while vastly different from Faskally Home Farm, had a fascination all its own. The Wharmley Guest House was, like Faskally, built of stone with a stone fence surrounding the courtyard, but there was no Maud and no John. In fact, we were the only guests.

It was dusk when we saw the little 'B & B' sign as we drove away from the area of Hadrian's Wall. We drove nearly two kilometres along a poorly maintained laneway to reach the guest house. In the courtyard, a tall, gaunt man left the piece of farm machinery he had been working on to talk to us. He raised his bushy eyebrows to reveal deep-set eyes as he replied to our queries about accommodation and an evening meal. He said, "We have a vacancy. We serve evening meals". After a pause, he added, "But we have no electric". I looked around at Annette and Nesta expecting them to say "let's go", but before they could speak the man spoke again saying, "The electrician won't finish his repairs until tomorrow. If you don't mind candlelight you can stay". When we enquired about cooking the meals without electricity, he told us that they cooked on a coal-fired stove.

As we ate our evening meal at a table set up in front of a fireplace with a rather meagre coal fire, our host told us of how he had unearthed two stone coffins in one of his fields. He had hit these obstructions on several occasions with his plough and had finally carried out his vow to rid himself of these annoyances. When he and his son dug them up, he found that his plough had partially removed the lid of one coffin. It was at this point that our host excused himself to go to the kitchen. He was acting as waiter and collected the beautiful Spode plates from which we had eaten our main course.

We looked around the huge room as we waited for dessert. The small fire and two candles were the only source of light so that the corners of the room were dark. The darkness only emphasized the dismal condition of the walls which were covered with very old and dark wallpaper. The wallpaper had been gold in colour with large sprays of silver ferns. Age and coal smoke had dimmed its brightness, and in the flickering light of the candles the ferns did, as Annette suggested, resemble the outspread arms of ghosts.

We talked little, but the little we talked was in hushed tones. The dowdiness of the room, the absence of electric light and Annette's whispered misgivings began to make me feel uneasy, although I knew these feelings were sheer nonsense. Still, the appearance of our host with his slow and methodical manner of speech and the strange non-appearance of anyone else allowed for some trepidation among all three of us.

A crash from the direction of the kitchen startled us and we had difficulty concealing our discomfort when our host returned, carrying a tray with three bowls of custard. He gave no explanation for the crash. Rather, he continued his story of the coffins just as though he had never left the room. He told us that on seeing what appeared to be human bones, he ceased his digging and went to Hexham to see the curator of the museum who then made arrangements to unearth the coffins and have them displayed.

We felt much more at ease and climbed up the long, curving stairway to get ready for bed. I expressed my amusement and chided Annette for having too vivid an imagination. Nesta, too, voiced her amusement, and her giggles almost convinced me that she had not been nervous at any time that evening. She confessed later, however, that she was happy there were three beds in the one room we shared that night!

We slept well. We had walked a great deal during the day so were physically tired, and with a chair propped against the door handle we had a feeling of security!

We awoke at daybreak, washed in cold water and proceeded downstairs to breakfast. With bright sun streaming in the windows of the dining room, all ghostly imagery disappeared. When the kitchen door opened to reveal a comely, cheerful lady, I sensed that there was a reserved cordiality in this house.

The breakfast consisted of hot cereal which warmed us nicely in the chill of the morning, and eggs, bacon and all the other foods that make up a good English breakfast. As we left Wharmley House, charming smiles and wishes for a pleasant trip came from our host, his gracious wife and their tall, handsome son.

We took a roundabout way to Newcastle, travelling to Durham to see its great Norman cathedral. Most intriguing was the demon's head which held the knocker on the massive north door. During the dark days of the Middle Ages, any fugitive from the law who could manage to grasp the knocker was granted sanctuary within the cathedral. Such legends stir the imagination and arouse feelings of sympathy for the poor devils who failed, by inches, to reach the door. Once inside, they would have been awed by the elegance of its choirs and columns, its towers and transepts. Today, visitors from abroad can seldom forego a visit to these medieval places of worship, whether it be for their religious significance or simply for their architectural charm. The Durham cathedral was only one of the many we visited during our several trips to Britain.

In Newcastle, friends of friends back home had reserved seats for us at the "Dagger Dinner" in Seaton Delaval Hall, a castle north of Tyneside. Part of the castle had been rented out to a company who served delicious meals to patrons seated on benches, while the serving "wenches" kept the wine and mead glasses brimming full. The "wenches" doubled as entertainers. They had such excellent voices that I wondered why they couldn't make their living singing instead of waiting on tables. But perhaps that is the fate of many superb artists.

When we turned our car into Kenning's Car Hire, the young lady behind the desk offered to drive us to the quay at North Shields. We accepted her offer gratefully and, once there, embarked on a ship bound for Norway. We opted for the cheaper sleeperettes instead of a cabin and found them to be much like airplane seats. It was false economy. None of us slept well, but seeing Annette and Nesta in a relaxed position which resembled sleep, I left to go out on deck.

The sea was rough and I noticed a great deal of shipping traffic. Clouds covered the moon and stars, and as the darkness intensified, the velocity of the winds increased. The height of the waves increased, too, and I felt that only the stabilizers with which this new ship was equipped kept it from tossing about like a cork. The siren sounded with a frightening blast as a ship passed on our port side. Shortly after, a further blast warned of the immediate presence of a huge freighter which suddenly loomed out of the darkness on our starboard side. This ship was so close that I felt a collision was inevitable, but we slid by it and I breathed a sigh of relief.

When we landed in Kristiansand, Norway, the next afternoon, we learned that there had been gale warnings the previous night; still, I didn't tell Annette and Nesta about my wanderings on deck. Although I had slept very little during the night, I did get some sleep in a lounge chair while basking in the sunshine that morning. I felt as fit as was possible with so little sleep and walked to the car rental agency, vowing never to take the so-called sleeperettes again.

We went from rags to riches; from those dreadful sleeperettes to a full-sized Mercedes Benz sedan! I had requested the smallest, cheapest car available, but the agent offered the Mercedes for the lowest price just to get it off his hands and back to Germany or France. He said that no one in Kristiansand would rent such a car.

Our experience of driving through Scandinavia was one of serenity. Norway and Sweden were similar to Canada, whereas Denmark seemed more European in character. All three countries appeared clean and wholesome. Food and lodging were considerably more expensive in Scandinavia than in Britain. Sometimes we wondered if we had chosen wisely by accepting the big Mercedes. How could proprietors guess that we were vagabonds looking for budget-priced accommodation? Another lesson: not all gifts are a blessing!

Germany was different. Almost everyone in Scandinavia spoke English, but in Germany we experienced some difficulty making ourselves understood and in understanding the proprietors of rental units. At one, the beautiful Pension Guildhouse near Saerbeck, the lady was explaining something to us in German and after some time I threw up my hands, indicating that I didn't understand. To illustrate how little German I knew, I said hopelessly, "Ein, Zwei, Drei" (One, Two, Three). The lady immediately smiled broadly and replied, "Ja, Zwei; Drei, Nein", at the same time leaning her head over her cupped hands. Then I understood that she had room for two but not for three guests. With more sign language and a few single words, it was finally decided that we could stay.

The room our German hostess led us to had twin beds, but it was so large that it could have held six or more, so we surmised that she intended to place another cot in it. She then took us to the dining room where several men were already seated. The puzzle was finally unravelled by one of the men who spoke English in a deep, guttural voice. He told us the establishment was almost full because of the many men in the area working on a major alteration to the telephone lines. He told us that the ladies were to sleep in the bedroom the hostess had shown us, and I was to share a room upstairs with one of the workmen. I thanked him for interpreting for us and proceeded to eat a cold evening meal consisting of a variety of meats, dark bread and sauerkraut. While it was tasty, the absence of something hot left a void in my stomach and I would have preferred hot tea in place of the cold beer that one of the men insisted I have. I attempted to reciprocate by offering to pay for a second round, but the English-speaking gentleman explained that none of the men drank more than one quart. Since one small bottle of beer is as much as I can normally consume, I sought the help of Annette and Nesta to finish my quart!

We sat in the dining room for a short time after the meal to watch television. We couldn't understand it, of course, but it was interesting to compare the picture, the colour and the expressions of the audience with sets and people at home. I soon diverted my attention to the construction of the building. There were blackout shutters which were pushed back in recessed slots between the outside brick and the inner wall, so as to protect the glass if a bomb should fall nearby. I asked if this was a pre-war building, thinking that such precautions must have been taken between the two great wars. My interpreter was as puzzled as I, for some aspects of the place seemed of an older era while others seemed so very modern.

Going upstairs to the room I was to share for sleeping was a rare experience. The treads on the stairway were made of solid walnut, as was the massive banister. Both were highly polished and beautifully moulded. I saw no scuff marks and wondered how much work it took to keep them in such immaculate condition.

I slept well and assumed that I had the room to myself since I neither saw nor heard the man who was to sleep in the other bed. Our breakfast consisted of the same cold meats and dark bread we had had the previous evening, but in addition there was a plate of cheese which was a fine substitute for the briny sauerkraut. The telephone workmen had left before we ate, so we had the dining room to ourselves. Our hostess knew at least one word of English, for she said "war" when I pointed to the heavy shutters at the window. I rationalized that this was an older building which had been very tastefully and expertly remodelled. It was clean, spacious, comfortable and less than half the price of the cheapest accommodation we had found in Scandinavia!

As we left, our hostess hugged and kissed each one of us, and smiled and waved as we drove out of the circular driveway. We all understood that language and mused about the goodness of people throughout the world. That German lady, being about the same age as ourselves, would have lived through the years of Hitler and World War II. The suffering caused by those horrible years was not of her making, yet she had had to endure many hardships and carry, in part, the guilt of her country.

We stayed only one night in Holland, having spent considerable time in that delightful country on an earlier trip. This time, we stayed at the Legerman Hotel in Gorichem, a hotel filled with wonderful antique furniture, clocks and china. It had a unique stairway, very wide with narrow treads and high risers which brought to mind the steep climbs of the Mayan ruins in Central America.

The highlight of our short stay in Belgium was Brugge, the "Venice of the North". It is so beautiful that we felt we could have spent a full week cruising its canals and another week strolling through the quaint, old streets, visiting the lovely, little shops and admiring the sculpture and wood carving in Notre Dame Cathedral. This is the city of fine lace. Little ladies, all of them old, sit in chairs on the sidewalks of streets near the canal area making lace of many varieties, but all of delicate beauty.

When we turned in our Mercedes in Calais, France, we calculated the distance we had driven and the money we had spent on petrol. We paid for the comfort of this big car. We had driven twenty-five hundred kilometres and had spent the equivalent of $200 for petrol. I had looked under the car more than once, thinking that there must be a leak in the tank!

The trip across the English Channel from Calais to Ramsgate was fast, noisy and uneventful. We had hurried to get window seats on the hovercraft, but we may as well have sat in the middle since the constant spray blocked out any view. The ferry across the channel is much nicer, unless you are interested solely in speed. Having only four weeks for the entire trip, we were, indeed, interested in speed, for we wished to see a little of London and some of the historic places along the south coast.

In Ramsgate, we rented another car, this time a small one, and took off for Dover and Folkstone. Just past Hythe, we stopped at Dymchurch and stayed in a delightful 'Bed and Breakfast' on Pear Tree Lane. Nearby was a Martello fortification built in the time of the Napoleonic Wars. Touring the structure and taking a second look at the outside made us aware of having been in a similar building before. After some thought, we remembered the Martello Tower, now a museum, in Kingston, Ontario, Canada.

We were fascinated with the railroad which runs from Dymchurch to New Romney. It is "Lilliputian" in terms of size of tracks, engines and cars, a must for any railway buff to see. Annette, always on the alert for unusual souvenirs, picked up a miniature railway spike near the tracks. We heard a shout from the direction of the little station and turned to see a man running towards us. From his frantic actions and shrill voice, I thought we were in imminent danger of being hit by an approaching train. However, this display of hysterics had nothing to do with danger from trains. Even though he was now only a few feet away from us, he shouted, "What are you doing stealing railway property?" It seemed so ridiculous that I laughed out loud. Nesta looked incredulous and Annette spluttered protestations about not being a thief. As Annette recovered from her disbelief, she said, "It was just lying there. How dare you accuse me of stealing?" Faced with a spirited lady who was not awed by his bluster and realizing that we were foreigners, he became most apologetic and breathlessly explained how the locals were always stealing things from the railway. He then insisted we take the little spike which is now displayed in our home in Canada.

On we went to Rye, the oldest town in England, and what a delightful time we had simply strolling the steep, cobbled lanes and sitting in the Mermaid Inn which is reputed to be the haunt of a multitude of ghosts. The English, of course, are fascinated with ghosts and the spirit world, and this area of the country attracts the believers more than most.

From Rye, we drove to Hastings to see the site of the Battle of Hastings which took place in 1066. Probably one of the most celebrated battles in history, it is remembered as the event which changed the course of Britain's history by establishing a foothold for the Norman Conquest. In the city, we asked directions to the site of the battle, and the reply was "Go to battle first". That made no sense to us at all and so we drove on, trying to find a sign which would point in the direction we wanted to go. Eventually, we stopped again to ask directions of a lovely and refined-looking lady who, after noting our consternation when she, too, said, "Go to battle first", added, "Battle is the name of the town near the actual site of the Battle of Hastings". When we looked at our map it was so obvious, but we had expected it to be at Hastings. Rather sheepishly, we thanked the lady and drove to Battle. Once there, we had no trouble finding the spot where the gallant Saxon, Harold, had died.

At Winchester Cathedral, we saw a sarcophagus of a Bishop Edgington. Since he died in the fourteenth century, long before old King Henry VIII made it possible for the clergy of England to take wives, he could hardly have been my legitimate ancestor, but I like to think that perhaps the old bishop was a bit of a rake and so I claim him as my many times great-grandfather!

We decided to get a 'Bed and Breakfast' in Horsham and travel by train to London. Rather than attempting to see London on our own in the short time we had left, we purchased tour tickets while in Horsham so as not to waste time on that chore while in the big city. We caught the London train at the Horsham station at 8 a.m. and were in plenty of time for the seven hour tour starting at 10 a.m. The cost of the train to and from Horsham, the tour and a lovely lunch at Dunsters Restaurant was £10 each. We had intended to return the next day to roam the streets of London at our leisure, but our feet were so tired from the tour that we altered our plans and drove to Bognor Regis, a seaside resort we had bypassed on the way to Winchester from Hastings. As we strolled along the soft sand of the beach, we noticed a policeman, a tall, young man immaculately dressed with freshly polished, black boots. He was standing with his legs apart and his hands clasped behind his back. He looked quite out-of-place on the beach, but he was performing a vital task. He very politely asked everyone approaching to skirt around an object that had been found that morning. It was a World War II mine! The policeman was waiting for a bomb squad to arrive. Needless to say, we left.

Our last 'Bed and Breakfast' in England was the Orford Farm near Wisborough Green on Route 272 in West Sussex. It was a little farther from Gatwick Airport than the accommodation at Horsham, but it was only half the price at £3 each and was so restful. The house was over five hundred years old with the remnants of a moat still visible. After a lovely breakfast, we walked around the grounds, putting in a little time before the short drive to Gatwick. We reminisced about the whole trip, but we talked mostly about the events of our short stay in Great Britain and vowed to return again and again to this enchanting land of our ancestors.

4

Madeira, Portugal, Spain and Morocco

In the cool early November evening, we felt elation in flying from Lisbon to Madeira, Portugal's island colony off the coast of North Africa. The flight was smooth, but because of the very short runway the brakes had to be applied strongly and immediately upon touchdown. Annette's purse went flying, expelling all the mysterious little things women deem necessary to carry. Although I have been successful in persuading Annette to restrict her packing so that each of us have no luggage other than a carry-on bag, she would never leave without a purse as well. Sometimes it can be stowed in the carry-on bag, but this time she had it on her lap, and precisely when the airplane came to a screaching halt the purse was open. We were a little slow getting off the airplane ensuring we had everything the purse had disgorged, but we had no trouble getting transportation into the town of Funchal. The moon was bright and in its light could be seen a host of beautiful flowers lining the roadway. What a lovely introduction to a lovely island!

We stayed that night at the Hotel do Carmo, and the next day, sought cheaper accommodation. Finding none to our liking, we walked the streets of Funchal, window shopping and eating hot, roasted chestnuts. While wondering what to choose from a menu in a restaurant, a Dutch visitor suggested we try the long fish, the Espada. These fish are caught in very deep water—eight hundred metres. They die from the change in pressure as they are brought to the surface, so no one has seen a live one. It doesn't matter—they taste superb!

We visited an embroidery factory where designs are printed on material which is then sent out to women in the small communities all over the island to do the detailed needlework. On its return to the factory, it is washed, stretched and ironed, all by hand. Looking at the beautiful lace work hanging in the store windows of Funchal, one marvels at its beauty but is deterred from buying because of its cost. However, when you realize the tremendous number of hours spent by the women in this industry, you can appreciate the necessity of the seemingly high prices.

We took a bus to Monte, a village up the mountainside dominated by a church with two impressive towers. We went inside this church which houses many beautiful old paintings and the tomb of the last King of Austria who had come to Maderia for his health. (He died there at the age of thrity-six after contracting pneumonia.) In that church, we met some more Dutch visitors, one of whom came to talk with us when she saw our small Canadian pin. With great emotion she told us of her first love—with a Canadian soldier near the end of World War II. She had loved Canadians ever since!

Rather than taking the bus, we took the sledge ride down the hill about half way to Funchal and walked the rest of the way. The sledge is made of wood with runners which glide over the smooth cobblestones. Two men dressed in traditional costume hold ropes tied to the sledge to keep it from plunging along at breakneck speed.

That same day, we went into a wine factory. After tasting three kinds of wine, we floated out declaring Old Maumsley to be too sweet and too potent. No wonder the old English sea captains, who frequently visited here, suffered from gout due to their heavy consumption of Madeira wine.

Seeing a statue of Christopher Columbus, we enquired about him and learned that he had married the daughter of the governor of Porto Santo, a smaller island just to the north of Madeira's main island. We decided to go there the next day. The water crossing is rough and many of the passengers on the small boat became seasick, so we looked the other way, only to see a repetition of what we saw before. I do believe Annette and I were the only passengers who didn't get sick. When we docked, everyone looked quite normal and went about their business more energetically than we did.

We liked Porto Santo and, on our return to Funchal, enquired about the possibility of renting a house or an apartment there, finally deciding to put an ad in the newspaper. A girl at the newspaper office knew of someone who had a place for rent on Porto Santo. If we would come back at 6:30 p.m., he would be here to talk to us. We walked the narrow streets, dodging the cars which were obliged to take to the sidewalks to pass. We looked at the bazaars and lace shops, bought some lovely pears and limes, and at 6:30 we made our way back to the newspaper office.

As we turned into the narrow street, we heard loud groans and saw a delivery van with its right front wheel on the sidewalk. Much groaning and a whining voice were coming from the front of the vehicle. A young man was bent over the form of an elderly man laying on the cobblestones. He pulled the old man's arm and pleaded for him to get up. Annette, always compassionate, bent over the old man as the young fellow turned away throwing up his hands in despair. When Annette asked, "Are you hurt?", the old man, in perfectly good English, blustered, "Go away, woman." Shocked by this reception, Annette turned back and said, "He doesn't want help. Why?" Another young, well-dressed chap who had arrived on the scene said, "Don't worry, he isn't hurt. He is trying to get money from the van driver by faking injury." This was a reasonable assumption, for even as he talked, the old man shifted his body farther under the van and, in between loud groans, called for the police to come. This, apparently, was too much for the van driver who offered the old man money which abruptly ended the incident. The old man got up and, continuing his charade, hobbled off around the corner. I hurried and got to the corner just in time to see him dash into a wine store.

We went into the newspaper office and encountered the same young man who had explained the rip-off to Annette. He identified himself as the owner of the house on Porto Santo. He further explained the event that had just taken place outside, saying, "The van driver was an easy mark for the old charlatan because he was afraid of losing his job if he was cited in an accident. The poor fellow had little alternative but to give the old man some money before the police came." We talked about the house on Porto Santo, and since he wanted to rent the place for a three-month period at least, we voiced our regrets and returned to our room. The price was reasonable at the equivalent of $500 per month, but we did not want a place quite that isolated for so long a time. The next day, we continued our search for accommodation and found something suitable, not on Porto Santo but in the old section of Funchal, at the Apartmento Hotel Reno.

Here we had an apartment with all facilities at a reasonable price, 750 Escudos ($15 Canadian) per day, and in a convenient location. It was in the centre of the Old Town, only two and a half blocks up the hill from the pier. We were on the top floor and could go to the beautifully tailored roof garden to look out at the numerous cruise ships in the harbour. At night, we could see the strings of lights indicating the roads up the mountainside. It was from this vantage point that we saw Madeira's fantastic New Year's fireworks display. Cruise ships fill the harbour, and the tourist hotels are jammed at New Year's because of this superb attraction.

We often walked to the Av. do Mar to board buses which would take us to all parts of the island, but we learned to purchase the tickets from a little hole in the wall first. This way, specific seats on the bus are reserved and hassles are dispensed with. At Cape Giaro there are spectacular views in all directions, and at Camara de Lobos there are outstanding views of the Cape. This was a favourite spot of Winston Churchill's, where he would set up his easel to paint the scene. In the heavily populated area of Camara de Lobos live the poorest of Madeira's poor. They occupy an area with a superb view or, rather, it would be were it not for their crowded conditions. Walking through the narrow streets to come to the best viewpoint of all, you are almost overcome by the smell of urine. Authorities have tried for years to relocate these people in sanitary, government-assisted accommodation, but they refuse to move.

One day back in Funchal, we spoke to a woman coming out of an impressive looking building to ask if it was a consulate of some sort. She informed us that it was a medical clinic run by the Red Cross. She thought we were Americans and, in her decidedly English accent, told us her name was Maria. She had unwittingly adopted her accent from the many English tourists she talked to. She revealed that she was an American, having been born in New York City. She had married a French-Canadian from Montreal who had retired from an active career in construction. At the age of forty-five, Louis had brought Maria to Madeira some fifteen years ago to live out their retirement in a place where the cost of living was very cheap. She said she revelled in the beauty of her surroundings at first, but her husband's life of idleness had made him very old and very dull. As a result, she had come to dislike Madeira and all it stood for. All she had left were nostalgic memories of New York and a husband who was feeble at age sixty. Apparently, either loyalty to him or lack of sufficient funds precluded any possibility of a return to North America. She begged us to accompany her to her home for further conversation over a cup of tea. We declined initially, but since we were curious about Louis we accepted the invitation. At times it was necessary to walk single file to avoid the cars on the narrow streets leading to Maria's shabby quarters above a pastry shop. The unpainted door had wide cracks in the wooden panels and the iron knocker, in the shape of a human hand holding a ball, was dangling uselessly. Inside, the well-worn steps creaked noisily as we ascended to a hallway showing some remnants of wallpaper here and there on the dull, gray plaster. At the end of an electric wire from the dirty ceiling hung a bulb with a drip of glass on the bottom indicating its age. I wondered if it still worked but, seeing no switch, I couldn't try it out and I felt Maria might feel embarrassment if I asked. Daylight from a small, grimy window provided sufficient light for Maria to find the door to her apartment.

"Louis, I've brought some people from your country, from Canada", Maria announced in what seemed an effort to arouse something of interest to him. Louis, sitting in an old chair whose upholstery was much the worse for wear, scarcely shifted his huge bulk. He removed his hand from the wine glass on the table beside him and extended it as I offered to shake hands. It was, indeed, like shaking hands with the proverbial dead fish. He made no effort to bend his fingers as I clasped that mass of pulpy flesh, nor did he make any effort to stand. As I bent over him, decidedly unpleasant odors came up to my nostrils. This man was a far cry from the muscular person who at one time had put together the steel girders in many of the skyscrapers of New York. The only muscles he used now were those needed to reach for the wine glass.

As we walked back to our lovely apartment at the Hotel Reno, I asked, "How does Maria stand living with that man? How can she put up with the smell of him?" Annette replied, "Well, Maria told me Louis' income is small and his addiction to Madeira wine takes a large portion of it. She also said that, as a side effect of an operation she had many years ago, she had lost her sense of smell!"

That evening, we ate in the Casa de Carochinka English restaurant and had roast beef and Yorkshire pudding. While it was acceptable, it did not reach the standards of the same dish served anywhere in England. As a general rule, I have found that local foods prepared in traditional ways are consistently good and always more reasonably priced. Although we occasionally ate lunch at one of the posh hotels, we usually ate in our apartment, at small restaurants in downtown Funchal or in the villages we travelled to by local buses.

Strolling the Old Town's streets after dinner, we stopped at a fruit stand and discovered a fruit new to us, the Anana, or, as the English named it, the Custard Apple. They are grown in Madeira, are the size of your fist and are an unappetizing green colour, but the inside is delicious. Just cut them in half and eat the sweet white pulp with a spoon. It is similar to custard, so the English name seems to suit. Then there is the soft drink called "Maracuja" which is made from the locally grown passion fruit and is very good.

The Portuguese and the English have always had a good relationship, and many English tourists still come to Madeira. Consequently, most companies do business in English as well as in Portuguese. Many Dutch people come, but the Dutch are so proficient in English that the shop owners are not obliged to learn Dutch. A fair number of German people come, and because they are not as fluent in English, their numbers are not great enough to induce the study of their language. So once again, we realize that English is close to being the international language. It is the language of the air and of the sea and certainly of commerce. We are spoiled and lazy insofar as linguistics are concerned. We can get by with our unilingual position, sign language and a few token words in local languages.

Funchal has a lovely opera house called the Municipal Theatre where I attended a performance of the Stockholm Sinfonietta and the Stockholm Philharmonic Brass Ensemble. I shared a loge with three German people, only one of whom could speak English, but the excellent music was the common language we could understand and appreciate.

Another common language is found in art. Funchal has a museum of religious art which includes some paintings by Flemish masters. The floors in the museum are unique. They are patterned of Tal wood, wood from an extinct Madeira tree. From our apartment we could look into the window of a nearby building and watch an art class in progress. We witnessed a further type of artistry when we watched a man repairing a sidewalk. Pieces of black and white marble were laid in an intricate design on black sand. Gentle taps with a hammer followed by sounder tapping with a wooden block and dusting, cleaning and sweeping completed the process. Beach rocks are used in other sidewalks, some of which are whole and others cracked in two pieces. On several occasions, we watched a man cracking these rocks and sorting them as to size and perfection. The huge piles all around him attested to the many hours he had spent at this rather mundane but perilous task. Amazingly, the thumb and fingers of his left hand were fully intact.

At dusk on December 10th, the Christmas lights were turned on and remained on every night until January 7th. They lit up the pier, the mountainside and the many trees of the Old Town area. But the climax arrived on New Year's Eve when Madeira put on a really spectacular display of fireworks. Skyrockets simultaneously leapt into the air from many positions over the mountainside, and at midnight a giant series of lights changed from 1980 to 1981. From our vantage point on the roof garden, we and the other guests of the hotel had a delightful and unimpeded view. All day long, we had followed folklore groups around to hear and see the music and dancing. During the Christmas season, similar groups had come to Funchal from the mountain villages. We delighted in their performances.

On two occasions, we went to the casino in Funchal to try our luck at the slot machines. While the casino was new, many of these machines were out of order and we wondered if some sharp Las Vegas operator had dumped a bunch of old machines on unsuspecting buyers.

We saw breath-taking scenery on the way to Porto Moniz. At one point the bus reached a point one thousand metres above sea level, yet we clung to the side of a mountain which dropped off sharply to the sea. The road continued on through many tunnels and under two waterfalls before reaching Porto Moniz where we had an excellent meal at the Cachalote restaurant.

The village of Curral des Freiras is situated in the crater of an inactive volcano. The bus ride to it is exciting and offers beautiful panoramic views, particularly from the rim of the crater.

We had seen no rain for nearly two months in Madeira, but the morning we left, there was a downpour. Our plane taxied to the end of the runway awaiting instructions for take off. A man seated across from us was reading a newspaper when, suddenly, he got up and demanded to be allowed to leave the plane. They actually turned back and let him off. A few others left with him, and the plane taxied back out again. Again, we waited. Apparently there were two pressure systems, both a High and Low (a phenomenon so rare that chances are it will never occur in that particular area again), directly over Madeira, and they were waiting for a change. When they revved up the engines in preparation for take off, no change in the dark sky appeared evident to me, but I simply refused to worry about it. My heart gave a little flip, however, when I saw the multiple yellow lines indicating the end of that very short runway and could still feel the wheels on the ground. There was no fence at the end of Madeira's runway. It merely fell off to the sea several hundred metres below and I swear that airplane was lower than the runway for a short period of time before it gained altitude and flew up through an exceedingly thick layer of black cloud to finally emerge into beautiful, bright sunshine! We did not see the sea again until just before starting our descent to Lisbon's airport.

From the airport we drove through Lisbon, following the Tagus river, and then, crossing the big 24 do Avril Bridge, we headed south. It was lovely weather, although a little cool this mid-January day. Of considerable interest were the large stacks of cork bark. The harvesting had recently been completed and it was now awaiting shipment to the factories. Apparently, the cork oak is one of very few trees which can survive after it's bole is completely debarked. It simply grows new bark which, after several years, is harvested again.

As the tree grows older, the larger limbs also produce a harvest.

We drove south, as far as possible, to Sagres and stopped at the OS Gambozinos, a four star motel. Behind this hotel was open farm land where shepherds, dressed in heavy sheepskin ponchos and carrying crooks, tended their animals with the aid of dogs. There were no fences, and the scene was reminiscent of pictures depicting biblical times. We went into Sagres to have a lovely fish supper with a bottle of wine and a huge helping of pudding for dessert, all at a cost of 380 Escudos ($7.60 Canadian) for the two of us. Back at the motel, we fell off to sleep in superior beds and in absolute quiet, for we were the only people there. As arranged, we were awakened at 9:00 a.m. with a knock on the huge, plank door. Shortly after, a pleasant woman in a black and white maid's uniform came in with our breakfast. As we sat down to eat, the maid opened the windows and the heavy shutters to let in the sunshine. In the cool morning air, the piping hot buns with hot coffee for Annette, tea for me, and hot milk for both of us, tasted especially good. The cherry jam, the orange marmalade and the cookies were wholesomely homemade. We decided to stay another night.

It was at Sagres where Prince Henry the Navigator established a school of navigation. Remnants of his instructive techniques remain and are of interest to any geography buff. Of special interest, in a frightening sense, are the furnas, tunnels or holes in that high rocky promontory, through which you could hear the water far below and through which a person could easily fall a hundred metres to the sea. In the distance, on the southernmost point of the escarpment, is the Carpo Vincent lighthouse. It is an easy flight of steps to see the three thousand watt light bulb which shines nineteen kilometres out to sea. The bulb is crystal, was made in France and lasts for a period of two years.

The next morning after another beautiful night's sleep and another lovely continental breakfast, we filled the little car with expensive gasoline and drove to Luz where we enquired at the Luz Bay Club about rental of a villa. It was 6000 Escudos ($120 Canadian) per week. We talked with a retired English couple who had a villa there. They spoke of the wonderful walks one could take from Luz. After a time, we realized they were talking about all day tramps of several kilometres. We went on to Praira do Rocha, a very pretty area of the Algarve and one where many tourists stay, but we continued on to Portinao and Albefeira which caught our fancy. At the Avis agency there, we had a soft tire replaced and asked about accommodation. They told us of a place "you can't miss", which we couldn't locate, and found ourselves on the road to Faro, the capital of Algarve Province, where I got a wonderful picture of a nun riding side-saddle on a donkey. The nun, dressed in full habit, had an umbrella over her to shield her from the sun. A little dog followed behind on the heels of the donkey.

Our last stop was at Monte Gordo, only three kilometres from the Guadiana river which forms the border with Spain. Once there, we checked into the Guadiana Apartmento Hotel. It was so new that parts of it were not finished, but the studio apartment we got on the sixth floor overlooked the beach and the ocean. We were so happy with it and with the price of 600

Escudos ($12 Canadian) per night that we contemplated staying for some time. Since there was no need to continue renting the car and Avis does not have a branch there, we drove back to Faro, turned in our car and took the local bus back to Monte Gordo. This journey proved interesting because the bus went in and out of the small villages along the way. It was an experience that paved the way for many jaunts by bus. One of our favourites was catching the bus in front of the hotel to go to Via Real San Antonio which is a pretty town on the Portuguese side of the Guadiana River. From there we often took the ferry across the river to the Spanish town of Ayamonte. The cost of this little excursion was 24 Escudos each, 9 for the bus and 15 for the ferry.

The first time we crossed the river to Ayamonte, the Spanish customs and immigration official was speaking sternly to a little, old Spanish woman in line just ahead of us. She was shabbily dressed in what appeared to be several blouses of grayish tones, a black skirt, brown lisle stockings and well-worn nondescript shoes. She was shaking nervously as she was ordered to step aside for further inspection. When we presented our passports to this fearsome official, he broke out into a broad smile and said "Ah, Kahn-Ah-dah!" As he handed our passports back with one hand, his other hand swept down in a flourish to welcome us. I felt like asking him to go easy on the poor, old lady who, by this time, was pulling out plastic bags of beans from the folds in her clothing. For curiosity sake, we compared the price of beans in both towns, and those in San Antonio were cheaper. We compared the cost of peanut butter, too, and that was decidedly cheaper in Ayamonte, so we brought that back to Portugal. We didn't have to smuggle it. No one ever looked at anything we had.

In Ayamonte, milk is delivered to houses by donkey. Two large cans, one on each side, are carried by the donkey up to the doorways, and the milkman ladles the milk into the housewives' containers.

Back on the Portugal side in San Antonio, we went looking for the storks for which the town is noted. Great shaggy nests can be seen on top of chimneys all over town, and while we were there it was nesting time. I was attempting to get a good picture of a stork on a nest when a lady asked if I would like to enter her place to take a picture from the roof. After the picture, we enjoyed chatting with her over a cup of tea which she insisted on serving us.

After two weeks in Monte Gordo, we left for Spain, taking a bus from Ayamonte to Huelva and another bus to Seville where we caught a train which would take us to Cadiz. The total cost of the bus and train rides was 767 pesetas (approximately $13 Canadian) each. While we wanted to see Seville, we knew we would be returning since we had decided to make Monte Gordo our headquarters for the remainder of the winter. After two nights and a full day in the colourful old port city of Cadiz, we decided to move. Upon checking out of the Hotel de Francia Paria, we were astonished to learn that they did not accept traveller's cheques. It was early in the morning, much too early for the banks to open. I put aside sufficient Spanish pesetas for the bus to Algeciras, then counted the rest of my Spanish money. After paying the hotel, I had 100 pesetas left, which was exactly the cost of a taxi to the bus station.

Fortunately, we found a bank close to the bus depot in Algeciras and we could buy our ferry tickets to Ceuta, that little area of Spanish territory in North Africa surrounded by Morocco. The ferry across the Straights of Gibraltar cost only 540 pesetas ($9 Canadian) each. We were pleased with the inexpensive transportation and accommodation, so far, and elated by what we had seen, but now we felt some apprehension in this land where the customs were so different from our own.

We left Ceuta after two days of surprisingly chilly temperatures. Early in the morning of the third day, we took a local bus to the frontier, had our passports stamped by the Spanish officials, then walked across to the Moroccan side past an area where a large group of Nomads were huddled behind cardboard boxes and pieces of plastic and brown paper, in an effort to ward off the cold wind. We were told they had been there in a sort of "No Man's Land" between Spanish Ceuta and Morocco for some time since neither country wanted them. The desperate look on their faces prevented me from building up sufficient nerve to take their picture, but their sorry state is forever recorded in my memory. As we approached the Moroccan Immigration and Customs building, we saw officials run to catch some of the women from the Nomadic group who were trying to run the gauntlet of guards. They were unsuccessful, and the guards were now herding them back wielding long clubs. This display did little to allay our growing apprehension, but our passports were stamped with scarcely more than a glance at us. We emerged from that building just as the bus to Tetuan was pulling away. We had been told of the early departure time and thought we would be able to make it, but we knew now that there would not be another bus for several hours. There were cars, the drivers of which declared them to be taxis and who offered to take us to Tetuan, thirt-five kilometres away. When there was only one such vehicle left, the driver, who already had two passengers, persisted in his efforts to convince us we would be quite safe. Annette refused to get in. I argued that one of the two male passengers, the old man with the djellaba and the fez,[4] was a kindly looking, old fellow. She mumbled something about these three men taking us off the road to rob us, and who would know what had happened. I admit I was apprehensive of this particular adventure in vagabonding and had set the stage for this feeling early that morning by transferring money, the majority of our traveller's cheques and my credit card to the terry-cloth sack under my shirt, leaving only our passports and a small amount of cheques in the big wallet stuffed in my deep pants pocket. In my little wallet was the small amount of Spanish and Moroccan money I had obtained at Algecerias.

Annette finally consented, and we got in the back seat with the younger, male passenger. The big Mercedes rolled along the smooth paved road for several kilometres at high speed. Without explanation, the driver slowed down and turned off on a dirt road. I

---

[4] *The djellaba is a full length robe with a hood attached. The fez is a round, brimless hat usually made of red felt with a black tassel. Also called tarboosh.*

could feel the tension as Annette clutched my arm. About a kilometre down the dirt road, the driver turned into a courtyard and stopped while another man got into the front seat. Back on the paved road, I noticed the speedometer showing we were travelling 120 kilometres an hour. Before we got to Tetuan, we stopped again to pick up another young man who sat on the lap of the man beside me. The driver appeared to be happy; he had a very full car! When we got out in the market place at Tetuan, everyone had smiles for the picture I took of the driver and the other passengers. Even Annette was smiling, and I have the picture to prove she was happy!

We stayed only a day in Tetuan and later wished we had stayed longer for we liked it better than Tangier, but our accommodation in Tangier was both superior and cheaper. At the Hotel Miramar, Ali, the manager, sat with us in the lounge where breakfast was served. He was a pleasant man who wore his fez outside which announced his Moroccan residency, but in his business suit he could have been a successful businessman from any European or North American city. Again we chided ourselves for having let our imaginations and suspicions of foreign people run wild on our drive from the frontier to Tetuan. Our pleasant chats with Ali were stepping stones on our road to tolerance and understanding. At the Hotel Miramar, we enjoyed a beautiful dinner which resulted in some added time spent in the bathroom the next morning. The salad, the crusty bread, the fish, the steak and the dessert were all excellent. It was the best meal we had had in nearly three months, but we should have known better. Was it the fish, the steak or the salad? No doubt, it was the water in which the salad was washed. It is definitely a mistake to eat raw vegetables in many parts of the word, certainly in Tangier!

We did enjoy the Kasbahs (market places) of Tetuan and Tangier. As you walk towards these areas, you are approached by someone who wants to act as your guide. You might as well accept, for he will stay with you until you do; but agree upon a price first and don't pay until you leave the area. Remember, too, that he probably gets a commission from the stores where you make your purchases, so don't agree on a high price for his services. Bargaining is an integral part of shopping in Morocco and exceptionally good buys can be made. Annette, who years before had declared her dislike of this method of shopping, has become so accustomed to it that, even in countries where prices are fixed, she reverts to this practice and often with considerable success!

Back in Spain, we took a bus to the Malaga depot. We wanted to go on to Nerja, nineteen kilometres farther along the coast but could see no bus destined for that town. A taxi driver who badly needed a fare told us there was no bus, yet we walked a block directly to the second bus station where we saw "Nerja" above a wicket. While we were in line to buy our ticket, the face of the taxi driver appeared briefly in the window. Our eyes met and he moved off, wondering no doubt how could he have thought of this old couple as a pair of innocents when they obviously knew their way around! And how did we happen to go directly to that other bus station? Actually, it was pure chance, for we were thinking of spending the night in Malaga and going to Nerja the next day when we spied the buses.

We had heard of the beauty of Nerja from friends, and we can now attest to it ,too. We spent a few days at El Capistrano Village and walked along the highway to downtown Nerja. The rocky coastline, the picturesque little beach and the caves are all pleasant memories of our short stay. Then it was off by bus along the coast to Motril and north through the snow-capped Sierra Nevadas to Grenada. Here we splurged on accommodation, spending 4000 pesetas ($67 Canadian) for a beautiful room at the Parador in the Alhambra. We stayed two nights so that we could fully take in all its beauties, and at no time did we regret coming to Grenada. Nor did we regret going back to Seville or to Huelva and Ayamote where we saw their attractions before returning to Portugal's Monte Gordo. We struck a deal with the people at the Guadiana Hotel to rent a studio apartment for at least a month at the rate of 500 Escudos ($10 Canadian) per day with once-a-week maid service rather than the daily service we had had during our previous stay. We stayed fifty days! The weather was more favourable here in the Algarve. It was warmer than the areas of Spain or Morocco that we had visited, and Annette was happy to be back on a beach where beautiful seashells were in abundance. She is an avid collector.

Monte Gordo is a little fishing village, and while tourism is expanding considerably, commercial fishing remains the principal industry of the community. I spent many hours watching these hardy people bringing in their catches, beaching their heavy boats and going out to sea. I wondered to what extent their sons and grandsons will continue in this strenuous occupation when they see easier ways of making a living. But perhaps the call of the sea is inbred in them.

Of considerable interest, too, are the clam diggers of Monte Gordo. They do not use a shovel; instead, they walk in the shallow surf and wiggle their feet in the sand to locate the clams, then bend down to pick them up.

We walked the length of the beach and suntanned on the balcony of our fourteenth floor apartment which faced the sea. While the wind on the beach was chilly at times, we could rely on the warmth of the sun on the balcony. When we left, both of us were well tanned and the picture of health. We visited all the towns and villages in the area by riding the local buses. We loved the buses of Portugal, for smoking is not permitted on them as it is in Spain. While the inter-city buses in Spain were superior to those of Portugal, the air was a constant blue-grey haze of cigarette smoke. We enjoyed visiting Vila Real do San Antonio and Ayamonte, on opposite sides of the Guadiana River. On one such jaunt we saw the annual Carnival of Ayamonte, and on another, decided on the spur of the moment to take the train from Vila Real to Faro. We bought second class tickets but, purely by mistake, sat in the first class coach. When the conductor collected our tickets he asked us to go to the adjoining coach which was second class. The two coaches were identical! Several days later, we went to Faro again, and again we bought second class tickets, and again we sat in the first class coach but this time purposefully. Again we were asked to move to the second class. The coaches were still identical!

We went by bus to Tavira and Luz, interesting little seaside towns similar in many respects, but each with areas of special interest. The cost of these little excursions was minimal, and we got the feel of the coastal area so much better than any organized tour could have given us. We were completely unhurried since we could spend a whole day in a little village and even venture back again if we enjoyed it.

Just a block behind the hotel was a market where we bought fresh vegetables from the local farmers and meat from the butchers. These people came to recognize us and would smile and greet us warmly. They amazed us with their knowledge of English as we looked over their produce, and gave us full value for the few escudos we spent there.

We met many people from England who were spending the winter at a caravan (trailer) site near Monte Gordo. Several of them told us that the charge for their caravan site with electrical, water and sewer hookups was less then their heating bill at home. Some rented out their homes in England while they enjoyed the warmth of the Algarve. One chap, a retired medical doctor with the peculiar name of Pillow, told me this story:

"A man came to me several years ago saying he had been a patient of Dr. Smith. I said "Dr. Smith is dead". The man replied, "Yes, I know, then I got Dr. Brown", whereupon I said, "Well, he's dead too". The man said, "Yes, I know. I've had a bad heart for years and I need a doctor. Would you take me?" I said "No"."

Dr. Pillow laughed slightly more than I did. Upon hearing the reason for my early retirement and of our travels since, he said, "You'll probably outlive all your friends and relatives who stay home and worry about your exploits." I still don't know whether Pillow was really his name or whether he really was a medical doctor, but his prophesy has been partly fulfilled.

I met so many English people here that I started a little game of guessing the area in England in which they resided by listening carefully to their accents. One fellow really fooled me. He came up to me while I was standing in front of the hotel contemplating in what direction I would walk the beach. This tall man with a great mop of curly, gray hair and a rather sharp nose asked if I spoke English, and when I nodded, he asked for directions to the post office. Rather than giving him "You Can't Miss It" instructions, I walked with him. (I didn't walk the beach at all that day.) I had incorrectly guessed his origin. He came from New Zealand, half a world away from any part of England. When he learned that we had been in New Zealand on more than one occasion, he insisted we have lunch with him and his wife. Annette joined in and we drove in Colin's car to the caravan park. He and his wife were nearing the end of a two year travel experience which had commenced immediately after his retirement. They had travelled extensively through North America in a motorhome they had bought in Los Angeles and sold in Boston. Then they had flown to England and had purchased the caravan and car they had now. Their intention was to ship them with all their other purchases to New Zealand where they intended to live out the remainder of their lives. The caravan was so crowded we had to eat lunch outside. Taking up considerable space was a large electric organ! He had bolted it to the floor, for it too would be going to New Zealand. They had bought the organ in England and had towed it all over Europe so that his wife could practise during their stays in caravan parks. They would drive through Portugal, Spain and France, then take the ferry across the Channel. From London, they would fly to India, Hong Kong and Australia for short visits before arriving home exactly two years from the time they had started their journey. When they left, we promised to visit them on our next trip to New Zealand.

The fifty days in Monte Gordo went by all too fast, but it was spring and time for us to go home. I enquired at the hotel desk about reasonable places to stay in Lisbon, for we wanted to see a little more of that delightful city before leaving Portugal. The manager called Lisbon and reserved a room for us at the Pension Residente Porte on Rua Pintlaro de Chagas near the Saldanka subway stop and close to the airport bus stop at Linha Verde. We enjoyed the bus ride over the rolling hills from Villa Real do San Antonio to Beja and marvelled at the beautiful spring flowers, particularly the Redbud and Wisteria growing wild along the way. We paid 750 Escudos ($15 Canadian) at the Pension Residente Porte in comparison to the 4,000 Escudos ($80 Canadian) per day price of the nearby Sheraton. We walked a great deal in our one full day in Lisbon, ate a wonderful fish dinner and gorged ourselves on the most appetizing pastries we have ever seen. We often think back on the beauty of those pastry shop windows. They alone are incentive enough to make a return visit to Portugal!

5

On A Slow Boat to the Persian Gulf...and Beyond

Climbing the gangway of the Hellenic Challenger in the port of Houston, Texas, seemed like a dream come true, especially after experiencing the disappointment of having our deposit returned by the shipping company. We had contracted to sail from Houston to Colombo, Sri Lanka on a Greek freighter whose eventual destination was Calcutta, India. When Colombo was deleted from their ports of call, they assumed we would cancel our passage. Frantically we made a decision when we received the bad news. We would disembark at whatever port the ship would stop closest to our original destination. It was arranged that we would leave the ship in Karachi, Pakistan, where we would find ourselves in the company of a king!

Now, as we neared the top of the gangway, a seaman offered to take our bags and to find the steward for us. No sooner had we stepped on board when Steve, the steward, appeared and showed us to the lounge. He served tea and called for his assistant, Niko, who scurried away to prepare our stateroom. The stateroom had barely enough space for the two single beds and the clothes closets and luggage storage. While there were private facilities—toilet, wash basin and shower—it would be difficult to classify our accommodation as first class, the designation given in Hellenic's brochure. The food, though, was very good throughout the voyage as we were soon to find out at lunch that first day on board. Steve showed us to one of two tables in the dining room and soon we were joined by the captain and the chief engineer, both of whom spoke English reasonably well.

The captain was of medium height and build. He had a full head of coal-black hair and a beard to match except for a few gray streaks which added character to his face. Under heavy eyebrows, his eyes seemed to shine with excitement and good humour as he talked incessantly of his friends, mostly female, in different ports around the world. We were amazed at the quantity of food he could consume, for he ate twice as much as I did and talked considerably more. And he seemed to relish the food but no wonder. First there was fish and crabmeat, lots of it and very good. This was followed by octopus soup. Now, I am not a lover of octopus, but that soup was so good that I felt like asking for more. I was glad I refrained, for the main course featured delicious, tender New York steak. A plate of several varieties of cheese and a large bowl of fresh fruit were placed before us after this sumptuous meal. The captain popped some pieces of cheese into his mouth as he rose from the table. He asked the chief engineer to introduce us to the other passengers and then excused himself, presumably to look after some pressing matter, and he hurried away.

The clean-shaven chief engineer continued with his lunch. He ate slowly. He ate possibly half as much as I did and, therefore, no more than one-quarter of that of the captain. He was of similar stature to the captain but of a decidedly different nature. He gave me the impression of being steady and reliable. In compliance with the captain's request, he introduced us to the four ladies and one man at the other table. All were experienced in travelling on freighters. Three of the ladies had spent many winters at sea. The other lady and the man were from Mexico. He was a medical doctor and a person of great linguistic ability, capable of speaking many languages fluently. He was an interpreter for his vivacious wife who spoke only Spanish. He had been born in Thessalonki of Greek parents, but the family had left when Pablo was young and they settled in Mexico. The parents had wrung out a living by selling fruits and vegetables in a Mexican market place while young Pablo worked at any job he could find and studied hard, eventually becoming a medical doctor. His industrious attitude prevailed throughout his life and, while he continued to practise medicine, he branched into real estate and development in Arizona, making himself financially independent. I liked the man immediately and, after several years, continue to keep in touch with him. He and his wife would come to share experiences with Annette and me for the remainder of the trip.

Of the three ladies, one was a spinster, one a widow and one a divorcee. Each had a separate stateroom and each of those staterooms had a generous supply of their favourite brand of liquor bought on a wholesale basis without tax or duty charges. It was bought to last their entire voyage of approximately 150 days. The youngest of the three, the spinster, must have been nearing seventy since she was a matron of a soldier's hospital overseas during World War II. She would not reveal her age. The eldest proudly announced that she was eighty-two, and that this was her nineteenth freighter cruise. Shortly after our voyage began, this little lady coyly invited me to play a game of cards with her. I barely won the first two games when she announced she owed me a little money, and she would have to try to win it back. I professed I was not playing for money and declined her payment, guessing she was setting me up for the kill later on. None of the other passengers would play with her, and when I asked if she was a card shark, they would only laugh knowingly. But she was a cute, old lady and in evident good health. We enjoyed her company.

The widow was a sweet, docile person who must have been a beauty in her day. She had children and grandchildren and loved them, but she was determined not to be a burden upon them, so she had been travelling on freighters every winter since the death of her husband with whom she had shared a wonderful life. She had a delightful personality, but she was convinced the ship's captain disapproved of her travelling instead of being at home minding the grandchildren in the style of eastern European grandmothers. She had met the spinster on an earlier trip, and since then they had arranged subsequent cruises together.

The spinster was quite the opposite of the widow. It was evident from the start that she still had the same thought processes as the matron of a soldier's hospital. Her hair was piled on the top of her head and held with two severe combs. Her head, with its multiple chins, rested on top of her torso since no neck was visible. Her large face was punctuated with rather small eyes set close together above a small, yet bulbous, nose. Her mouth was large, and incongruously from it came many a hearty laugh, usually heard at the end of one of her stories. When she was reading, however, she demanded silence, and she read a great deal, so I tried to have my reading time coincide with hers. Only occasionally did I look up to see the Mexican doctor plodding through a huge medical journal and the spinster, with her half-lens glasses down to the bulb of her nose, deeply engrossed in a novel.

At the evening meal that first day, we were first to arrive in the dining room and sat at the second table, thinking someone else would be chosen to sit at the captain's table, but Steve told us we were to sit there and sit there we did for the seventy days we were on board. And the other passengers sat at the other table. We all had the same food, but often Greek beer would be served to all four people at our table and water served to the others, although it was maintained that everyone, passengers and crew, ate the same fare. The ship's officers, other than the captain and chief engineer, ate in an adjoining dining room, and the rest of the crew ate on a lower deck.

The other passengers had boarded at New York since they had paid the $7,000 each for the full cruise from New York to India and back to the first U.S.A. port. Houston was to be the last port of departure in the U.S.A. when we made the booking; since we were going to Karachi only, we were to board the ship there. Our fare was $2,000 each. In our innocence, we thought we had to be in Houston at the time the ship arrived there. We had no way of knowing it would be in port eight days.

The last passenger to board was a bachelor who had been on twenty-three previous freighter cruises. He was truly a lover of the sea. Like the spinster, he would not divulge his age, but he was not like the spinster in disposition. He was the only smoker among the passengers. He smoked one big cigar a day and always went out on deck choosing a spot where the wind would carry his smoke away from the ship. He was the most inoffensive, passive and silent person I have ever met. He did not ignore other people and would answer their questions in a soft, slow voice, but he never opened a conversation nor raised his voice. He was a loner. He had apparently learned to let the world go by and had no desire or conviction to change it. He had an aura of contentment. He loved to watch the loading of the ship, so we found something in common.

I spent hours watching the stevedores on the dock and on the ship. Some operated the big fork lifts, some operated the little fork lifts, and others operated the huge cranes on the dock. Even the ship's own cranes were operated by the stevedores. These were used mainly to load the thousands of bags of wood fibre plaster bound for Jedda, Saudi Arabia. The ship's cranes were operated, too, when the frozen foods, also bound for Saudi Arabia, were loaded into the refrigeration hold of the ship. The large dock cranes were operated when long pipes to be used in oil drilling were loaded. The first mate had the responsibility of working with the head stevedore to balance the loads put on the ship. This can be an extremely crucial caution, for if a freighter is loaded haphazardly it may fare badly in a storm at sea. Days passed and each day resulted in the loading of plaster, heavy cable, pipes, boxes of pressed turkey and boxes of oxtails. There were cranes loading cranes and other heavy equipment on board, and just as we thought the ship couldn't handle any more, along came containers which were piled on deck two deep. Surely, we thought, this would be the last, but then we learned that the ship would stop at Galveston to take on five thousand tons of rice. Apparently, there was still some room in the holds.

While we were still in Houston, we had an opportunity to visit the Seaman's Club one night. The club is run by Catholics, but a van sponsored by Baptists took us there. Apparently the Catholic bus had been barred from the docks for some reason, although no one could remember why. While there was little or nothing for people our age to do at the Seaman's Club, it was interesting to see the faces of the seafarers from many parts of the world. We also walked some of the streets near the docks. We were advised not to do this at night since it was an area where many hold-ups and murders had occurred in the past. We were somewhat amused to see, on the corner of 75th Street and "O" Avenue, two buildings of contrasting interests. One was the "Port O' Call Seaman's Mission" with a huge mural of man torn between the path to heaven or the path to hell. The other building had signs "Totally Nude Girls", "Dancing", "Bar" and "Girls, Girls, Girls"!

One evening, we were on the bridge deck watching the preparations for departure. The pilot was on board and on duty in the wheelhouse. Suddenly the horn blew with a terrific blast. Annette had been the cause—she had accidently leaned against the red button! Fortunately, the captain was beside her and he assured us all that no harm was done. We were ready to get under way. We headed for the turning basin and saw the numerous oil refineries and smelled the terrible pollution. The captain invited me into the wheelhouse and I could hear the pilot say "Port 10" and the helmsman reply "Port 10" as he swung the wheel over, then "Starboard 10" or "Amidships" would come from the pilot and the helmsman would echo these directions each time. The captain told me that such directions took place on ships all over the world because English is the language of sea navigation.

I mentioned my concern with the overloading of the ship, since it had appeared there was precious little left on the graph, indicating a full load. The Captain told me that it would be alright when we were out at sea, that a ship rides higher in salt water than in fresh water.

If you've never been to Galveston, you will be fascinated by it on your first trip. We had been there before, yet Galveston was still a pleasure to us. There is an air about it of years gone-by, despite the new highrises and the huge seawall. It was to be our last place to walk on land, other than a cement dock, for forty days.

We left the port of Galveston and anchored in Galveston Roads, a 'parking lot' for freighters avoiding the high costs of docking while they secure the cargo on deck and prepare for the ocean voyage. On the first day at sea, the captain explained the chartroom and showed me how to plot a course. Every day thereafter, I would go to the chartroom shortly after noon hour to obtain our longitudinal and latitudinal position. On a large chart put up in the lounge I would move a pin indicating our progress. Old Paul, the veteran freighter passenger, also went to the bridge every day and obtained the nautical miles travelled in the previous twenty-four hour period which averaged 315. He put this information up beside the chart. It was not until we were about to leave the ship in Karachi that I learned Old Paul, as we affectionately called him, had done this, as well as showing the ship's position on the chart, for most of his previous voyages. Yet he had not complained nor even mentioned this fact to me during the entire voyage.

The captain took me down to the engine room and I marvelled at the big German-made 8,200 h.p. MAN engine, nine cylinders with pistons so large a man can get inside them. It drives a shaft of solid steel fifty-one centimetres in diameter, which in turn drives the propeller. Piston rings are normally replaced every three thousand hours, and while this is being done on one piston, the engine continues to run on the other eight cylinders. This engine burns twenty-two tons of fuel oil per day, so it is costly to have delays. The captain altered course on more than one occasion which added considerable time to our crossing, but he was nervous about our load. A huge crane destined for Yanbu, Saudi Arabia, had been loaded on the deck and had shifted during heavy seas in the mid-Atlantic. So instead of going straight towards Gibraltar, he headed towards the Canary Islands, then turned north past Madeira where we hit some swells. The ship rolled at the precise moment I was about to sit in a lounge chair. I held onto the chair as I went for a ride on my rear across the floor of the lounge. It was so gentle I was not hurt. I almost enjoyed it. We continued to experience the same swells until we came close to Gibraltar. We all felt relief when we passed the "Rock", but the crew reminded us that the Mediterranean can be rougher than the Atlantic.

One day, Steve and Niko gave us an exhibition of Greek folk dancing which seemed quite strenuous. They were both a little breathless as they finished. Niko said he would be in better physical condition soon since he had to leave the ship to enter the Greek army. All young men are required to serve for three years. Steve, on the other hand, mentioned that he would be retiring in three years. At forty-two, he seemed too young to retire, but he reminded us that he was often at sea for twenty months at a time and worked every day.

The chief engineer, the quiet, soft-spoken man who took everything in stride, told me the engine of the ship was a continual problem. This became evident when we were adrift for many hours in the mid-Atlantic and again in the Mediterranean Sea for engine repairs. The captain was always excited and distraught during these periods, while the chief engineer was completely unruffled. Meanwhile, two black balls were run up the mast, the signal for other ships to stay clear of a vessel without power. I asked the chief engineer about the problem, but he didn't give me any concrete answer. He just shrugged and said the Hellenic company had pulled the old ship out of the "graveyard" and the refit was poorly done. This made us wonder about other aspects of the ship!

There was no lifeboat drill during the seventy days we were on board. The other passengers, all experienced in freighter travel, were not only shocked at this but also at the lack of cleanliness of the ship and crew. The old ladies evinced their disapproval when Annette cleaned an area of the deck just outside our staterooms. The captain heard about it, and in a very short time the bosun and some of the crew were hosing down the decks!

As we neared the eastern end of the Mediterranean, the speed of the ship had to be drastically reduced due to very strong winds which sent great sprays of water over the decks. The captain altered course again to avoid the storm centred around Crete and Cyprus. He stayed close to the shores of Libya as we celebrated Christmas Eve with Greek sweets, nuts and wine and the singing of Christmas carols. On Christmas Day, there was so much food and wine of such excellence that we gave up all resolves to restrain our intake. The ship was rusty, it was greasy and dirty and the crew was much the same, but the steward and his staff spared no expense or effort in providing the best in gastronomical delights. This applied not only for the Christmas season but for the whole voyage. And the captain was very cautious in avoiding storms, so we felt safe on our dirty old "Tramp Steamer" as Annette dubbed it one day in the lounge. The other passengers, without exception, said that, except for the food, it was the worst ship they had ever been on. Even Old Paul nodded assent.

As we anchored off Port Said, Egypt, and waited to form a convoy to go through the Suez Canal, a chandler ship came alongside. On board this little ship were the people who determine the position the big ships will take in the convoy, and from it a long pole was thrust upward to the lower deck of our ship. At the end of the pole was a bag into which the steward placed a carton of American cigarettes and a bottle of whiskey. This little bribe ensured us a favourable position in the first convoy. A pilot soon came aboard and we moved out before other ships that had been at anchor when we arrived!

After we moved into line at Port Said, we anchored in the middle of the channel. Swarms of little boats headed for us and the other big ships. These little boats held merchants and their wares which they spread out on the decks for passengers and crew to choose from and purchase. The wares were as varied as the old-time general store. Besides all kinds of crafts, there were brilliantly coloured ladies' garments and even hardware items. Of special interest to us were the

Arabian headgear, beaded belts and costume jewelry. These merchants are enterprising people when it comes to selling and stealing. The captain had warned us to lock our stateroom doors and to be vigilant at all times, and this proved true when we saw the smiling, polite and gracious hawker, from whom we had bought many souvenirs, emerge from the area of the staterooms which were on a higher deck from where he had laid out his goods. He rushed down the ladder and into the small boat waving good-bye with a lovely open face. But these are not the only con-men in Egypt. As well as the pilot, there is a "guard" whom the big ships are obliged to take on to guide them through the canal. This guard exacts a toll from the hawkers as they board the ship. Without a "donation" from the hawkers, the guard would send them back to shore.

Then there is the regulation that two small power boats must be hoisted on deck to be lowered with lines to take to shore in case the ship becomes disabled during its passage through the canal. The two men, who came aboard with the boats, put up a tent over their boats and slept there. The smaller of the two was caught by Niko, the assistant steward, trying the door of our stateroom. We had kept it locked as had the other passengers, but later a careless member of the crew reported the loss of some jewelry he had bought for one of his girlfriends. At Suez, near the end of the Canal, the little boats are lowered to the water, one at a time. When the second one was almost at the water, the same little man who had tried to enter our stateroom brought out a knife and cut the nylon rope above the swivel hook. At Suez, an official came aboard to give clearance for the ship to proceed and blatantly asked for his present. In total on the trip, seven bottles of whiskey and fifteen cartons of cigarettes were given out as bribes!

As we came through the Gulf of Suez, we could see the glow of the gas burning off the oil wells. As we came into the Red Sea, it was breaking day. I had been awakened by great showers of sparks going by the window of our stateroom and had got up to see the ship's smoke-stack burning like a chimney fire. The chief engineer shrugged and said, "No problem". Later, as we neared Yanbu, the Saudi Arabian port where the huge crane was to be unloaded, the radio man failed to contact the pilot on shore. These were new waters to this crew. The captain had never been east of Suez and was nervous about dealing with the Arab nations. His nervousness was compounded by his decision to proceed inside the reef, and he reacted violently when his first mate pointed out the error. The captain's temperamental personality was revealed when he snatched a pair of expensive binoculars from the hands of the first mate and threw them over the side. As he turned he saw the look of amazement on my face, and his remorse was immediate. He apologized—not to his first mate, but to me!

They finally located the navigational markers they had sought when they returned to the open sea. Since our radio was out of order, signals were sent up the mast, and another ship close by transmitted our plight to the shore. After seven hours of laying to, a pilot boat arrived and the pilot agreed that someone on shore must have seen our yellow and blue flag indicating a request for a pilot. He was not very complimentary of his employers but stayed because the pay was exceptionally good. The pilot, who was British, declined the offer of a bottle of Scotch whiskey because he said the Saudis would throw him in jail if they caught him with it. He also informed us that an armed guard would be stationed at the gangway to ensure none of the passengers or crew would go ashore. And sure enough, a guard armed with a sub-machine gun came aboard with a ship's agent, who inspected the crane, and an official customs man, who sealed the door of the cupboard containing liquor with a wide band of sticky tape on which there was a considerable amount of Arabic writing. The door also had a huge padlock on it. All this to ensure no spirits would be consumed by anyone on board while the ship was in a Saudi port. The older ladies had anticipated this action. They had been in Moslem ports in Africa so had experienced this denial of what they considered their rights. Accordingly, they had brought along empty Listerine bottles which they had filled with their bourbon the night before. They had their "Happy Hour" in their staterooms.

The next morning, fascinated with the guards on the dock, I was about to take their picture when shouts and waving of the sub-machine gun convinced me I should put my camera out of sight. A guard came up the gangway with his finger on the trigger of his gun and ordered all cameras and binoculars to be left in the stateroom. So I have no pictures of the spotlessly clean and excellent new dock areas of Yanbu, but later on at Jedda, our next stop on the Red Sea, I took some surreptitiously.

Docked behind us in Jedda was a ship that had gone through the gale in the Eastern Mediterranean area, the storm we had sought to avoid by hugging the coast of Libya. The Penny S, a ship of Panamanian registry, had severe damage to the cargo on its deck. Four containers, which had been piled three deep, had crashed inward onto new cars and trucks on the deck, and nine containers had been lost over the side, taking the ship's railing with them. While the stevedores were busy unloading our ship for the five days we were in port, we saw no similar action on the Penny S, so evidently the controversy of unloading damaged goods can result in costly delays. I took a picture of the Penny S from inside our ship—through a doorway to the deck!

It was in Jedda that we experienced our first confrontation with the captain and the ship's agents. The captain issued an order to the effect that the crew could leave the ship for a period of three hours and that the passengers would not be allowed to leave. I was upset because we had visas for Saudi Arabia, so I wrote a letter to the Canadian Embassy in Jedda and demanded that it be posted. This created quite a stir and I was called into the captain's office where I was told my wife and I would be allowed to go ashore for a period of three days in accordance with the visa stamped in our passports. We planned to go the next morning. Both the captain and the agent seemed relieved when I agreed not to send the letter to the Canadian consulate. We had no intention of staying ashore three days since we could have only one visit and we knew how expensive the hotels were in Jedda. In any case, we simply wanted to see the place. The next morning as we were preparing to leave, I was again called into the captain's office and the ship's agent triumphantly pointed out that my visa had expired and, therefore, I couldn't go ashore. True enough, because of the many delays, firstly in our departure from Houston and in the extra long sea voyages, we had arrived in Jedda after the date stamped on the visa by the Saudi consul in Ottawa. I resolved that in future I would read every word of a visa as soon as I received it. Some of the other passengers, particularly the doctor, were disturbed by not being able to see the city of Jedda, but Old Paul didn't say a word. He was content to smoke his daily cigar out on deck, moving occasionally as the wind shifted so as to ensure his smoke didn't offend anyone.

I took another forbidden picture of the dock area as a pure white pilgrim ship came in to dock across the harbour from the freighters. These ships arrive from all over the Moslem world bringing pilgrims to Jedda. These pilgrims then take land transportation to Mecca, a scant sixty kilometres east.

The frozen food, pressed turkey, oxtails and rice were unloaded. The stevedores, engaged in unloading the rice, worked and looked like slaves. They appeared to come from many eastern nations. Some were Filipino, and from one of these I bought a hook which they use to grab the burlap bags of rice down in that sweating hold. We talked with several of them and all expressed, in good English, a desire to go to North America. One especially handsome young man, Mario, was quite persistent in wanting to marry one of the older ladies, the widow. Perhaps he saw the vestiges of the beauty she once was, or more likely he saw a ticket to the land of his dreams. He had never been anywhere except Jedda and the Philippine town in which he was born where he had been recruited for labour by the Multinational Recruitment Group of Saudi Arabia. This company sends recruiters to Bangladesh, India, Pakistan, Philippines, Sri Lanka and Thailand to round up labour forces for the oil-rich nation. Mario and all the other Filipinos in his group were in Saudi Arabia on a block visa. They were not treated as individuals. They ate and slept on an old ship anchored in a remote part of the harbour, and in the three months they had been in Jedda they had not been allowed away from their place of work or the harbour area. These were modern-day slaves. No wonder Mario schemed to find ways to leave. His dream was to be a card dealer in Las Vegas!

Annette was now anxious to leave Jedda, too. Her elbows were becoming sore from leaning on the rail watching the stevedores at work. She longed for some physical activity after so many days of idleness. She also longed for some good old apple pie, so she asked the captain if she could make one for the passengers. Abiding by the tradition that everyone on board is entitled to the same rations, he agreed, on the condition that she make a pie for all the crew as well! Appealing for help in peeling the large number of apples such a large pie would require, Annette ran into opposition from the older ladies. However, Ruth, the doctor's wife, enthusiastically accompanied her to the galley. There was no shortening, only butter with which to make the pastry. Since there was no temperature gauge on the oven, the cook would put his hand in that chamber periodically to determine the heat. Finally he announced it was ready and he assisted in getting the pie into the oven. This was no ordinary pie. The only dish considered big enough to provide a serving for thirty-eight people measured eighteen by thirty inches! It was not a pie up to Annette's standards either, for the crust was not flaky and the apples were underdone, the result of wrong ingredients and the absence of a heat regulating device. Nevertheless, it was a welcome change from the Greek diet and the making of it provided Annette and Ruth with a welcome change of scene.

On the morning of our last day in Jedda, I was standing on the lower deck watching the activity on the dock when the armed guard, who was seated at the bottom of the gangway, motioned for me to come down. I had made that a special spot from which to take in the comings and goings of the dock workers. Each day I had noted the presence of the guard and each day he had looked in my direction. I now wondered what was on his mind and, curious and a little apprehensive, I descended the gangway. He questioned my nationality, finding it hard to believe I was a Canadian on a Greek freighter. It seems he thought I was a member of the crew, for he wondered when I would be taking shore leave. Just then, the ship's electrician came down the gangway for his three hour respite in town and I asked him if he would bring back a one riyal coin for my collection. The guard dug in his pocket and came up with a one riyal banknote, but I explained that I collected only coins. He dug in his pocket a second time and brought forth two one-quarter riyal coins which he insisted I take. Although of considerably less value, I could find only three one cent Canadian coins. He would accept only one of them, the shiny one. I asked him about prices of some goods in Jedda and, as an example, he told me that gasoline was .20 a litre and drinking water was $2.00 a litre!

As we pulled out of the harbour, I took more pictures from my hiding place inside. No one was sorry to leave and head south into the Red Sea.

A stiff headwind, created by the mountains on each side of the narrow passage, is common through the Strait of Bab el-Mandeb. We had passed islands belonging to Ethiopia on our starboard side and Al Hudaydah, Yemen, on our port side. Now as we came to the Straits, I gazed at Barim Island, the guardian of the southern entrance to the Red Sea. We saw no activity on Barim which used to be administered by England. It is now dominated by the U.S.S.R. since the island belongs to Democratic Yemen. Then, on our starboard side was Djibouti where the U.S.A. have naval and air force bases. As we came into the Gulf of Aden, we saw a low flying airplane coming straight toward us which created considerable excitement and tension among passengers and crew. I had my camera so I waited for the plane to come into the frame. At the last moment it veered off and we noticed that it was American. The captain told us he had been told to expect inspection in these waters, and shortly thereafter, the menacing shape of a warship came into view. It was coming up fast on our port side with the shores of Yemen in the background, so we assumed it was Russian. The captain excitedly ordered a Greek flag to be run up the mast and was surprised to get the warship's reply showing that, like the plane, it too was American. They apparently monitor all traffic in and out of the Red Sea.

We had three memorable nights of travel in the Gulf of Aden and in the Arabian Sea. After the excitement of our inspections by the American military, we had calm seas and idyllic, clear, starlit nights. We sat out

Robbers Bridge, Lorna Doone country, Exmoor, England.

The Old Mill 'Bed & Breakfast', Lake District near Kendall, England.

Piper at Glen Coe, Scotland.

Brugge, Belgium, "The Venice of the North".

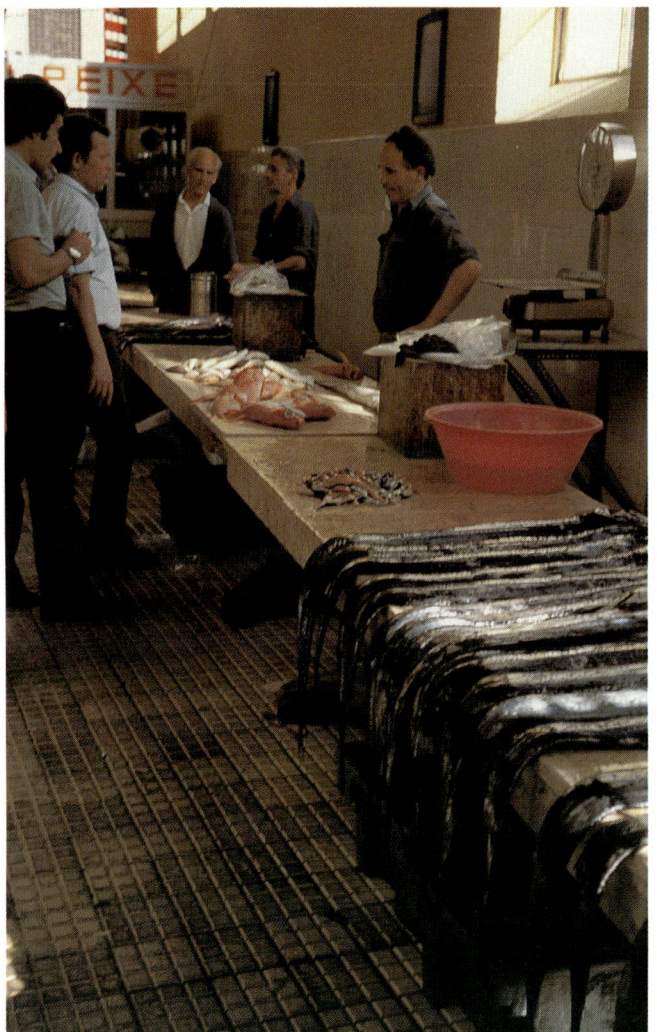

The residence of Christopher Columbus in Porto Santo, Madeira; built before 1492.

Funchal Fish Market, Funchal, Madeira. Note Espada (the long fish caught at depths of 800 metres) in the foreground.

Splitting rocks to lay sidewalks in Funchal. Madeira.

Annette with taxi driver and other passengers after wild ride to Tetuan, Morocco.

Street scene in Tetuan, Morocco.

Cork trees south of Lisbon, Portugal.

Shepherds near Sagres, Portugal.

Sardines at Portimao, Portugal.

Milkman's donkey in Ayamonte, Spain.

Cemetery in Ayamonte, Spain.

Annette (in disguise) with Egyptian hawker aboard the Hellenic Challenger.

Pilot coming aboard at Port Said, Egypt.

on deck for long periods at night with the Mexican doctor and his wife, gazing at the sky which appeared to hold so many more stars than the sky we see at home. Their brilliance bedazzled us, and as we reclined in our deck chairs, Dr. Pablo showed brilliance in his knowledge of the constellations.

We came into the Mina Quabos area late at night in mid-January and anchored there until early the following morning when the pilot brought us into port. All the passengers were convinced there would be no trouble going ashore here in Oman, particularly because the pilot had told us it was a free country and we could take pictures of anything. We were surprised, therefore, when the captain came to the head of the gangway and told us no passengers could go ashore. The entire crew would be allowed ashore in shifts for a period of twelve hours. When we questioned his authority, he said it was the immigration officers who had given the order. When he stopped me from taking a picture, my anger mounted and, seeing a Dutch ship docked next to ours, I descended the gangway and walked toward it. An officer of the ship, dressed in smart, very clean white shirt and shorts, replied to my questions in excellent English. While his ship no longer carried passengers, he told me that if it had, they would be allowed ashore. He suggested I take my passport to the guard at the port's gate where he was sure I would have no trouble. On the way back to our ship, I asked a Pakistani on the dock and he confirmed that all I needed to go into town was my passport. The steward had taken our passports for safekeeping when we boarded the ship in Houston, so back on the ship I went to the captain's office to demand it be returned to me. The captain had left the ship to go to the agent's office in town, and the second mate was in charge. He told me that all passports had been left with the immigration office in the port. Off I went, but this time accompanied by Annette, the Mexicans and one little old lady, the eighty-two year old divorcee. The other older ladies couldn't be found, and Old Paul declined to join this little, mutinous group. He resignedly accepted the captain's order. We marched to the immigration office and with little trouble obtained our passports. On we went to the gate, where the guard looked at only one passport—mine—and produced a paper for me to sign to the effect that I was responsible to ensure the return of five people within twenty-four hours! As we walked into town, a car coming toward us stopped. It was the captain and he was quite perturbed at our presence. I very briefly told him the sequence of events in the past two hours, and as we continued into town, he got back in the agent's car.

Muscat was so different from anything we had seen on any of our previous trips, and the five of us felt like children let out of school. Other than my short visit with the guard on the dock at Jedda, none of us had been ashore for forty days!

We were back on the ship in plenty of time for the evening meal. The captain did not appear, and when I told the chief engineer of our adventures of the day, he smiled whimsically and, with a circular motion of his index finger, indicated he thought the captain was a little insane. Later, I was called into the captain's office. He vowed it was not his fault, but as he admitted his fear of the Arabs, great tears flowed down his face. I felt compassion but worried a little as to his stability. I left his office thinking we would not meet with any further obstacles in going ashore at the ports we were to visit in the Persian Gulf.

To relieve the tension of my interview with the captain, I thought I would relax with the English language newspaper I had bought on shore. I was paying scant attention to what I was reading, thinking back on the day's events and thinking of the dress conditions of our ship as compared to the Dutch ship and to those of the Omanian Navy. I had learned that day of the make-up of the Omanian Navy wherein the officers are British and the other ranks are Omanian. It was still daylight when I had seen one of their ships steaming out to sea and I was reflecting on this strange aspect of its crew when I read of the possible bombing of a tanker off Iran's Kharg island. The reporter speculated that the fire on board the tanker may have been caused by something other than an Iraqui bombing mission. So much for relaxing while reading a newspaper!

The next day as we sailed towards Dubai in the United Arab Emirates, only the chief engineer appeared at our table in the dining room, so we knew the captain had not gotten over what he probably considered was a challenge to his authority. It was only then that we learned that this was his first voyage as captain, although he had been qualified for this position for many years. As we docked early the following day, we wondered how the captain would conduct himself here. Would he assist us in going ashore or would he put barriers in our way? The answer was not long in coming, for the agent came aboard shortly after we docked, and I was called into the captain's office. Sensing a further confrontation, Dr. Pablo accompanied me, and this time it was the agent who said the passengers could not go ashore because of immigration rules. After a rather heated argument, I said we would test that by going to the immigration office and, furthermore, I would tell them of our conversation. The agent asked that I give him half an hour to try to make arrangements. I consented. In less than fifteen minutes he was back with immigration officials, including a photographer who took our pictures and gave us several free prints. What a happy time!

The Mexicans shared a taxi with us, and off we went to see the sights of Dubai. Our taxi driver was also our guide and he took us to the Suq, the old town of colourful shops and more colourful people. Beggars, black-clad women, turbaned dark skinned men, oil-rich Arabs, water taxis, push carts and powerful Mercedes cars all blended into a colourful melange to enthrall and delight us. We ate different food—food cooked in something other than olive oil—and while not as good as the ship's food, we relished the difference. We drove through the new part of the city, past embassies and very rich homes. Near the President's Palace was a huge compound of four houses of similar structure. They were the dwellings of the president's son who has the four wives he is entitled to under Moslem law.

Our next port was Bahrain where we had no confrontation of any sort. We left the ship in the morning and returned in time for the evening meal. We took a taxi, again sharing it with our Mexican friends, and toured that little island nation. We saw some of the industry of Bahrain—the making of traps for fish and crabs and the construction of a dhow out of oak and mahogany. The relatively new museum of Bahrain contained antiquities dating back five thousand years. These had been recovered in recent excavations. The pride of their heritage showed on the faces of the museum's curators as we complimented them on their recent work. The ladies were fascinated with the large array of gold objects in a great number of stores dealing solely in gold, but my interest tended more to getting a picture of a man smoking a hookah (the water pipe) and of a mosque with a massive dome covered in gold leaf. At specific angles, the sun's reflection on this dome formed a distinctive cross and I mused that there would be many Christians who would see some significance in this. We went in to see the elegance of the Regency International Hotel and to get our English language newspaper. We saw the old ladies. They had spent their entire shore time in this hotel sampling the bar's offerings. Old Paul had shared a taxi with them but was nowhere in sight. When we returned to the ship, we found him on the bridge deck smoking his beloved cigar.

At Damman, Saudi Arabia's new port on the Persian Gulf, four big wooden cases weighing five tons each were taken out of one of the holds, the one at the ship's stern. These cases were marked "HANDLE WITH EXTREME CAUTION" and the port authorities made the ship fly the red danger flag. The silent one, Old Paul, commented that people from the atomic centre in Oak Ridge, Tennessee, were in Saudi Arabia. I mused again...was there a connection? Was this part of the cause for the captain's extreme behaviour? There had been rumours among the crew of other goods with mysterious markings taken off in Jedda—they thought they were guns of some sort. Our captain seemed more friendly the next day and came into the lounge to show us a magazine he had received by the mail from his wife in Greece. The Saudi officials had opened the magazine and with a black brush had inked out the bare legs of girls in the advertisements!

We stopped briefly at another Saudi Arabian port, Al Jubayl, before going up to Kuwait where we tied up to piers in the middle of the harbour for unloading onto barges. We were the only people among the crew or passengers who had visas for Kuwait, and the astuteness of Kuwait's representative in Ottawa came to mind when he designated six months validity time. If only we had paid more attention to the visa for Saudi Arabia we would have seen more than the docks of Jedda! The agent, a Pakistani, told Dr. Pablo that the immigration authorities would not allow him in, but he insisted on trying so he came in the water taxi with us. The ship by this time was riding high in the water, having unloaded most of its cargo, so the extended gangway did not reach the water taxi. It was an exceptionally long step onto a moving deck, quite a feat for senior citizens, we thought. The agent was severely criticized by the immigration authorities for bringing Dr. Pablo and ordered him returned to the ship. We were kept waiting nearly an hour while ledgers and books were brought down from files, our names entered with much rubber stamping by several clerks. We finally got out on the street and took a bus downtown. The singularly different-looking people looked at us as though we were very strange indeed, but as strangers in their midst, we made a determined effort to look at the sights outside the bus and thus enjoyed the ride. Kuwait did not strike us as being as colourful as Dubai or Bahrain. In the market place, the merchants displayed their wares in neat, little shops in the new concrete building that had replaced the ramshackle booths of the former Suq. We went to a money changer since the banks were closed and obtained a set of Kuwait coins. We went to see the beautiful water towers of Kuwait which store desalinated sea water. This is an immensely costly procedure, but this small oil-rich country deemed wisely to invest some of its huge profits in such a worthwhile cause.

When we returned, the stern and foreboding faces of the immigration officials turned to smiles when my wife commented on the beauty of the small, glass tea cups from which the officials were drinking tea. They very graciously asked if we would care for some tea and it was served to us with great flourish. It was very sweet but good and we expressed our delight. The atmosphere was one of relaxed pleasantries as we talked of travel and New York while the clerks got down ledgers and books and rubber stamped numerous things, including our passports. The head official expressed his sorrow that we couldn't stay in his country the full two weeks allowed by the visa and hoped we would return someday! We didn't tell him we would never be able to afford the exceptionally high accommodation prices in their luxury hotels.

We took the same old water taxi to the ship and had less trouble making the first step of the gangway. We wondered if the ship's crew had done some work on it or if the change in tide had affected it. Our Mexican friends were out on deck to greet us. They had been concerned for our safety. The old ladies, like Old Paul, had nothing to say. It was time for Old Paul's cigar so he vanished, but the old ladies had a look on their faces which depicted envy, jealousy or anger. These experienced freighter passengers had not thought it necessary to obtain visas; I thought back to our Freighter Cruise Services in Montreal and realized I had chosen a better agent than they had.

We arrived in Karachi, Pakistan, in January after a voyage of nineteen thousand kilometres and seventy days. The agent came aboard and we received the letters our family and friends had written to us in care of the agent. We sat up until after midnight reading our mail, so we slept in and didn't leave the ship until after lunch. We said our good-byes to all and took a taxi uptown to the General Post Office to mail a parcel home. We were left with only our carry-on bags.

The Hotel Northwestern is a very old hotel, built in 1906 by the British and never altered in any way since that time. Dr. Pablo had read about it in a book on older hotels throughout the world. The manager/owner was determined to keep this delightful old stone structure intact. He told us he would not let it go the way of the former Palace Hotel which had been torn down to make room for the modern Sheraton Palace Hotel. Shortly after checking in, we went to a travel agency to enquire about planes to Bombay and Colombo. While there, a young man helped us by interpreting the heavily accented English of the travel agent we were speaking to. This young man was learning the travel business and, as such, was serving an apprenticeship and earning no money for many hours of work per week. We met him later in the afternoon near our hotel and made arrangements for him to drive us around Karachi the next day. His name was Mohammed Ali. He looked too young to drive, although he said he was twenty-one.

That evening, we ate supper in one of the hotel's two dining rooms. We declined to eat in the European-style room after looking at the menu which showed how expensive it was. We ate, instead, in the Pakistani restaurant where the food was good and downright cheap. We ordered the chicken we had seen roasting on a spit in the courtyard, and we had the bread baked outside in an oven which resembled a beehive. We had seen the dough formed into the shape of a large dinner plate and slapped against the side of the oven. By some miracle, it stuck without falling on the flames below, and it came out a golden brown. These large pieces of doughy bread accompanied each meal and served not only to fill the cavity in our stomachs but as a substitute for utensils in picking up food or gravy. Only once during our five day stay did we eat in the European room. And when we did, we thought the meal was inferior as well as costly.

Breakfast the next morning was served to us on our balcony overlooking the beautiful garden. The waiter had knocked on the door precisely at the time we had specified the night before, had taken our order and had returned with our breakfast in precisely fifteen minutes as promised. We had boiled eggs, toast and marmalade, and a huge pot of tea. The little waiter bowed and deferred to us in such a manner as to suggest we were on a par with English gentry. The order of things and the treatment afforded us never varied. Although our quarters were very old and the plumbing very basic, we began to feel like gentry or perhaps a senior officer in a respected British regiment taking a breather with his lady in the city of Karachi. We had more room than all the staterooms on the ship put together, and the ceilings were so high we could have had staterooms piled on top of one another. The exotic birds flying in the mature trees outside our windows delighted us and the orderly garden below the balcony was filled with flowers and pathways. Our accommodation at the Northwestern cost slightly less than $4 per day!

Mohammed Ali arrived in his car, and off we went to see the Mosque Tuba and the Mausoleum honouring Mr. Jinnah, the father of modern Pakistan. These exceptionally beautiful structures are considered holy places and they exercise a requirement for all visitors to remove their shoes. The shoes are guarded by young people who expect a coin on your return. There are so many desperately poor people in Karachi that you tend to reflect on the disparity between the costs of such buildings and the welfare of the people, but you put such thoughts aside in the excitement of camel rides on the beach! Have you ever ridden a camel? It is rather frightening at first. You feel your back will break when the camel gets up and when it kneels to the ground. In between, when you are actually riding, you are so high up and the camel's head is so low you feel you have no control over the animal. The gait is strange also, being very different from that of a horse.

Mohammed Ali wanted us to meet his parents and his sister who lived in a fairly modern apartment building. We had tea and pastries and were invited to stay with them. We declined and returned to our hotel, but not until we promised to come for supper in two days time. Those next two days were spent riding around in motorized rickshaws or three-wheeled taxis. The drivers are extremely competitive, each trying to beat the other to fares or to run a red light. One driver we had was obliged to stop periodically to put water in his vehicle, and after each such occurrence he seemed more determined to make up the time he had lost. At the end of the day we wondered how we could have been so reckless to have entrusted our lives to such daredevils.

The Bohri bazzar was undoubtedly one of the best market places we had seen for colour, quantity and good prices. There were stalls which specialized in bracelets—thousands of them of varying colours and sizes—and other stalls which dealt only in strings of beads. There were numerous stalls from which clothing could be bought and still others with brass or wooden bric-a-brac. A man walked around with a pole upon which several exotic birds, mainly parrots, were tied. I enquired about the cost of these beautiful feathered creatures and found the price quite astounding at less than $2 for the most expensive one. A man with very dirty hands and feet and dressed only in a sweat-stained pair of shorts carried a goatskin filled with water. Another fellow, only slightly cleaner looking, tended a table on which sat a large container of pomegranate juice. Both men had a single drinking glass with which to serve their customers!

We were fascinated to see a camel pulling a large cart loaded with hay past the Sheraton and the Intercontinental hotels. We went into the Intercontinental where Air India had an office and bought tickets for Bombay. As we entered the office, we were still trying to decide on whether to go to New Delhi or Bombay, but we decided on Bombay and then on to Sri Lanka, the route we had originally planned. We were already more than three weeks behind the tentative schedule we had set for ourselves, and a trip to New Delhi would set us back even further. We thought, we'll do that on another trip. As we were coming out of Air India's office we saw the old ladies from the ship. They were perfectly sober since no liquor is served in the hotels of this Islamic country. They didn't stay to talk but hurried to catch a taxi which would take them back to the ship and their Listerine bottles.

The old ladies would have envied me that evening, for I was given a drink of Canadian Club whiskey. How it was obtained in this land that prohibits the consumption of alcoholic beverages was not a question I would dare to ask, and even though I seldom drink that beverage, I felt obliged not to offend my host. Annette was not offered any; ladies simply do not consume alcohol.

Our host's wife kept in the background, but Mohammed Ali's attractive and exquisitely dressed sister came into the room with a fine looking, little boy of about five years of age. He immediately went to Annette whose kindly manner never fails to attract children. As he sat on her lap, his large black eyes glowed with happiness as she told him stories about our grandchildren. It was only then, when our host told Annette the little boy on her lap was a prince, that we learned we would be dining with royalty this evening. Shortly after, Sultan Chandio, the nawab of Sind Province, appeared at the door. An imposing and regal looking man of perhaps sixty or more years of age, he carried his huge frame directly to a large chair in a corner of the room. Oddly, perhaps because of his kingly bearing, the chair seemed to take on the semblance of a throne. We learned later that a nawab in Pakistan is the equivalent to a maharajah in India or a king in Europe. Haji, the little prince, ran to him and the affection of father and son was touching. Haji is not likely to become the nawab, however, since the current nawab has several older sons.

We talked of many things, including life in Pakistan under the British raj, but he seemed most interested in his latest pursuit. He had just returned from a hunt in northern Pakistan where he had shot more than one hundred deer. He invited me to go along on a hunt with him when we next visit Pakistan. Annette was not invited to participate because, as he said, "Ladies don't care for such activities, but she will stay on at the palace in our absence".

At precisely 11:00 p.m., Sultan Chandio stood. All others in the room arose in unison as though pulled by the strings of a puppeteer. Our host hurried to assist the nawab in donning his coat. Mohammed Ali's sister tended to the dressing of the little boy. Mohammed Ali opened the door. Out of the shadows of the night appeared two swarthy-looking men both of whom looked inside, nodded to the nawab and escorted him and the prince down the steps and into a waiting vehicle.

We flew out of Karachi the next day and arrived in Bombay two hours later. I should have called the Sea Palace Hotel with whom we had made a reservation through the Air India office in Karachi, but we hurried to the taxi stand and the first taxi in line took us approximately fifty kilometres to the hotel which is near the famous Gate of India. Along the way, we were forced to keep the doors locked and the windows up, although the heat was suffocating. At every traffic light, women would thrust deformed children to the windows of the taxi and beg for money. The squalor and poverty of great masses of people is shocking to the senses and we felt like asking the driver to run the red lights.

It was nearly 10:00 p.m. when we arrived at the Sea Palace Hotel. Foolishly, I paid the driver, and he took off. The desk clerk said the hotel was full and declared no reservation in our name had been received, so we found ourselves walking the dimly lit streets of Bombay looking for accommodation. Annette went to one hotel and I went to another across the street, but both were full. As I emerged from the door, a little girl of about ten or eleven pulled my sleeve and asked if I wanted a room. It was nearly midnight when we finally got a room, the last one available in the Garden Hotel on a street behind the Sea Palace. The room itself was large and quite attractive, but we had to share a bath that was filthy. We used the air conditioner which we found out later was the only one in the hotel. We also found out the reason they had this room left was because it was the best and most expensive. The air-conditioner cooled us off sufficiently that we could avoid attempting a shower in that terrible bathroom.

We slept well and the next morning, after a good breakfast a few blocks away in the beautiful Taj Mahal Intercontinental Hotel, took a tour of the city. We saw the colourful Jain Temple, the place of worship for a comparatively small group of people dedicated to non-violence, and we saw through the foliage of lovely trees, their Towers of Silence where the flesh of their dead are eaten by vultures. We toured a house where Mahatma Gandhi had lived, saw the sacred cows roaming at will and saw nearly-naked men laying on the sidewalk staring at the sun. We were taken to a market place crowded with people and were advised by our guide to guard our wallets carefully. The poverty, the masses and, particularly, the missing noses and hands of sufferers of leprosy was overwhelming. We decided to gain back some of our lost time and fly on to Colombo, Sri Lanka.

We arrived in Colombo at midnight. The customs and immigration procedures were mere formalities. As we were emerging, a man came out of a booth with a sign which read "Travel & Tour Agent". He tried to sell us a tour. I said I would be looking into that the next day, but that all I wanted right then was a nice bed to sleep in. He said his men would take us to the Lake Lodge Guest House and would pick us up the following morning and we could all talk about a tour. I thought this man came on too strong, but I accepted the long ride to the city and the lovely room at the Guest House.

After breakfast in the dining room of the Guest House with a beautiful view of the lake, we were taken downtown to the office of J.N.W. Lanka Tours where the head man, Mr. Wasser, commenced to pressure us into taking a ten day tour which would take us two thousand kilometres in a car with a driver and a guide. The cost would include our ride to and from the airport, all our accommodation, breakfast each morning, entrance fees and photography fees at sights where such charges would be levied, and a wildlife safari. I could see the cash register running out of space for the dollars this would cost when he announced the price would be $410 in U.S. funds. Holding my breath to hide my amazement, I accepted with a nod and we were soon on our way in a station wagon with our guide and driver on one of the most pleasant adventures of our life. What a contrast to Bombay! No one was subservient, in the manner of the waiters in Karachi, and no one begged for money. Everyone was polite and pleasant with us. It was such a refreshing atmosphere, at that time in early 1983, that we were shocked at the discord between the factions in subsequent years.

Sri Lanka is a photographer's dream...the rice fields, bullock carts piled high with coconut fibre, water buffalo, the immense reclining Buddha of Polonnaruwa and the impressive ruins at Anuradhapura which somehow reminded us of the Mayan ruins in Central America. When we learned that the two sets of ruins were built at approximately the same time, we mused on the possibility of man progressing at the same level at distances too far for any cultural or physical exchange. The stellae and structures seemed similar, although the subjects in the carvings differed.

We were intrigued with a scarecrow—so different from any we had seen at home. Our guide Zarook told us it was really a replica of a god to keep wild elephants out of the rice fields. Then there are the spices, the rubber trees and the tea pickers. There are places to buy these products, and we got so many packages of tea and spices we decided to send another parcel home when we got back to Colombo. But we had Kandy to see next.

Kandy is perhaps the most beautiful city in Sri Lanka and we were most fortunate to be there when the great parade of elephants took place to celebrate their Independence Day. After four hundred years of colonial rule under Britain, Ceylon, as it was called, gained its independence on February 4, 1948. It was at Kandy that we saw a splendid cultural dance exhibition and an astounding display of firewalking quite different from that practised in Fiji. The Royal Botanical Garden in Kandy is very beautiful with an extremely large and diverse display of orchards among many other exotic flowers, shrubs and trees.

The safari started before dawn. We boarded a bus that would take us for a full day of sightseeing through the National Park in the southeast sector of Sri Lanka. We did not have to wait long for excitement. A big elephant, the only one we saw that day, was crossing the red dirt road as we came around a bend. He was a big bull with huge tusks and it was evident he was in heat. We had not known that in elephants it is the male who comes in heat. The bus driver stopped and the big bull commenced to feed on the branches of the trees beside the road. I could lean out the window to take pictures and my excitement rose when the bull decided to charge the bus. I got some good pictures but could have got better ones had I not lost my nerve and pulled my body back in the bus. Fortunately, the bull stopped before crashing into the vehicle, but even the driver had left his seat. I had occupied the seat directly behind the driver! We did not dare move until the elephant lumbered off into the jungle. Someone announced we had been there thirty-five minutes!

We saw many other animals and a great number of birds to complete our day. We spent that night and the next day at the Polhena Reef Hotel at Polhena, Matara, on the south coast, a beautiful spot next to beautiful Indian Ocean beaches. We could have spent days there, but on we went to Colombo. On the way, we stopped several times for Annette to shop for gems, batiks and carvings. We had to purchase sufficient goods to warrant sending a parcel, she reminded me.

All around the island, we stopped to refresh ourselves with coconut milk. Zarook would select four coconuts from little roadside stalls, and the proprietors of the stalls would deftly slash at the top of the coconuts with machete-style knives until an opening appeared. After one or two episodes of the milk running down your chin and onto your chest, you learn to tip it just right. It is surprisingly cool and refreshing, and so cheap. In Colombo, we almost felt outraged by having to pay more than twice as much as in the countryside for the same thing.

Back in Colombo, we started thinking about how we would get to New Zealand which had been our only planned destination after leaving the ship. We enquired about ships to New Zealand or Australia, but it would entail so much time that we discarded any further thoughts on that mode of travel. Mr. Wasser did not handle overseas flights, but Zarook and a driver took us to a travel agent who did, and we decided on a flight to Singapore and then to Perth in Western Australia. We had thought of going to Singapore and then to New Guinea and Cairns in Queensland, Australia, but found that there were no direct flights from Singapore to New Guinea. We would have had to fly from Singapore to Djakarta, Indonesia, and stay there overnight to catch a flight to Port Moresby, New Guinea. Since we would be required to stay in Djakarta, we would need a visa and that could take nearly a week since it was now a Friday, their office would be closed until Tuesday, and they simply could not be rushed. Well, we thought, it would be nice to see Western Australia anyway, so the decision was made to go to Perth from Singapore.

There was a further hitch—the travel agent would not accept traveller's cheques. Off we went to a bank to get $1300 changed into rupees. We asked for banknotes in large denominations, but they gave us over 20,000 rupees in ten rupee notes! I counted, Annette counted, and Zarook counted. Then, on Zarook's instructions, I stuffed the twenty bundles of bills under my shirt and went to the doorway while Annette went down the steps in front of the bank and our guide ran to get the driver to come around the corner from his parking space. Feeling as though I was a feature player in a scene from a Laurel and Hardy comedy, my stuffed shirt and I made our way down the steps and into the car whose door was held open by our guide. We sped off to the travel agent and he counted and Zarook counted. I didn't, but somehow I ended up with more rupees than we needed, so we went on another shopping spree which meant we had to get a bigger box than Zarook had previously obtained for us. He helped us pack, and at the post office he slyly put the stamps over the heavy cord "to discourage postal clerks from opening the parcel". We thought of the parcel we had mailed from Karachi. Could that have been opened? When we finally left Sri Lanka, I gave Zarook a further tip which was accepted in his polite and pleasant manner.

Singapore was celebrating the Chinese New Year when we arrived, and it was difficult to find a reasonably priced room. Since so many places of business would be closed for a four day period and since we had been in Singapore before, we decided to stay only two days. We had to go back to the Raffles Hotel though and to the Jade Restaurant in the Shaw Shopping Centre, two of our favourite eating places. We noticed the tremendous changes at the airport. Ten years before, Singapore's airport had been drab and very ordinary. Now it was transformed into the most beautiful and different airport we had seen.

The long flight to Perth, again on Singapore Airlines, was made tolerable by the relatively few people aboard the Boeing 747. For the first time I slept a little, stretched out over three seats, which helped considerably since we did not get to bed until 3:00 a.m. Our flight had arrived at 2:00 a.m., and a taxi driver suggested the Travelodge motel. On the way there, I noticed a vacancy sign at the City Waters Lodge and told the driver to pull in there. What a lovely place for a very reasonable price. We had an apartment there with all facilities for a week at $25 per night. Just behind was the Sheraton at $75 per night, and that was without kitchen facilities! We completed this around-the-world trip with extended touring of Australia and New Zealand.

6

Australia

Our first visit to Australia was in January 1973. We had exchanged the remaining New Zealand money into Australian money at the airport in Auckland and had boarded a DC 8 to fly across the Tasman Sea to Sydney. It was evening when we arrived and we sought out advice on where to stay from the Traveller's Aid booth, explaining our need to have clean accommodation at cheap prices. The lovely, little lady at the booth told us the bus drivers were on strike, so she arranged for us to share a taxi with two other people. Fortunately, those people had little luggage; otherwise, we would have had to wait for the next taxi. Our luggage filled the little trunk and we had some on our laps. We still had so much to learn!

The driver took us to the Imperial Hotel in Kings Cross. As we got out, the driver, a very young lad, told us this was a rough neighbourhood. In the darkness of night it looked fine to us, and the clerk at the desk was very pleasant. Our room was spacious and clean, all the plumbing worked well and the beds were very comfortable. The cost for the two of us was $11.50 (Australian) per day and that included a full breakfast and an excellent evening dinner! We had intended to stay in Sydney about three or four days, but after two days of excellent food and very comfortable beds, we reasoned that now was the time to really see the city. We stayed two weeks!

We walked a lot—to Hyde Park and around the new Opera House. What a beautiful sight it is, from a distance or close up. What a great disappointment we had when we learned it would not be opening for some few weeks. We walked to Pitt Street and then to Australia Square where we took the elevator far up to the top of that round building to get an excellent view of the city and the harbour. The city was in the midst of a building boom with great highrises under construction all over the downtown core. We rode buses to the ends of their routes which was cheap in comparison to other modes of transportation but rather pricey to ride long distances since they charge additional fares for each section beyond the inner core. Much the same thing applied to the many ferries we took, but of course you should expect to pay more the farther you go. One particularly nice ferry and bus jaunt is the one to the zoo. When you disembark from the ferry, a bus takes you to the top of the hill, you enter the zoo and walk back, downhill all the way. The zoo is interesting with native animals so different from those we are accustomed to. Of particular interest was the platypus, but even more intriguing was the recently opened Night Environment House where nocturnal creatures could be seen in a nature-like setting.

We rode in a car to Hornsby, Woy Woy and Gosford, accompanying people we met in the dining room of the hotel. This couple, a man and his mother, had rented a car and had invited us along for the ride. He was on holidays from New Guinea, and his mother had joined him in Sydney from her home in Adelaide. Colin, about forty, had been in the highlands of Papua, New Guinea, for twelve years teaching the natives the three "R's". He told us there had been no registration of births so he would look at their teeth, as horse dealers look at the teeth of horses, to judge their approximate age. As we left Hornsby, the last suburb of Sydney, the countryside along the Pacific Coast Highway showed its beauty, and the pretty little community of Gosford was a delightful spot to spend a few hours away from the big city. We returned on the electric train, a fast ride through lovely country and long tunnels until we approached the highly industrialized areas, to Sydney's Central Station.

Back at the Imperial Hotel we looked out our window and realized how clean the sills were. We also realized we saw no smog over this big city and detected no foul-smelling fumes. The same applies to the cities and towns of New Zealand, and the probable reason is the lack of smokestacks, for very little heating is required. Of course, it was midsummer down under. One newspaper headline screamed out in large red letters "ITS TOO DAMNED HOT - TO HELL WITH CELSIUS - ITS 104°". Below this, in smaller black letters, "40° Celsius". Australia and New Zealand, like many countries of the world, were ahead of Canada in going metric.

Sydney is a very large city, but we felt we had seen a large part of it in the two weeks we were there, so we didn't mind leaving to fly on to Bali, Indonesia. We did voice our desire to return to Australia some day to see more than Sydney and the immediate area around it.

It would be a full ten years before we would return. We had left Australia in February 1973, and we returned in February 1983 after a night flight from Singapore. But the second time, we landed in Perth, Western Australia. Although we were tired, we felt fortunate to be in nice accommodation at the City Waters Lodge on Terrace Road, and we went to sleep with pleasant thoughts of being back in Australia again. It was nearly noon hour when we awakened and made a hot drink with the complimentary tea and coffee. Then we went out into absolutely beautiful weather. Perth was having its coldest spell since 1926, and the Aussies were complaining of the chilly breeze, but to us it was a refreshing change from the hot tropical weather we had left in Singapore.

We walked a great deal in the downtown core, eating in little tea houses and delighting in the small stores of London Court and other similar shopping areas. We rode on a bus to Kings Park, high on a promontory overlooking the city and the wide expanse of the Swan River. We rode buses to Freemantle, the main seaport of Western Australia, and to Cottesloe, a pretty little town with wide boulevards and beautiful flowers.

At Freemantle, you can board a boat to take you to Rottnest Island, thirty-two kilometres away. The island is only ten kilometres long and four kilometres wide and does not have automobile traffic. Bicycles are the means of transportation and most visitors hire them to see the beauty of the island. There are only twenty-five kilometres of roads, so it is possible to see most of the sights in one day, but it is such a peaceful spot you may want to rent a holiday cottage or stay at the hotel lodge. There are beautiful beaches, lovely trees and wildflowers. The mauve coloured Rottnest daisies are a special delight, but possibly the one different thing that brings people to this island is the small wallaby called quokha. The island was originally named "Rottenest" after a Dutch mariner found what he thought was a nest of rats. They were actually these small, friendly wallabies and the Aussies have dropped the first "e" in the name to come up with the interesting "Rottnest".

We went to the government travel agency to buy tickets for the train to South Australia and to Alice Springs, and as we were walking along St. George's Terrace, Perth's main business street, we saw a small store called The Flight Shop. We went in and asked about prices for flights home from Brisbane with stop-overs in New Zealand and Hawaii. One airline would not accept us on their cheap flights because we were asking to leave Brisbane twenty-nine days hence instead of the required thirty days. Another airline accepted us so we got our tickets immediately—Brisbane to Sydney, Sydney to Auckland, Auckland to Honolulu, then to San Francisco, Chicago and Toronto with the requested stop-overs in New Zealand and Hawaii. The cost? $840 each. That was a big spending day, but we were now fairly well set on the route we would take for the remaining laps of our second round-the-world trip.

The Australian trains must surely rate among the best in the world. Admittedly, we splurged in getting the nicest compartment available where we had very large beds, toilet, wash basin and a shower with hot and cold water. It was air-conditioned and equipped with venetian blinds. A smartly dressed conductor for each car saw to it that we had tea and cookies served to us before retiring for the night. The urge to splurge was brought about because we had not spent as much as I had expected in Sri Lanka or for our flights back to Canada, and we were elated with the outstanding beauty of Perth. We anticipated a lovely time in Australia.

At Kalgoorlie the next morning, we had a long stop, long enough to leave the train and take a tour of this active gold mining town. The food on the train was unbeatable—thick juicy steaks, luscious seafoods, roasted leg of lamb, attractive salads and vegetables, and lovely puddings and pies—and our table companions, the same for every meal, were an interesting couple from England. He was a medical doctor who had lectured on cancer in universities in many countries and had retired when he found that he himself had contracted the disease. He had met his lovely wife in Kenya where she had been born, the daughter of a prominent English adviser to the ruler of that country. They had travelled extensively, but this phase of their life seemed to be drawing rapidly to a close since the doctor was finding it increasingly difficult to get around. When we said goodbye to them in Port Augusta, South Australia, we wondered how much farther he could go.

Along the way, we had seen hundreds of kangaroos. When we first spotted them, I rapidly took several pictures. They became so numerous we almost got to the point of not looking at them. We enquired about their great numbers and were told about the large bush fires in South Australia forcing wildlife to move, so we saw many more of them than we would have under normal circumstances. We stayed in Port Augusta overnight to catch the train to Alice Springs the next evening. An Aussie we had talked to on the train from Perth drove up in his Volkswagen van as we were walking and invited us to go for a ride into the countryside. As we drove towards the Flinders range of mountains, we saw an emu on our left. I wanted a picture so asked Neil, our newly found friend, to stop. By the time I had got out of the van, the emu had crossed the road in front of us, miraculously got through a high fence and was well out of range of my camera lens, but it was a wonderful spectacle to see the speed of that huge, flightless bird. A little farther along we saw a much slower animal, the bob-tailed goana. I had no trouble taking its picture, although its ferocious appearance resulted in a picture taken at ten feet instead of five!

Our dining companions to Alice Springs were of a very different sort from the English doctor and his wife. The woman was just plain and fat with straggly blonde hair. The only words she uttered were to the waiter when she ordered from the menu. She avoided our eyes by staring out the window. She stared out the window even when she ate, yet she didn't spill a drop of food and finished before us and the man who sat beside her. She left the table immediately. The man who sat across from me talked. He said one word at a time and it was always a long slow "Yeas". Somehow this was not conducive to a lively conversation, so Annette and I found something to talk about. The next morning, the woman left the table after a hasty breakfast while the man surprised us by talking almost continuously. He was a station master at Alice Springs and was most informative about the area through which we were passing. He seemed to be catching up for the few words he spoke the evening before. Despite his volubility, he finished his breakfast before we did, excused himself and left. Neither one showed up for lunch and since the train arrived in Alice Springs shortly after, we never saw either one again.

After a cup of tea at the Elkira Motel, we walked to the Minerals Building where we noticed the temperature was 45°C. Inside the building, air-conditioned by solar energy, the temperature was 24° C. On we went to a very superior panoramic painting of the area, the Henk Guth display. Attached to this display is a museum of aboriginal artifacts. We went to the CATA office in Alice Springs to arrange some tours of the area. In particular, we wanted to go to Ayers Rock which lies some four hundred kilometres to the south-west of Alice. The coach (bus) was waiting for us early the next morning. On the way, we stopped at a camel farm. I reached to get my camera and discovered it wasn't there, nor was my cap which I have needed so badly for the past ten years (ever since my bald head was sun burnt on the slopes of the volcano in Hawaii). Another Canadian couple from Calgary, Alberta, offered me the use of a second camera they had, another young fellow offered me his hat, and the bus driver offered to radio back to the motel to have them send the camera and my cap on the next airplane to Ayers Rock. Everyone was coming to my aid when suddenly I remembered putting both items in the pocket of the seat on the bus where they would be handy. Sheepishly, I went back on the bus to get them. Everyone was so nice. They didn't even laugh!

Our next stop was at Mt. Ebenezer where I took a picture of a windmill. It was motionless in that still hot air with the temperature at 47° C. I enquired if the windmill ever went around and the reply included information about its cost which astounded me—$50,000 to drill an eighty metre well and install the windmill. While it was a fairly large structure, the cost seemed unreasonably high to me. We travelled on along the red, sandy road which appeared to have been made simply by bulldozing the desert, creating ditches on either side. There was no gravel or pavement, and as we sped along, the tires threw up a cloud of red dust. We made a few other stops, some of which were for picture taking. Getting out of the coach was like walking into an oven, so we soon began to relish the anticipation of a nice air-conditioned restaurant in which to have the promised champagne lunch. We pulled up at the Olga mountains, and in the sparse shade of scattered eucalyptus trees, the driver set up folding tables. A slight breeze was blowing in that strangely beautiful setting, and we had a lovely lunch of ice-cold asparagus tips and other delicacies, along with copious amounts of champagne. We soon forgot about the air-conditioned restaurant. Some of the people even undertook a fairly strenuous hike, after which we drove on to the Chalet, our accommodation very close to Ayers Rock. We were assigned our rooms, and I was not long getting to the shower. I turned on the cold water tap. It was warm. I turned on the hot water tap. It, too, was warm. It took some time for cooler water to come through the pipes, but I don't know when I have appreciated a shower more.

Sunsets and sunrises on Ayers Rock are pretty sights even if there is some cloud cover, which there was when we were there, but according to the slide show we saw before retiring for the night, sunsets and sunrises can be spectacular after a rainfall. The Rock flames like a ball of fire and must be a sight never to be forgotten. Unfortunately, the right conditions do not occur with any degree of regularity, so only a few people travelling there can view it at the height of its splendour. I did something I am loathe to do under normal circumstances and bought a transparency in flaming colour, knowing there was little likelihood I would return to Ayers Rock.

Half of those on the tour were young and very fit persons, and they managed to climb to the top of Ayers Rock. All were warned not to go unless they had good walking boots, yet a couple in sandals went along. They returned with bleeding toes from the strap rubbing continuously while descending the very steep pathway. Those of us who didn't attempt the climb were driven completely around the Rock to view the irregularities formed by erosion, and we were taken on a short hike to view a wave-like formation in the rock which was considered a place of great importance by the aborigines.

We took another tour by coach to Ellery Creek, Serpentine Creek, Glen Helen and Ormistar Creek. The heat was bothering Annette so much by the time we got to Glen Helen gorge that she elected to stay in the air-conditioned coach. This was a pity, for the Glen Helen was the most beautiful sight of the day. I felt fortunate that the temperatures, in excess of 45°C, didn't bother me. I hate cold weather and feel the chill so much each year as November approaches. Here, my wife would ask at regular intervals, "Are you warm enough, Bob?" My answer was consistent—an amused grin.

Another day and another tour. This time the heat abated somewhat, and we both could enjoy a bush walking tour several miles north-west of Alice Springs where we would spend some time with the driver/guide Rod Steinert and several aborigine people in their natural environment. Rod had a genuine love of these people, and it soon became evident why such an affection could grow. We watched two women dig into the base of the witchetty (mulga) bush to look for a swelling in the roots which indicated the presence of the witchetty grub, a large white grub they relish. The aborigines and Rod ate them live, after which Rod said we all would have them for lunch. This, of course, produced protestations as well as laughs of disbelief. But we did eat them, or at least six of us did. The aborigines cooked them in hot ashes. Annette was the first to try them and upon declaring them to be tasty, I followed along with four others, all Americans. The remaining six of our party, all Europeans, steadfastly refused. One rather formal lady from France thought it was disgusting and openly said so. Others simply laughed and shook their heads. Way out in the outback, we did have a nice lunch of barbecued steaks and a salad. To top it off, we had a hot cake which Rod had mixed with flour, raisins and other ingredients and had baked in a dutch oven which he had placed in a bed of hot coals in a hole in the ground. Covered with a sweet syrup, the cake was so good that our little group devoured it in very short order. Rod and his native friends smiled with satisfaction as they listened to our praises. Some of them gave us demonstrations of spear and boomerang throwing at which they excelled. It was a pleasant experience.

That evening we decided to fly to Cairns near the top of Queensland and so we said good-bye to the Canadian couple from Calgary. They were planning on taking the bus south to Coober Pedy where opal mining is the chief industry. We also said good-bye to two little, old ladies from Adelaide who had been on some of the same tours that we had taken out of Alice Springs. They talked so sweetly to each other and called each other "Dear". While they often had differences of opinion, one or the other would smile sweetly and concede the possibility of the other being correct on any given point. Everyone thought they were cute, but as we said good-bye to them, separately, each one told us what a "bitch" the other was! Mildly shocked at this disclosure of their true nature, we gasped for breath and laughed. Each of them laughed, too, for I'm sure they were fully aware of the impression they had created. Whenever we spoke of them afterwards we called them "The Arsenic and Old Lace Ladies", whom they resembled in appearance and demeanour.

I took a picture from the window of our Trans-Australian airplane of the copper, silver and lead mines of Mt. Isa on our flight to Townsville, Queensland, and I took several pictures of the Great Barrier Reef on our flight from Townsville north to Cairns. What a beautiful sight to see the varied colours of the reef from the air, and the pilot told us it was an exceptionally good day visually.

Cairns was hot and humid, so it was a relief to take a boat the next day out to Green Island, a part of the Great Barrier Reef. This is truly an island paradise even though part of it may be a little over-commercialized. We took the last boat back to Cairns as coal-black clouds approached on the horizon, but it didn't rain. The multi-coloured water with the mountains and black clouds provided the right ingredients for excellent pictures.

We gorged on seafood during our stay in Cairns. At one meal, I had Barramindi fish with a sauce of prawns and cream, cooked celery, string beans and potatoes with a sauce of herbs and spices. Annette ordered Seafood Sailor—crumbed reef fish, prawns, scallops in a large shell and chilled shrimp with salad and tropical fruit. Every day we ordered different meals, but all were seafood dishes and all were very good.

The day before we left Cairns, we booked on the Kuranda Tourist Train, an old coal burner which took us up to Atherton Tablelands through beautiful mountain scenery. At Kuranda, a bus was waiting to take us to Burringa Lake Park. On the way we stopped to view huge termite hills which, curious as they may be, are so ugly in comparison to the ecstatic beauty of the large butterflies of the Park. The iridescent Blue Ulysses and the Green Birdwing butterflies were in abundance. Both were mating with their even larger, black females, but I didn't know this when I used up half a film attempting to get pictures. They light on a leaf, you are awe-struck by their beauty, and then (just as you are pressing the button on the camera) they fly off to another leaf. Annette laughed so much at my antics of which I was completely unaware that I began to wonder if it was she who was going crazy! Finally we both laughed as we made our way to the restaurant overlooking the pretty little Burringa Lake to have better Devonshire Tea than we had had in Devon, England. When we left to return to Cairns, the black clouds rose again on the horizon. Still, it didn't rain.

Since we wished to leave Cairns the next day before the car rental agency would be opened, we arranged to have the car delivered to the motel that evening. If we had not done so, we would have had to stay in Cairns much longer. We left early in the morning, just as the black clouds opened to start a particularly heavy rain storm. We drove south to Townsville in pouring rain and barely made it through deep waters at a dip in the road where a car was stalled in the other lane. I drove very slowly in order not to create a wash and made it through. As we passed the other car, we could see no evidence of anyone inside and could see no one on the road in that rather desolate stretch of highway. We had no trouble farther on, and shortly after we left Townsville we ran out of the rain. We had not intended to drive a great distance, but because of the downpour we had continued on to Proserpine. This turned out to be a stroke of good luck since, from Proserpine, it is only a short drive to Shute Harbour where the launch "Whitsunday Princess" takes on passengers and cargo for Daydream Island and Hayman's Island.

We spent a full day on these glorious islands, two more pieces of paradise. What a beautiful planet we live on! Not so beautiful were the great numbers of kangaroo bodies along the road, killed the previous night by speeding cars. We managed to avoid hitting them, but then the fanbelt of our Ford Falcon broke near Mac-Kay. That, combined with a high consumption of petrol, influenced us to change cars at the same rental company's agency in MacKay. We had been given the bigger car, although we had contracted for a small one. It was certainly more comfortable than the replacement we got, a Dhaihatsu Charade, but the Dhaihatsu used less then half the amount of petrol and it was fun to drive. Annette preferred to drive it over the Ford, so I drove considerably less than before.

We stopped in Gladstone for the night and learned that the heavy rain had hit Proserpine and, therefore, the dream islands that day. We also heard that the Cairns area was in flood, the highway was closed, and the Kuranda train tracks had been washed out in several places. We had left Cairns just in time, and fortune continued to smile upon us as we kept ahead of the rain. When we stopped at Noosa Heads, we went to an information booth where we were directed to a motel which offered housekeeping accommodation at the rate of $50 for three nights. This suited us admirably since we had read of the attractions of this area and had tentatively planned to spend some time here.

The Noosa Heads Park itself is a picturesque place, and nearby at Buderim we visited a ginger factory where we bought a good supply of ginger chocolates to satisfy a mutual passion. We toured the factory and saw their film about the growing, harvesting and processing of ginger. Nearby, too, was the town of Caloundra where the English doctor we had met on the train was visiting relatives. He and his wife had extracted a promise from us to call them there and we fulfilled that promise. What a delightful time we had with them and a fine old gentleman, her uncle, who had left England to seek a warmer climate. He certainly had found it here in his home on the Sunshine Coast.

We thought of that lovely home and these lovely people several times as we flew out of Brisbane on the first leg of our long journey home, and we speculated on the idea of leaving our cold climate to live in a tropical paradise. We have never had quite enough incentive to do so. The distance from children, grandchildren and old friends has been the deciding factor. And, too, the love of our own country, despite the chill of its winters, has contributed to our decision to return home each spring.

On another, later visit to Australia we had the roughest airplane ride we have ever experienced. It occurred in March as we approached Hobart, Tasmania, on our way from Melbourne, Victoria. We had wanted to cross Bass Strait on the overnight ferry, but they were fully booked so we flew, getting a 30 per cent senior citizen discount on Trans-Australian Airlines. The plane dropped as a front was going through, and the recovery from that drop was very rough. A young mother sitting beside us had turned down a lovely meal since she couldn't handle it with an active little boy on her lap. Annette, having finished eating, offered to hold the child to allow the girl to have a nice meal. It had just arrived, and she was about to eat the first bite when the plane started its violent movement. The tray landed on the floor. The little boy threw his arms around Annette's neck, and I could see his eyes grow large with fright. Everyone was silent. Fortunately, the seat belts had just been fastened since we were near the end of the one-hour flight; otherwise, some people could have been thrown from their seats. The pilot apologized for the discomfort and told us the extreme turbulence had come as a surprise to him and his co-pilot. He made a perfect landing.

We went to Tasbureau after taking the bus uptown. The people in this agency were friendly and worked hard to get accommodation for us in this small city full of tourists from Melbourne on this Victorian holiday weekend. They got a room for us in the Hadley Hotel, a fine old place built by convicts in 1848. It was built for a man named Webb who called it The Bedford Arms. It was an exclusive place for the elite and the chief resort of the local military officers who entertained their ladies in the large ballroom. Webb died in 1881, and John and Mary Hadley bought the hotel and changed its name. By 1895, they had tired of the hotel business and offered Hadley's as first prize in a lottery. The winners declined taking possession, accepting the alternate of £13,500. So the Hadley family retained the hotel until 1931 when a farmer bought it and again offered the hotel as first prize in a lottery. Again the cash prize was preferred, but this time the winner received £200,000. There have been several owners since that time, but this hotel which nobody wanted has hosted many distinguished guests including royalty. It was in one of the royal rooms that we stayed at a cost of $40 per night. All the other rooms were occupied and the other hotels and motels in the city appeared to be fully booked. Comparatively speaking, we were splurging again, but the money we spent for two nights there was well worth it. Just down the hall was the room in which Amunsden, the Norwegian conqueror of the South Pole, stayed and communicated his exploits to the world in 1911.

We walked the few blocks to the hotel with our carry-on bags over our shoulders. A pleasant young man stopped his bicycle on seeing our Canadian flags and told us he was from Vancouver. He was taking his PhD in Marine Biology at the university in Hobart. He loved the city and the people but was happy to speak with fellow Canadians, even senior citizens.

The day we spent in Hobart was a Saturday, market day, and a more pleasant experience would be hard to find. Not only was there the usual market produce but there were flea market stalls as well. Best of all were the many musicians. There was a harpist with a harp he had made from African mahogany, a boy of about thirteen doing a masterful job of playing the violin, a couple singing and playing a guitar and a French Horn, a trio of one violinist and two Mongolian bagpipe players, and finally a chorus of university students singing, a capella, old English folk songs. It is in Hobart where John Woodcock Graves, the composer of "Do Ye Ken John Peel", is buried. Hearing this song, so robustly performed, took my thoughts back to my school days and to the beautiful Lake District of England. I took pictures of the performers and later took many pictures of the beautiful flower arrangements in front of the old State Parliament Buildings and of many of the stone cottages throughout the Battery. These attractive residences, built by convicts for the freemen of the early settlement, are now greatly in demand by young professionals who work hard and spend considerable sums restoring them to their original elegance.

Down at the dock, we saw the Icebird, a German vessel used by Australia for research in the Antarctic. It had been on its way to the Antarctic to pick up sixty-eight scientists when mechanical troubles developed and it had to return for repairs. We noticed that the life-boats were enclosed, the theory being that survivors of a shipwreck would die of exposure in open boats. From the dock, we could see a race of sailboats. It seemed their numbers must be in the hundreds. Never had we seen so many assembled and sailing at one time. When we walked back up Murray Street to the hotel, we felt we had had a wonderful day.

We rented another car, getting a full-sized Holden, the Australian General Motors product, for the price of a Mini with the option of changing it for a car with better petrol consumption if we wished. But we kept that lovely car for the full two weeks and drove nearly four thousand kilometres into literally every corner of Tasmania in complete comfort and without any trouble. The roads of Tasmania are well maintained. While there are stretches of sharp curves in some of the coastal and mountainous areas, the surfaces are good and they are well marked. Taking normal precautions makes for a very pleasant driving experience. One hazard to be aware of is the driving habits, not of the Tasmanians, but of the vacationing mainlanders who are accustomed to driving fast on endless stretches of straight roads. And, as in New Zealand, Australians drive on the left in the English fashion.

After picking up Annette and our luggage at the hotel, I drove to the Botanical Gardens. These are worth the visit although they don't match similar gardens of some other cities around the globe. Driving through Hobart was no trouble for it is not a big city and the traffic is not too heavy. The Botanical Gardens are on the northern outskirts so were on the route to Port Arthur where we planned to spend the first night. Port Arthur was a penal colony built by convicts sent to Australia by the British. It is said that, in order to obtain stone masons, trumped up charges would be laid against tradesmen, in Scotland particularly, and long sentences of penal servitude in Australia would be meted out for the most minor misdemeanors. To Australia's credit, they do not try to hide this segment of their history; rather, they are restoring some of the ruins for viewing and turning jails and torture chambers into museums as testimonials of their past. And they are wise enough to realize that these are great tourist attractions. We spent the night at Tanglewood

Host Farm where we met Jock Leadley, the father of the owner of the establishment. Jock had done some of his flying training during World War II at Dunnville, Ontario, Canada, just fifty-five kilometres from my hometown of Simcoe. We talked for a few hours that night about those years and concluded we must have seen each other at the Dance Pavilion in Port Dover on the north shore of Lake Erie. Now we were half a world and almost half a century away.

We drove up to Palmer's Lookout for a panoramic view of the former penal colony, including the Isle of the Dead where nearly two thousand convicts were buried in unmarked graves and where one hundred tombstones mark the graves of free men. Annette felt uneasy about going there, but I boarded the little schooner, The Bernadeen, to visit that place so gruesome at one time but now so lush with greenery and pure of air that it seems idyllic. In the building called "The Asylum", the normal entry fee was halved because we are "pensioners". Here we saw a series of slides showing the actual buildings inside and out before the fire of 1884 which destroyed the church, and the fires of 1895 and 1897 which destroyed the hospital, all of which are believed to have been deliberately set by local residents ashamed of their predecessors. Now people come from many parts of Australia and from other countries to trace their ancestors, whether they were jailers or convicts. "The Asylum" escaped the torch of the arsonists, and much of the building is intact, including the "Separate Prison" (where convicts were put in solitary confinement) and the chapel with its isolated, individual stalls which required the convicts to stand throughout the long mandatory church services.

Before dawn the next morning, I braved the chilly air to go outside, hoping for a view of Halley's Comet. But, while some stars were visible, most of the sky was dark. During the night the wind blew a hard driving rain against the window of that old house high on a hill. Although our room was cold, we had plenty of down-filled comforters to warm us. I had willed myself to wake early, but when the comet did not appear I went back to bed. When I got up to stay, I went into the bathroom to find someone had taken a hot shower before me. On the steamed-up mirror over the wash basin were the words "I love Jacob". I told Annette about it and she said she had caught sight of a fortyish-looking woman in the hall who looked well scrubbed. We wondered if she had meant "I love Jock", our host. But at breakfast, which Jock cooked while Inge, a Danish girl who had arrived late last night, sat and talked with us, we learned she pined for her absent lover Jacob in Denmark. Good old Jock came in with the slightly over-cooked eggs and bacon—he was filling in for his son and daughter-in-law—and sat down to talk with all of us over hot tea and coffee. Every five minutes he got up to put another stick of wood in an old wood stove which produced a cosy atmosphere. Inge was travelling alone and intended covering as much of Tasmania as possible in just a few days. We wondered how much she saw last night since she arrived shortly before midnight, but she was a happy sort and waved merrily as she roared off in her little rental car. The itinerary she had drawn up for the day was staggering.

When we left, we had no definite plans for the day but took side roads from Eagle Hawk Neck to go down to the Blow Hole, the Tasman Arch and the Devils

Kitchen, all of which are fantastic rock formations. From there we drove inland to Richmond, a charming old town which has the oldest bridge in Australia. This old structure, built of stone by the convicts, appears to have waves in it. Apparently, this was built before the conscription of skilled stonemasons who would not have erred in this way to produce such an intriguing effect. From here we went to Brighton where we saw many native fauna at the Bonoran Park Wild Life Centre on Briggs Road. We saw wombats, cuddly wooly things which the owner held for a picture, kangaroos with little joeys in their pouches, the quilled echidnas, a huge emu which seemed threatening as it roamed freely around us, and the ugly "Tasmanian Devils" from whom we were protected by a sturdy wall. The devils are truly frightful to look at. They appear to be menacing as they approach the wall with teeth bared. We were told they eat all parts of the animals they kill, hair and bones included. Their bite has been measured to exceed the strength of any animal alive.

It was at this wildlife centre that we stayed in a colonial cottage. It was a charming, four-roomed freestone and timber cottage, built by convicts in 1830 and faithfully restored. An unobtrusive addition containing a lovely bathroom has been added and the kitchen had modern conveniences, but the rest of the cottage was authentic and the small fireplace lent great comfort as we sat before it in comfortable rocking chairs. We could have stopped right there to enjoy the serenity of that old house which had a sweeping view of the Jordan River and the rolling hills beyond. However, we had to leave after one night. It was booked up for weeks ahead. We had been fortunate to arrive just minutes after a cancellation.

It was still chilly in the southeast of Tasmania, so we took heed of the weather forecast and drove west. I had no warm clothes so stopped at New Norfolk to buy a wool sweater made in Italy, here in this land of millions of sheep! I needed more Australian money so went into a bank in that small town 'down under' and cashed $500 worth of Canadian dollar traveller's cheques. There was no difficulty; the service was immediate and efficient. Later on, I changed $100 in Canadian currency with the same pleasant efficiency. Try changing Australian currency in small town banks in Canada or the United States. In Canada, they have to send them to their foreign departments at head office and there is a hefty charge for this service. In the U.S.A., as they refuse your request, they look at you as though you are guilty of some crime. I know these things because I once inadvertently brought home $90 in Australian currency. I had put it in the wrong compartment of my wallet and overlooked it when we left Australia.

We ate lunch at Tarraleah where huge pipes, carrying water from the high dam above, follow the road. Tasmania produces a lot of hydro-electric power. To do so, many rivers in the southwest are dammed and this has led to many confrontations between the engineering establishments and the environmentalists. While we were there, just such a confrontation was taking place with the environmentalists establishing themselves in the tops of huge trees destined for felling before the proposed construction of yet another dam. The environmentalists won that battle, but the feeling was they were fighting a losing war. Of special interest were the great huan pines, trees of very dense wood due to their extremely slow growth. They are a national and, particularly, a Tasmanian heritage, for they are unique and strangely attractive.

We kept driving west through desolate-looking country near Linda and the yellow rock of Queenstown. When accommodation was unavailable there, we drove on to Strahan on the southwest coast. I had driven fast, unusual for me, on a newly surfaced road and it was this factor which enabled us to get a room at Strahan Lodge, a beautiful old frame structure. As we signed in, another couple drove up looking for accommodation. They were turned away since the lodge was full. Then, on the advice of our hosts, we drove downtown to make reservations for a jet boat trip up the Gordon River the following day.

It was a beautiful day. In this part of Tasmania, which has a very high annual rainfall, the sun shone brightly in a pollution-free atmosphere. The trip through McQuarrie Harbour, up the Gordon River to the Franklin River and back to Sarah Island was an experience long to be remembered. Our boat "The Wilderness Seeker", not quite as large as the largest jet boat in Australia, was capable of going through shallow rapids to get far upstream and, therefore, we had wonderful views of the wilderness in this section of Tasmania, many areas of which have not been fully explored. The sun's rays seeking their way through the moisture laden trees created stunning effects for scenic pictures of shorelines and mountains mirrored in undisturbed waters above the rapids. Even with a hundred people aboard, with the engine stilled, the silence was so pronounced it seemed the world had at last stopped revolving. No jets passed overhead to disturb the peace and, in that brief moment of absolute silence, life seemed unthreatened by the potential horrors of nuclear warfare. Strangely, it was this subject that was brought up by some English people on board shortly after the engine was re-started and we had headed back downstream. Several Aussies, including a retired army officer, Eric Phillips, and his wife, joined in the conversation and they all echoed the fear of a possible nuclear disaster as a result of the arms race. They were not fearful for themselves, but all, being parents and grandparents, were fearful for the coming generations.

At 3:30 the next morning, the retired army officer, Annette and I were wandering around outside, half dressed, to view Halley's Comet. I have never seen a sky so clear, so full of stars, and our view of the Comet was perfect. We thought of an older friend of ours who had seen Halley's Comet seventy-six years before and who, but for the infirmity of her husband, would have been with us to see it again. She has one great satisfaction to override her disappointment of not seeing it this time: when she was a little girl, the comet was much larger in the sky. Scientists estimate the 1986 display was only one-tenth the size of that in 1910. Nevertheless, it was a thrilling finale to our stay in Strahan.

Later that morning, we drove north on a beautiful new road to Zeehan, passing great sand dunes beside the Southern Ocean on our left and lovely mountain scenery on our right. Particularly beautiful was the scenery of Hellyer Gorge, and the mining museum of Zeehan was very interesting. We came upon the Phillips again in Somerset, and the four of us decided to get accommodation at Kentford Park Host Farm near Yolla. After securing our rooms, we drove to Stanley on the extreme northeast corner of Tasmania where we viewed Circular Head or, as it is more commonly called, "The Nut", a great soaring headland jutting out into Bass Strait. Not far away, the ladies had fun picking strawberries which we had as dessert back at the farmhouse. Shortly before, we had stopped at Wyn to eat an excellent meal of wild duck in a pub among some of the friendliest people in the world. We were tired from our sightseeing and our middle-of-the-night wanderings to see the comet, so we all retired early. The next morning over a superb English-style breakfast, our hosts Lorna and Bob Cooper were advising us about other host farms in the north and east of Tasmania. The Phillips decided to move on, but we opted to stay another night with the Coopers and planned to meet the Phillips again at Bonnie Doone Host Farm, at Sheffield, the next evening. While Annette prepared to wash out our clothes, I accompanied Bob Cooper to the barn where he started up the Massey-Ferguson tractor made in Canada many years ago.

I stood on the running board beside him while he drove over much of his farm. This man was partially paralyzed. He had been thrown from a horse thirty years before and had broken his neck. Miraculously, he had survived and, after months of medical treatment, had returned to farming. For some time, they had been providing bed and breakfast accommodation, a place where people could take interesting side trips to the west and northwest coasts of their island state, or just relax in the slow pace of life on the farm, as we were doing. The rural vistas were superb as Bob drove the old tractor to the top of a big hill and, as I turned to the north, I could see Table Cape and the waters of Bass Strait beyond. That evening, we ate a big meal of food grown organically on the farm, after which Annette and I went for a walk up the country road where we saw a sheep with a hind leg entangled in its tether and in a fence. Annette went to its rescue and, after its initial fright, it allowed her to free the leg. The stoic look in its eyes was somehow amusing to me or was it the struggles of my farm-reared wife? It was amazing how intricate the tangles were. Annette's scolding of the sheep didn't jibe with her good samaritan deed when, time after time, she had to change her attention from tether, to wire, to leg.

The next morning after another big breakfast, we went out in the orchard with Bob to pick delicious plums to take along with us. We were sorry to leave these friendly people, but we headed the car towards Paradise. On the way, we took a circular route along the coast through Burnie, Penquin and Forth, then down a small road to the west side of Lake Barrington, up to Cradle Mountain and past the Wilmot dam towards King Soloman Cave, a lovely display of stalagmites and stalactites. Just before Sheffield is the small community of Paradise, high on a hill with a splendid view of a jagged mountain range.

The Phillips were already at Bonnie Doone Farm when we arrived in the early evening. We stayed up talking with them and our hostess until well after 10 p.m. They told of their experiences of the past two days, and we did the same while our hostess, a lovely lady recently widowed, told us some of the history of her husband. As a young man, he had emigrated from Scotland after a sad love affair. He had been a lawyer in love with a beautiful lassie who jilted him in favour of his brother. In his grief, he left Scotland and never had anything more to do with his family there. Tears came to the eyes of this gentle lady as she told this story, and we felt compassion for her since we could sense the loss of her husband only a few months ago was still prominent in her thoughts.

Our breakfast the next morning was different but delicious. Fruit, muesli and hot, freshly made scones with butter, homemade jams and copious amounts of whipped cream were greatly enjoyed before the Phillips took off in their little car and we took off in our big, comfortable Holden, for which we were paying a cheaper rental rate. We made no plans to meet again but didn't discount the possibility since we both were going around Tasmania in a clockwise direction.

At Deloraine, we stopped at an attractive old building, the Bowerbank Mill, an early colonial corn flour mill built in 1853. The brick smokestack soared high into the sky above the three storied, stone structure which is now a lovely gift shop and museum. We went through the small community of Perth and up to Launceston, an attractive town. Well to the east, at St. Columba Falls, I walked what seemed miles to view this impressive cataract. Annette stayed behind after talking with some old ladies who were still puffing to get their breath on their return. I stopped four times coming back. Going there was relatively easy, it being all downhill, but coming back was indeed a different story. I made my four rest stops at places I could sit and see those lovely falls from different viewpoints. I was none the worse for the climb, and we went on to St. Helens on the east coast where we booked in at the Artnor Lodge Guest House at 71 Cecilia Street. It was basic accommodation but very basic in price, too, and was immaculately clean. The rooms were quiet, facing on a central courtyard. Breakfast was served in a delightfully bright room, and since breakfast was not included in the cost of the room, we could order and pay for only what we ate. We were late in eating breakfast that morning, so we ordered a big one. We had talked with the host the night before about Halley's Comet. He had loaned us a good pair of binoculars to use and told us where to use them—right in front of the guest house—so we got up at 3:30 a.m. and were treated to this great sight. In addition, the Milky Way seemed to stretch across the entire sky, and the planet Venus showed brighter and more colourful in that crystal clear atmosphere than I had ever seen it before. Again, we thought of our friend who had seen Halley's Comet so many years before as a child in rural Manitoba. We resolved to write to Helen to tell her how appropriate it was to view the comet in St. Helens, Tasmania.

That day we drove on many roads around the area to Bingalong Bay Road, to Humbug Hill and Skeleton Road, up the Bay of Fires Coastal Reserve to Big Lagoon and The Gardens, and to a dead end road where a large sign read "Trespassers Will Be Prosecuted. Dogs Will Be Shot". We turned around.

When we returned to the Artnor Lodge Guest House, the Phillips emerged from the unit next to ours. Fortunately, we liked these people, for they kept choosing the same accommodation we did. This time, we planned to meet at the next place the following evening, but now we ate together and reminisced at the Bayview Inn. We met again at Coles Bay in The Chateau located in Freycinet National Park. The owner of The Chateau, Mrs. Joan Brand, had relatives in Vancouver and on Salt Spring Island in British Columbia, so we had a nice chat about those places. The National Park has many scenes of outstanding beauty, and The Chateau itself is in a setting most pleasing to the eye. We ate the evening meal of roast lamb in the company of the Phillips, but later, in the lounge, we talked with several other people from many, many parts of the world.

When we left The Chateau the next morning after a big breakfast with the Phillips, we bade them a final farewell since they were returning to Hobart that night and flying back to Sydney the next day. There would be no more chance or planned meetings, so we exchanged home addresses and promises to write. We also went to Hobart, but continued on to the south to Crooked Tree Point Tea House, three kilometres south of Cygnet. The Tea House had lovely accommodation on the Huan Estuary. It was so lovely that we stayed two nights so that we could see as much of the surrounding country as possible. We went down in the Hastings Caves which were nicer than the King Soloman Cave we had seen earlier. We drove, as far south as it was possible to go, to Catamaran and Cockle Beach. When we saw a car we were almost startled, for the traffic was practically non-existent. On we went to Bruny Island, to Kettering and Sandfly. We wondered how this community got its name as we saw no sandflies or mosquitoes.

We drove to the top of Mount Wellington, from sea level to 1260 metres, where the view of Hobart is so outstanding you realize what a dramatic ride it was up the mountainside. There are few places in the world where a similar view is possible, and every visitor to Tasmania should ensure this drive is included in their itinerary. From there, we drove west to the Gordon River Dam which is only twenty kilometres, as the crow flies, from the spot we had reached in the jet boat out from Strahan. No road or trail has been forged through this wilderness. Returning by the well paved road, we stopped at the beautiful Russel Falls. There was not a great volume of water, but the width and constancy of the water made for a delightful scene. They could easily have been named Bridal Falls, for the whole thing looked like a veil of pure white.

We spent the night at Hamlet Downs Host Farm, hosted by a young English couple who had left prestigious but tension-filled jobs in London to emigrate to Australia. While travelling around Tasmania, they had stayed here, fallen in love with it and made an offer to the owners they couldn't refuse. Two happier and more serene people I have never seen. Knowing their great love of animals, neighbours had given them the joey of a mother wallaby found dead on the highway. Fiona treated it as a baby, and we saw the demonstration of affection Peggy, the joey, gave Fiona as she gave it a bottle. The sheep, Marco, was just as affectionate, and baby ducks in a cardboard box were displayed with great love. A ferocious looking German Sheppard, Lady, was as gentle as a kitten, and even Annette, normally fearful of this breed, petted it. This young couple had an innate presence of gentleness which transmitted to humans and animals alike.

Breakfast the next morning was the biggest and best breakfast I have ever eaten. In front of us was a lovely fresh fruit salad and pitchers of apple, grapefruit and orange juices. Several boxes of dry cereals were on the dining table, and Fiona asked if we would like cooked cereal. We declined, but accepted fried ham and bacon with poached eggs. Potatoes, beans and tomatoes were available and, since they had already been cooked, we accepted a small helping. We finished up with tea and coffee, and chose slithers of cheddar cheese from the many varieties on the tray. On the sideboard was a huge bowl of fruit from which we were invited to select whatever we wished to take along with us. I felt as though I wouldn't require food for a very long time, but that evening, at Prospect House in Richmond, I ate again.

We had tried to return to the charming, little colonial cottage at Brighton for our last night in Tasmania. It was occupied, however, so we went on to Richmond which is not too far from the airport where we could turn in the car. Prospect House is a large mansion built at a later date than the bridge in this town, the oldest bridge in Australia, but it was built by skilled, convict masons as were the stables where we slept. We didn't sleep in a manger though! The stables had been very attractively turned into deluxe accommodation. In the courtyard, there was a walnut tree. Walnuts had fallen from low hanging branches. I ate one and, thinking it tasted different from the walnuts I was accustomed to, ate another. I still didn't care for the sharp taste, so I walked away. Later on, I decided not to go to the dining room for the evening meal and went to bed early. I awakened violently ill. I thought I was dying and Annette thought so, too. My initial thought was the huge breakfast I had consumed at Hamlet Downs Host Farm the previous morning, but it was not that. Fiona was very clean and so was all her food. We learned that the walnuts were to blame for my troubles. Why didn't I suspect it when tasting the first one? Instinct, if not brainpower, should have warned me about those sharp tasting walnuts. As morning came, some of my strength returned, but I didn't think I would be able to fly to Melbourne that day. Fortunately, our flight left at noon hour, so when I felt better by mid-morning, we were able to leave.

We stayed a week in Melbourne at the Kingsgate Hotel and from there we walked the streets of the city's downtown core. We had taken a bus from the airport and had transferred, at no added cost, to a shuttle bus which took us the extra ten blocks to the hotel. We took in the sights of the Bourke Street Mall and looked up at the very tall Rialto building where parachutists jumping off the roof had broken glass windows in abortive falls. That same day, the Police Headquarters building was damaged severely and a policewoman killed as the result of a car bombing. It was stressed in the papers that this was not a terrorist action but a reprisal by thugs. Both daily papers bemoaned such violent action, declaring Melbourne had lost its virginity, so to speak.

We continued to walk the streets and take cruises on the river. While preferring Tasmania to Melbourne, we enjoyed our stay in this city until our departure on a plane that would take us back to New Zealand.

7

Italy and Greece

Ah, Naples! Sorrento! Capri! No wonder Italy produced so many composers of romantic music and so many fine voices to sing of its charm.

We arrived in Italy by air from Amsterdam. Even though I was tired after the overnight flight from Montreal, I chatted with an old chap in the Amsterdam airport. He was waiting for a flight, as well, but he was returning to England, his home for all of his eighty-five years except for this brief excursion to Holland. He told me he had been a church organist most of his life, and he whispered in conspiratorial tones that he had played by ear all that time. With a twinkle in his eye, he said he didn't think he had sinned too badly in not telling church officials that he couldn't read music! But music was his life, and he envied our trip to Italy, for he had always cherished a desire to go to the San Carlo Opera in Naples. Now that we were in the Naples area, we looked forward to attending the opera, but we were soon advised that the season had not started. Would we ever realize this dream? Would we ever come back to Naples, would we come back to Sorrento and to Capri? We certainly preferred this part of Italy over Rome, but no doubt the weather had something to do with our assessment of Rome. It was cold and damp in these early days of November.

We arrived at the Leonardo da Vinci airport at mid-morning, and it took a good hour to get to the centre of things and look for accommodation. We obtained a small amount of Italian currency and bought bus tickets for 5,000 lira ($5 Canadian) each for the ride downtown. We got off the bus at the main depot, looked at the pouring rain and decided to make hotel reservations at an agency in the bus depot. The Hotel Augustea on Nationale Street cost 75,000 lira ($75 Canadian) per night which included breakfast—the usual bun with tea or coffee that they call "continental".

This hotel is rated as a two star hotel, just one above the basics. It had comfortable beds and a bathroom with facilities that worked, although we pondered as to whether or not they were old enough for Caesar to have cast his eye upon them. Annette inspected the beds and found the linens acceptable, but the blankets were badly soiled so she demanded cleaner ones. Three other sets were brought out before she was satisfied. Our plan was to spend the first night in this hotel and look around for better and cheaper accommodation as we have done in many other places. We simply could not find anything better in that area of Rome. Later we learned, from people on the same city tours we took, that three, four and five star hotels cost up to 300,000 lira ($300 Canadian) per night in downtown Rome. One chap even came back to the Hotel Augustea with us to obtain a room there, since he was paying twice as much for similar accommodation. He couldn't get in, though, for all the rooms were full. Needless to say, we did not move from the Hotel Augustea!

We slept long and well the first night in Rome, so we were in good shape to take two tours of the city the next day. The prices of accommodation and meals were so high that we decided to stay in the city for as short a period as possible. This decision was partially influenced by the weather which was decidedly cold, so we spent another exorbitant sum of 50,000 lira each for two conducted tours. In fact, everything seemed expensive in Rome except the little snack bars where the pizza, cheese sandwiches, salami sandwiches, local beers and pastries were not only reasonably priced but were exceptionally good. Our decision to cut our stay in Rome short was aided by the fact that we couldn't use our Visa credit card. Apparently, only the deluxe hotels accept Visa or other credit cards.

On the morning of the third day, we walked to the railway station where we purchased first class tickets to Naples where the weather was supposed to be nicer. The tickets were 19,000 lira each. This seemed reasonable since second class was only slightly less at 14,000 lira. Why go with the common herd for the sake of five more Canadian dollars? Sometimes we like to splurge! And too, we might as well have the extra comfort for a rather long train ride.

We had two hours to wait until the 11:45 a.m. departure, so we sat in the station and watched the inevitable bum beg cigarettes from whomever he could. He put one in his mouth then begged a light from a smoker. He sat down nearby, crossed his legs and placed the corktip on his knee. He talked to the cigarette or to the smoke curling up from it. He became oblivious to everyone and everything around him. He was transfixed by it. He had taken only one or two puffs of that cigarette! Finally it had burned down to the cork and he gently placed it on the floor in front of him. He continued to talk to it for some time after—until the cleaner came along and swept the butt into his dustpan. The spell having been broken, the bum got up and went the rounds of begging again. We were cold in that unheated waiting area so we went to buy a hot chocolate which cost 1,750 lira ($1.75 Canadian) each.

Our tickets stated that the train to Naples would be on binario (platform) 5, but the train on platform 5 was going north instead of south. Our train to Naples was on platform 8. We were advised by a young man in a rather elaborate uniform that this change was for today only. I didn't bother to tell him that I probably would never be taking the train from Rome to Naples again.

We were rolling along and well out into the beautiful countryside, feeling quite proud of ourselves for getting on the right train and for having opted to get first class tickets with our very comfortable seats, when the conductor came along and requested additional money—8,300 lira ($8.30 Canadian) each. The first class tickets we had bought allowed us in the first class car, but now we had to buy our seats! I confirmed this with a very pretty, dark-haired girl sitting nearby. I asked if she spoke English and she replied in the affirmative, saying she had been born in England and had lived there for over twenty years! It seems she had been travelling through Italy with a girl friend some ten years previously when she met a handsome, young Italian man, fell in love and married. She was now travelling alone to go to a small town south of Naples to attend the wedding of another girl friend. Sandra, in assuring us the conductor was not overcharging us for the seats, acknowledged that many things in Italy were different. After the blush of romance had faded from her marriage, she had become disenchanted with her husband and all things Italian, but she was now resigned to her changed lifestyle.

We decided to continue south of Naples, thinking it might be warmer farther south and, since we wanted to see Mount Vesuvius and Pompeii, we thought we would take advantage of Sandra's experience and change trains with her in Naples, then go on to Sorrento. There was no first class to Sorrento. The train was more like a streetcar, but it was a much shorter distance and the train was fast. It seemed almost no time had passed before Sandra left us to depart at Castellammare di Stabia. Very soon after, we were in Sorrento. The cost of this train was only 2,000 lira. We compared that to the cost of rental cars, about which we enquired after our short walk downtown. We thought we might rent a car for a period of about four or five days to go to points of interest in and around Sorrento and perhaps to Brindisi on the Adriatic coast. We were astounded at the cost—600,000 lira ($600 Canadian). With a laugh, I told them I wasn't interested in buying the car. He laughed, too, and said business was slow! We enquired at another rental agency which confirmed these outrageous prices, so we knew we would be using public transportation. We then went to a travel agency to arrange a tour of Pompeii and Mount Vesuvius the next day at a cost of 32,000 lira. It proved to be well worth the price.

Pompeii, twenty-three kilometres southeast of Naples, was destroyed during the eruption of Mount Vesuvius in 79 A.D. It had been badly damaged by an earthquake just seventeen years earlier and the town was still in the process of repairing the damage when the eruption occurred. It took only two days for the town to be completely buried under pumice and ash. We know a considerable amount about the event, partly because of the account written by Pliny the Younger. His uncle, Pliny the Elder, died in a vain attempt to save some of his friends. Many people suffocated in the ashes. By pouring plaster into the hollows left by the bodies when they decomposed, archaeologists have recreated the last moments of many of the victims and these plaster casts can be seen by visitors to the site.

The streets were paved with large pieces of stone, and in many places the deep tracks of wagon wheels are clearly visible. In the past, lead pipes carried water from the aqueducts to the buildings, and these are still visible. Temples, theatres, sport fields, public baths, bakeries, taverns and other shops are well-defined as are the brothels, which house paintings of erotica that are still in amazingly good condition. Exquisite paintings on the walls of prestige houses are likewise in a state of extraordinary preservation. It was a wonderful experience, but we felt a tinge of sadness, thinking of the people struggling to save themselves from such a traumatic occurrence.

Vesuvius has erupted many times since it wreaked its havoc on Pompeii in 79 A.D. The volcano, twelve hundred metres above sea level, last erupted in 1944 and, at that time, Pompeii was covered with a foot of ash. Now you can hike to the rim of the crater. This hike and the previous walk through the ruins of Pompeii proved the necessity of ensuring that good walking shoes are worn on any vagabonding trip. A cable car had been available to take people to the top of the crater, but some time before we were there it had been struck by lightning and had not been repaired.

We spent a day on the famed Isle of Capri which is an hour's ferry ride from Sorrento. You can get to this beautiful island on your own, although guided tours are available. From a distance, the precipitous appearance of the island gives one the feeling there could scarcely be a landing spot, but as we drew nearer, we could see the docking area nestled in a small verdant area at the base of sharp cliffs. From this lovely harbour, you can take short buses up to Ana Capri. Not only are the buses short but the wheel bases are even shorter, enabling them to get around the hairpin turns in their steep ascent. If you can, put the natural nervousness out of your mind and gaze out at the beautiful scenery instead of staring at the road. The bus will get you there, and when you get to Ana Capri (Ana is Greek for "above"), you will be glad you did.

From the end of the bus line, it is an easy walk to St. Michaels House, the former residence of an English doctor who was a devotee of Franz Liszt. The famous pianist and composer used the piano in the guest house for practising on several occasions. The shops are interesting and walking the streets is a pleasant experience. The late Gracie Fields, the English music-hall singer, had an attractive home here, as did other celebrities and personages of great wealth. Regretfully, we had to leave without seeing the Blue Grotto. It is necessary to stay overnight on Capri and to make arrangements with people who will take you in small boats at low tide into this fairyland of beauty and enchantment. Nevertheless, Capri will remain a highlight of our short stay in Italy. Also, we were pleasantly surprised to find we received a better rate of exchange for our money at a bank in Ana Capri than we had anywhere else in Italy.

Sorrento itself is a pleasing little city. Local buses are cheap and the shops are interesting and not overly expensive. There are several factories which specialize in the production of furniture with beautiful inlaid patterns. Tourists are allowed to watch some stages of this workmanship. While we had no intention of buying, we found great pleasure in viewing these lovely pieces.

We stayed three nights in the Hotel Dania paying 50,000 lira per night. It was certainly superior to our accommodation in Rome and was more reasonably priced, but the breakfast (included in the price) was still the same spartan fare they call "continental"—buns, jam and tea or coffee. They were closing for the season so we moved downtown to the "City Motel" which cost only half as much. This place, while very basic, was clean and had the added advantage of being very close to all the shops and the railway station. We thought we would take a room at the back which would be quieter than in front over the main street, but the back room was chilly since it had no artificial heat and no sunshine. The room in front was much warmer and much larger, and certainly much more interesting. We watched an old lady work at her treadle sewing machine in the window of a building directly across the narrow street. As darkness fell, she moved the old machine in towards the centre of the room under an electric light bulb dangling from the high ceiling. With the full length windows devoid of drapery, her poorly furnished home was fully visible. On the floor above her, another old lady seemed to enjoy a peeking game as she parted her long-faded curtains every few minutes to look up and down the street. When I caught her looking directly at me, she withdrew hastily and the parting in the curtains henceforth was narrower than before!

I didn't count the number of steps in that one flight to the "City Motel" above street level, but they seemed almost endless. Below us was the Standa (grocery supermarket) where we bought salami, biscuits, nuts, chocolate milk, beer and wine. We felt like true Bohemians in our garret eating this fare, but we thought we had to start economizing or our cash would get dangerously low before the time of our departure for Athens. After all, we had spent a considerable amount of money in just one week and there were five weeks to go! Still, we couldn't resist buying some cameo rings from a jeweller just down the street. He would take Visa, but for cash he lowered the price from an average of 20,000 lira each. We got five of them for a total of 25,000 lira ($25 Canadian)! He seemed to be more interested in talking about the problems of the world and about his philosophy of life than in making a large profit. I am always amazed at the knowledge of people around the world and their awareness of the political and geographical situations of other countries. This interesting Italian gentleman, whose name was Cuomo ("spelled like the Governor of New York", he said), seemed as delighted as we were to have solved the problems of the world in less than an hour! Why can't the politicians be as smart?!

On the train back to Naples, we talked with a young girl in a school uniform. She was full of the spirit of youth and enthusiastic to talk with us in her very passable English. Like the jeweller and like countless other Europeans, this young teenager had a very good command of English and had a smattering of several other languages in addition to her own. How inadequate I felt. Coming from a country with two official languages and I am unilingual! In such situations, I feel almost ashamed, and yet I know how lucky I am that English is so universally used. A friendly man, having heard our conversation with the schoolgirl, volunteered to show us where to catch the train to Bari and Brindisi. Our tickets read binario (platform) 13, so we were waiting there when another chap came up and told us that, for today only, they had changed the Bari train to another track. That had a familiar ring to it and we surmised that there were many "for today only" situations in the train stations of Italy. This chap took Annette's bag and wanted to take mine, but I declined. He took us to the right train and to the right car. He refused a tip of 600 lira and, by his demeanour, I could tell he was displeased. He finally accepted 1,000 lira!

From our first class seats in the first class car, we viewed the lovely farm land in the valleys and on the hillsides, the numerous vineyards and market garden plots. We saw no cattle. We had to change trains in Bari, but nothing could have been simpler. It entailed only a short walk directly across the platform to the waiting train. On arrival in Brindisi, we walked about one kilometre to the port. It was only 4 p.m., so we had ample time to stop for a meal in one of the many eateries along the way. On this street there were many agencies selling tickets for the ferry crossings and most of them accepted credit cards. We breathed a little easier and felt confident again as we went through the formalities of the steamship line stamping our tickets and the police stamping our passports. On the ship, the Greek authorities again stamped our tickets and passports and assigned us a cabin for the overnight journey across the Adriatic Sea. We sailed at 8 p.m.

Three young men from Lebanon talked with us. They said they were working in Greece and had come to Italy for a holiday but had to leave since the Italian authorities would not allow them to stay more than four days. They seemed disturbed that the Greek authorities on the ship had kept their passports, but they professed they would have no trouble getting them back when they disembarked in Greece. They asked at what port we would be leaving the ship. When we said Patras, they said they were getting off there too. They went on to suggest we share the cost of a taxi to take us the two hundred kilometres to Athens. We were non-committal since, despite their apparent openness and fine appearance, something was telling us not to get that cozy with young men from the Middle East. So the next morning when they approached us again in the snack bar, we said we might go with them but that we first wanted to check the cost and times of the bus. They said they would, too, and that they would meet us on the dock since they would be the first off the ship. We were somewhat relieved when they didn't show up, and because of this we actually watched for them, knowing now that the Greek authorities had not allowed them to leave the ship. What would they have done when the ship returned to Italy? Would the Italian authorities allow them to disembark, and if so, what then? They had told us they could not go back to Lebanon, that they would be in danger of losing their lives. What could these young men look forward to? What was the actual purpose of their trip to Italy? More important to us, perhaps, was what had prompted them to ask us to share a taxi with them?

The bus to Athens cost 1020 dracmas ($10.20 Canadian) and took us on a pretty drive alongside the Korinth Estuary. We crossed a bridge over the impressive Korinth Canal—a deep ditch canal built in the late nineteenth century and a remarkable feat of engineering. At the bus station in Athens, we enquired about a local bus to the downtown area and got one to Omonia

Square where we found a hotel, the Hotel Astey, which accepted our Visa card. All hotels in Omonia Square are reasonably priced and while the Hotel Astey is not the cheapest, the fact that they accepted the credit card was inducement enough for us to stay there. The rate quoted was 2400 dracmas for two people and this included a continental breakfast. We stayed three nights and our bill was only 6730 dracmas ($67.30 Canadian). Perhaps the manager gave us a slight reduction because his wife was a Canadian. She was a lovely girl from Vancouver, British Columbia. Both of them were so nice, we told them we would come back to their hotel on our return from the Islands—and we did.

Underground at the square, which one reaches by escalator, are many shops and banks. I cashed traveller's cheques at the National Bank of Greece and got a favourable rate. Also underground is a post office and the entrance to the Metro (subway). The subway charge is 30 dracmas (.30 Canadian) except for early morning, before 8:00 a.m., when it is free! Near the hotel was a travel agency which sold ferry tickets and also accepted the Visa card, so we bought our passage to Patmos which cost only 2800 dracmas ($28 Canadian) each, including the cost of a cabin. Although we would be arriving at Patmos at 11 p.m., we thought it advisable to get a cabin for the ten hour voyage.

We checked out of the hotel the next morning and, knowing exactly where the Metro was, walked the short distance with our carry-on bags. We got off at the end of the line in Piraeus, the principal port of Greece. Here we had to enquire where to find the ship whose name was on our tickets, and then we had a ten minute walk along the quay. The "Alkeos" was a nice ship with comfortable cabins and a surprisingly cheap dining room. At lunch we met an interesting young couple with two sweet, little children. They were speaking English so we took the opportunity to ask them about the island of Patmos. The husband was Greek and the wife was Scottish, from Glasgow. They lived on Patmos so were well informed as to its attractions. They said their little boy spoke English and also Greek, but with a "Glasgie" accent! Arriving in Patmos, we wondered where we would be able to find accommodation, but the young couple pointed out a lighted sign just fifty metres from where we disembarked. It was the Hotel Rex. We were in bed with the lights off by 11:25 p.m.!

In the morning, we saw the beach of the island of Patmos, the most northerly of the Dodecanese group. What a lovely restful spot! We went to the police station near the dock which is the accepted place to find out about accommodation. The friendly policeman made a telephone call and, very shortly after, a man arrived and took us in his car to view his rental units. We thought the previous night's room charge was reasonable at 1300 dracmas, but this large efficiency he showed us was only 800 dracmas ($8 Canadian) per night. The notice posted on the door showed the summer rate was 2400 dracmas. We shopped for groceries, and our host took us, our bags and our groceries up the hill in his car. We bought a fairly good supply of groceries, for we intended to stay about two weeks. We bought heavy things, such as bottled water, bottled wine, shelf milk, canned Coca-Cola, canned beer, potatoes and onions, as well as lighter-weight types of groceries. We took advantage of the car ride to stock up since we proposed walking to the stores to do any subsequent shopping.

Our host pointed out the Sacred Cave where Saint John supposedly wrote his *Book of Revelations* and we found out the next morning that we could lie in bed and see the sight. The cave is covered by a chapel and that is topped by stonework to carry the weight of three large bells. In the afternoon, while sitting outside the door of our unit in the lovely, warm sunshine, we saw a priest ring the chapel bells. Every afternoon thereafter, the same ritual took place. Above the Sacred Cave, at the top of the mountain, is the monastery build to honour Saint John. The monastery has its own bells and these are very large. We heard their deep tolling on two occasions during our stay on Patmos and were told they were tolling because someone had died. Inside the monastery, there is a wonderful display of ancient treasures in the form of scriptures, hand-written in the sixth and seventh centuries A.D. Also on the side of the mountain, we could see a very large theological college where boys, aspiring to become priests of the Greek Orthodox church, come from many parts of the world to study. Our host, Antonis, told us there were four hundred churches on the island of Patmos which has a resident population of twenty-five hundred! He pointed out that the great majority of these were little chapels, built all over the hillsides as well as in the three small communities of Patmos, Scala and Campos.

From our unit, we could see farmers on the terraced hillsides with bags over their shoulders, walking along stone fence rows picking up almonds and gathering figs. We were there for the fall plowing which is done with a light-weight plow pulled by two donkeys. Nearly every morning we were awakened by the cry of the plowman. "Ehhh, ehhh", he would call, either to urge on the little beasts or to keep them in line. And every plowman had the same call!

We often saw an old lady, in her grey skirt, blue sweater and white kerchief over her head, lower a bucket into a well or cistern to get water to moisten plants. At one point, we saw her spread out a large white cloth to collect the kernels of the grain she threshed by striking it with an old-fashioned flail. Another man came regularly each day to milk his goats and left sitting sideways on his donkey with the milk pails slung over the donkey's back. As he passed by our quarters, he never failed to smile and lift his hand in greeting. The whole scene was so peaceful that we felt as though we had been transported back many years in time.

Our daily walks to downtown Scala to replenish our larder were always interesting. We found new routes to take through streets and alleys so narrow that not even small vehicles could navigate them. We learned a Greek word—"Kalemetta"—which we would say to people on the way downtown. Sometimes they would reply with the same word, but often they would reply "Good morning!" Each day I would buy the *Athens News*, a nice little newspaper which was the only English language reading material available at that time of the year. We saw a shop with a sign in the window advertising English language books for sale, but the shop was closed as are so many when the tourist season ends. If I had known, I would have bought some reading material in Athens where lots of it is available at the kiosks in Omonia Square. Although the tourist season was over, we met a few other vagabonds, although none from North America. They were from other parts of Europe and all were younger than ourselves. Still, we enjoyed their company, chatting and sipping the strong coffee in the many coffee houses still open.

There was a liquor store in the square with more varieties of spirits than we had seen anywhere else. The proprietor, a dapper old gentleman, told me that the Dodecanese Islands enjoyed special status and could sell spirits without charging taxes so that prices for these goods are very cheap; yet we did not see one drunk person in those islands nor in any other part of Greece.

We met Anna, a little lady who lived in a two room house of white-washed stone and plaster. Living with her was her aged and obviously ill mother who was sitting in a very uncomfortable-looking old chair beside a bare and decrepit dining table. The old lady was garbed in a long, black dress with long, puffy sleeves and a high collar buttoned at the neck. Around her shoulders was a black, lace shawl which was held tightly together by her poor withered hand. Anna had the typical white kerchief, blue sweater, grey skirt and black stockings, denoting her social status, but she was so gracious that she invited us into her humble dwelling and brought, from her little garden, sprigs of an aromatic herb which she presented to us with a delightful smile and a slight bowing motion. She could speak no English and we could speak no Greek, but using sign language we told her our names and she told us her name and (with the aid of a family picture) the names of her family. As she pointed out her father, she indicated he was dead and then she pointed to her mother, in the picture and in the chair. We speculated on how long it would be before the bells of the monastery would toll for the old lady who was struggling for every breath.

There is a hospital on the island and it is reported to be very efficient. Fortunately, we didn't have to put it to the test since we were healthy for the full nineteen days we spent on Patmos. We had intended to stay no more than two weeks, but we became so enthralled with the place that we extended our stay, even though the weather turned unusually chilly and we had no means of heating our quarters. After a hot shower, we would pile on the extra blankets our host had left with us. We had scoffed at the possibility of using so many blankets; now we were happy to have them. In such a relaxed atmosphere, we slept like babies until the warm sun awakened us in the morning. We came to rely on it, and rely we could, for it shone every day.

On the first day of December, we left Patmos, reflecting on the many peaceful aspects of the island and on the people we had met. We thought about one old farmer we had talked to—an Italian who fled his homeland when Mussolini was strutting around prior to World War II. This intelligent man had foreseen the events which would follow the military build-up in his country and in Germany, and had come to Patmos to find peace. We were amazed at this seemingly simple farmer who grew cabbages and cried out "Ehhh, ehhh" to his donkeys, yet spoke Italian, Greek and English so well. We wondered, as he conversed with us in our language, if he could converse with peoples from other foreign countries, people from Germany and Holland for instance, who visit Patmos in fairly large numbers.

The big ferry, the Ialyssos, took us to Leros, Kalymnos, Kos and Rhodos. Although it was a ten hour trip to Rhodos, we did not take a cabin so the fare was only 1560 dracmas each. The hotel we got in Rhodos was 3800 dracmas, expensive by Greek standards, but by the time we got a taxi from the port it was 1:00 a.m. We were tired and decided to look for cheaper accommodation the next day. After a good night's sleep, we went to the Tourist Bureau where the employees were pleasant and informative. We walked through the old town, using a map obtained at the Tourist Bureau. The walls of the old town, which were used as fortifications at the time of the Crusades, are in excellent condition and, for a small fee, you can walk a fair distance on them.

That afternoon, we decided to take the bus fifty kilometres down the coast to Lindos. This attractive, little village nestles at the foot of the ancient Acropolis which is on the crest of an imposing promontory with a dramatic drop-off to the sea. A short, immaculate old man with a well-tanned head, completely devoid of hat or hair, grabbed our bags as we got off the bus and, without asking if we had reserved any accommodation, insisted on taking us to one of his rental units on the beach. The price, he said, was very cheap at 2,000 dracmas per night. We glanced in every direction and saw no hotels of any description so said we would look at his place and decide then, even though he repeatedly declared his rentals were the only ones available at this time of year. As we followed, I wondered why I had considered this little man to be immaculate since his suit-coat and pants were mismatched and his shoes, although well polished, were severely worn by much walking over the cobblestones of the narrow, winding ways. Passing an open area sloping sharply away to the sea, a voice from high above asked, "Do you want a room?" When Annette called back to ask the price, the reply came down: "1,000 dracmas". The old man dropped our bags and, flinging his arms about, went into a tirade of what must have been cursing at the young man who now became visible as he leaned over a stone retaining wall, partially covered with lush greenery. Annette was already starting up the rock stairway when the old man picked up the bags and turned to go back up the hill from where we had come. I hurried to catch up and held his arm firmly. He dropped the bags to the cobblestones with a pushing motion and said with disdain, "Wife!" After a scornful glance at Annette, he stretched his little body to its fullest, then looked at me with an air of haughtiness and contempt. Containing my amusement, I gave the old man 100 dracmas. After all, he had carried our bags some considerable distance and we may not have come this route if not for his insistence. He grudgingly took the bill and left, mumbling to himself, as we climbed the steep steps to the beautiful accommodation we were to stay in for the next three nights.

Our room overlooked the beach of a sheltered, little bay below and the blue Mediterranean beyond. High cliffs and barren mountains to the right and left, with the Acropolis above, completed the scene. And the view at night from the balcony of our room was quite spectacular, too. Looking at the sky on those cool, clear nights reminded us of the great starry display in the sky over the Arabian Sea when we sat out on the deck of the old Greek freighter on a previous voyage.

We had dinner that first evening at the beach restaurant, the only place to eat out at that time of the year. We ordered fish caught in the bay that day. It was very good, but we were somewhat shocked when we got the bill to find we were charged for every item on the plate, and the little fish cost 600 dracmas ($6 Canadian) each. Why did I let the waiter talk me into ordering three of them? Thank goodness Annette is not a great lover of fish and was firm in ordering only one! It is a curious thing that fish is so much more expensive in this maritime country than in some land-locked places. It is especially odd since grocery items and fresh fruit and vegetables were very reasonable. We did not know at the time that the restaurant would be closed the next day and would remain closed until the next year's tourist season began. Consequently, we had to return to our bohemian style of eating for the next three days since this beautiful room was not equipped like our place in Patmos.

The next day, we rode donkeys up to the Acropolis. You may walk to the Acropolis, but the route entails a considerable upgrade, and when you enter the main gate many steps await you. We were glad we had chosen to ride, even though the donkey I was riding had a tendency to rub up against the stone walls along the way, presumably to rid himself of the foreign matter on his back! When we arrived at the top, the owner of these little beasts informed us that Annette's donkey was old and gentle, but mine was young and obstinate. From the ancient Stoa, just inside the main gate, an impressive stairway of seventy-six steps leads up the Propylaea of the sanctuary of Athena, to whom this fourth century B.C. temple was dedicated. Down below, you can see a small harbour, the place where Saint Paul is said to have landed when he came to Rhodos. There was a considerable amount of restoration work being done at the Acropolis, but it did not impede our wanderings. There was only one other couple within the Acropolis while we were there, so we took our time climbing the stairways. Although we must have climbed about two hundred steps altogether, the majesty of the place and the superb view made it worth the effort.

Back in the city of Rhodos, we left our luggage at the Tourist Information Centre while we walked around the marketplace across the street. There, we had the best tasting pizzas we have eaten. They were small, square in shape, and had just been made. When we finished eating them, we went back to get more and found they were all gone and no more would be made until the next day. We had eaten those delicious pizzas in the park with many eyes upon us—the eyes of hungry cats. In many parts of Greece, and of some other Mediterranean countries, wild cats abound. At times they can be quite aggressive with each other. The island of Rhodos has its fair share of them.

On the way back to Athens, we stopped off in Kos for a few days. Kos is the island noted for its ruins of the fortified castle of the Knights of St. John of Jerusalem, for its abundance of fresh water springs and, most particularly, for being the birthplace of Hippocrates, the father of medicine. The castle was built in the fifteenth century; however, due to many Turkish raids, several modifications were made up to the early sixteenth century. Kos has been under many rulers since early times, but at the time the Knights of St. John obtained it, Kos had been under Roman rule for several centuries. The Turks finally captured Kos in 1522 and held it until 1912 when they surrendered it to the Italians. It was only in 1947 that Kos and the other Dodecanese Islands were returned to the rule of Greece.

In the museum, visitors were allowed to take pictures of the statue of Hippocrates, and the lighting was such that I could take a picture without the use of a flash. I had left my flash in my bag at the hotel, so I simply pressed the camera against a pillar with the time set at one-thirtieth of a second. The picture has a nice, soft look, so I am happy I forgot my flash. It was the only time I would have used a flash during our stay on that island, for most of the ruins have no roofs to shade them from the sun. The fourth and second century B.C. Greek buildings and temples, silent witnesses of ancient times, make Kos a paradise for photographers. The Askilpeion, four kilometres from town, is a sanctuary where an order of priests practised medicine in the manner advocated by Hippocrates. There were other medical centres at Asklipeion where different methods of cures for various illnesses were experimented with, so it is fitting that the Foundation of Hippocrates is located on this island of Kos. The Foundation is an international medical centre created in 1960 and devoted to the cultivation of the science of medicine as Hippocrates conceived it.

I took pictures of the plane tree, under which Hippocrates is said to have taught medicine. While it is an extremely old tree, it is most unlikely that it was there in 460 B.C., the year Hippocrates was born. However, like the Loch Ness Monster in Scotland, it is an intriguing legend.

We stopped briefly on the island of Kalymnos which is famous for its sponge divers, and on the wooded and fertile island of Leros, before returning to Patmos for another look around that peaceful little dot on the map of Greece. We found it as enchanting as before and felt real regret when we left for Athens in mid-December to return to the Hotel Astey for a two night stay, thus ensuring that we would not miss our flight back to Montreal. Our flight to Montreal and the subsequent bus ride to Ottawa were routine, but we returned home feeling pleased about a thoroughly interesting and enjoyable trip.

8

South Pacific

On another excursion, we decided to spend some more time in our favourite of all countries, New Zealand. In the early planning stages, we looked into a cruise of the Society Islands—that part of French Polynesia which includes Tahiti and Bora Bora. Later, in our quest for different islands, we included the Cook Islands, a little closer to New Zealand.

The inclusion of an organized cruise was a very definite splurge on our part. While we enjoyed it, it was doubtful we enjoyed the added costs. Perhaps everyone should take at least one cruise of this type, enjoy it and learn from it...learn that you can go to the same places on your own for a fraction of the cost!

We went to a travel agent who made the bookings for us. She booked the cruise which would take us from Tahiti to the islands of Moorea, Raiatea, Bora Bora, Tahaa and Huahine in one week. We would be cruising on board the Majestic Tahiti Explorer operated by the firm Exploration Holidays and Cruises of Seattle, Washington. They invite a comparison in costs between their small ships which carry only eighty-eight passengers and the large cruise ships carrying seven hundred passengers. Their costing readily shows they are less expensive and they pride themselves on the fact that their ships can enter secluded lagoons and go behind the reefs where the big ships cannot. The ship's ability to make bow landings allowed passengers to go on beaches directly from the ship, but being of shallow draft the small craft was tossed about in a mildly rough sea between Huahine and Moorea. We had the cheapest stateroom available, but the best for rough seas—a centre stateroom on the lower deck. To get to it, we had to descend a stairway from the Explorer's dining room on the main deck. During the night of rough seas, several of the people who paid considerably more than we did for their staterooms on the upper deck or bridge deck came down to sleep on the dining room floor! We slept very well! And during the days and evenings we sat on the same sundeck, in the same Vista View lounge, and ate the same food in the same dining room. Still, we could have toured those same islands for much less using the ferries which ply the same waters.

The travel agent had booked our flights to Los Angeles and Tahiti in conjunction with onward flights to the Cook Islands, New Zealand and Tasmania. Since we would be arriving in Tahiti at 2:15 a.m. and since we were splurging on a cruise anyway, we decided to pay the extra money for being met at the airport and be driven to an expensive hotel. It is certainly the way to relieve yourself of any responsibility, but it also relieves you of a considerable amount of money. We did not return to the airport that way, nor did we stay at the Hotel Tahiti when the cruise was over.

The cruise was to start in mid-afternoon of "Day 1", so we had a day and a half to wait before boarding and took advantage of this time to see some of the attractions of Papeete and the island of Tahiti. We changed a little money at the hotel and took the bus downtown where we got a better rate at the Caisse. It was very simple to compare costs since one French Polynesian franc equals one Canadian cent. The bus (Le Truck) fare is only 90 francs, but taxi fares are quite expensive. It is best to establish a price to get to any particular destination before entering a taxi. Most things in Papeete seem to be expensive. The residents have taken full advantage of the reputation of Tahiti and its outer islands of being the most beautiful in the world, and the prices reflect their greed. A further factor in the explosion of prices is the explosion of the nuclear tests done by the French government in the nearby Marquesas Islands. As a result, thousands of French troops are stationed on Tahiti, and the military and construction workers spend their money freely, helping to send prices higher and higher.

Still, everyone dreams of visiting these enchanting islands someday. Sailing vessels and yachts from countries all over the world moor in the lagoon at Papeete. We talked with a Canadian couple in their early sixties who had sailed in their ten metre sloop from Victoria, Bristish Columbia. They had arrived several months before, had been to many islands in the group and had no plans to move on; yet they were interested in first-hand knowledge of what was going on back home in Canada. "We'll go back—someday," Don said, as he turned to gaze dreamily at the peaks of Moorea across the bay. We left them, knowing it would perhaps be a long time before they would see Victoria again.

I lost my cap at the Hotel Tahiti. The bus-boy, who insisted on carrying our bags, expropriated it in lieu of a tip. I bought the cheapest cover I could find for my bald dome and had to pay the Canadian equivalent of $9.95. A cup of soup at the hotel restaurant was $4 and the entree of beef was $11. The pineapple sundae was $5, so this meal of meagre portions cost $40. On a shore excursion from the ship, we experienced another example of how they fleece the tourists. During an island bus tour of Bora Bora, our group stopped for a lunch at the Hotel Marman, the cost of which was included in the price of the cruise. However, drinks other than coffee were not included, although no one was advised of this beforehand. Being assured the ice was pure, we ordered iced tea. The two glasses of slightly coloured iced water cost $7.

The only other Canadian among the eighty-eight passengers aboard the Explorer was the travel editor of a large Canadian newspaper who told us of an experience he had in Papeete. He was struggling with two suitcases when some young people, boys and girls, offered to help and even offered to drive him to his hotel. He was thinking how nice they were and then was shocked when they demanded $25 for the transportation. Their formerly friendly faces turned into menacing stares until the money was given.

What a difference we found on the island of Moorea! We left the ship at 10:00 p.m. on "Day 7", after the fabulous Captain's Farewell Dinner. Since "Day 8" consisted solely of getting off the ship in Papeete at 7:00 a.m., we looked around Moorea for accommodation during our docking at the Hotel Bali Hai, and found exactly what we were looking for. Just across the road from the Bali Hai was Motel Albert where we obtained a nice unit on a high piece of land for $22 per day. It had all the facilities including a small kitchen, where we prepared our own meals for the next few days with groceries purchased at reasonable prices from a nearby shop. On the table in the fully screened porch overlooking the great profusion of tropical flowers, tended by Albert himself, was a huge bowl of fruit grown on the premises. Each day the fruit we ate was replenished at no charge. We were relaxed and happy sitting on that porch eating the delicious fruit and looking beyond Albert's flowers to the thatched units of the hotel below and to the exceedingly beautiful volcanic peaks of the legendary Bali Hai.

Some other passengers from the ship left it when we did, but they did not stay at Motel Albert. One couple had prepaid for a week's stay at the Hotel Bali Hai and occupied one of the thatched units we could see from our vantage point high above. They had paid $1,890 for seven nights of accommodation only. Admittedly, it was pretty with the thatch inside and out and one of the most unique bathrooms I have ever seen. Since the unit was built on stilts over the water, glass floors in the bathroom seemed especially daring. The whole unit had many mirrors and tropical plants which enhanced its size and atmosphere. Unfortunately, they were bothered by water rats running along the beams and into the thatch of the roof. We felt compassion for them and brought some of our free fruit to them which they accepted with the expressed relief of not having to order dessert in the hotel's dining room. Not having kitchen facilities, they were forced to eat at least one meal at the hotel and found it very expensive. The Sandbergs were not rich people. They had spent considerable money, taking the best stateroom on the ship and the most expensive hotel in Moorea, on the one great trip of their lives. They could not cancel at the hotel and move up the side of the mountain beside us since they had prepaid on a package deal. As they sat under the clothes they had washed out in their lavish but impractical accommodation, they felt somewhat dejected, particularly when they realized they were paying twelve times the cost of our unit.

In the unit next to ours was a young doctor from Philadelphia. He had quit his job in a hospital six months previously and decided to see some of the world before marrying and settling down to raise a family in the respected tradition of his forebears. He was running out of money so he said with a sigh, "I suppose I will go home soon, but I will always dream about the South Pacific." As he was speaking, the very attractive daughter of Albert and his Polynesian wife walked by!

In another unit, larger than ours, six young people lolled on their porch and as we passed, one called out, "Are you the other Canucks?" They were all recent graduates of universities in British Columbia. They were taking time off, "to relax their brains," they said. Some were going back to university to get their Masters degree and others would be looking for employment. The unit they were in was new and very nice. It rented for $45 per day—$7.50 for each of the six of them. They loved it. We were proud of them and thought again how we may have done the same thing if conditions were similar when we were young.

We shared the cost of a rental car with the Sandbergs and leisurely drove all over the island, and when we left Moorea to return to Papeete, they accompanied us. The bus to the ferry cost .75 each and the ferry ride to Tahiti cost $6 each. These are the prices the natives pay to go from place to place and they are the prices vagabonders pay. Our ride across the Sea of the Moon, as the waters between Moorea and Tahiti are called, was just as pleasant as in the Explorer and infinitely cheaper!

At the dock in Papeete, we said goodbye to the Sandbergs, and with our carry-on bags over our shoulders, we walked a short distance to get on Le Truck to the airport. We talked briefly with the Canadian newspaper man whom we bumped into in the airport. He said he was going home to the ice and snow of Toronto. We were going to the Cook Islands. We met an American couple from California who were destined for the Cook Islands, as well, and we learned from them that the immigration authorities there require the name of the hotel you have booked. Since we had not booked in advance, we put down on our landing cards "Edgewater Motel", the accommodation where the California couple had made reservations. However, a gentle, soft-spoken chap on the plane suggested we stay at the Kii Kii Motel, so we went along with him and obtained transportation in the Kii Kii's little bus. The chap turned out to be Dr. Jochen Biersack, a research scientist from West Berlin. I had several delightful conversations with this intelligent man who had come to this beautiful island of Rarotonga to advise the prime minister on the pros and cons of burning wood for energy.

Another intelligent man was the prime minister of the Cook Islands. This stalwart-looking fellow, whom we met in a restaurant, was a medical doctor by profession and had worked for NASA in the U.S.A. in the early years of rocketry. He had been responsible for monitoring the physical condition of monkeys sent up into space, But he, like many other Cook Islanders, felt the call of the islands and returned to his homeland.

One evening we met another such man. He appeared to be preparing to go fishing, but he already had some fish more than half a metre in length. Annette approached him to enquire if he would sell any of his fish. He smiled and advised her the fish he had were only bait. Just then, an old pick-up truck drove up, and out of it came a man with a dirty shirt and even dirtier yellow shorts. Two lovely ladies came from the truck as well, but they were dressed in clean and pretty loose-fitting dresses. The younger man with the fish introduced the man in the dirty clothes as his uncle, the governor-general, and the ladies as his aunts, one the governor-general's wife and the other, her sister. We laughed in disbelief but soon realized this was indeed the Honourable Tangaroa Tangaroa, the Queen's representative in the Cook Islands. The fisherman, the governor-general's nephew, was the chief surgeon here. He had obtained his degree in New Zealand and had a practice in Auckland until he, too, felt the call of the islands and left what he described as the rat race of a big city to go home. We had an extremely pleasing and casual conversation with the governor-general and the ladies, sitting there on that lovely tropical beach while watching the doctor go out beyond the reef to fish for the big ones.

We rented a car from a young fellow who took us to the police station to get a Cook Islands driver's licence, a requirement for driving the thirty kilometres around Rarotonga. It was handy to see this Pacific paradise and to go to town for groceries, for here we had accommodation with full kitchen facilities. The one bank in town happily cashed our traveller's cheques into New Zealand currency. Although the islands have independent status in the Commonwealth, the same as New Zealand or Canada, the Cook Islands still use New Zealand currency as they did when it was a protectorate of that country. We bought some pearls brought up from the sea by the famed divers of Penrhyn, the northern-most atoll of the group. These would be special souvenirs which would take very little room in our bags and add very little weight.

One Sunday we went to church. We had heard of the beauty of the hymn singing of the London Missionary Society so we went to a church founded by the society, which began its work in these islands in 1823. The rich, full resonance of their voices thrilled us immensely and their smiling welcomes were a delight. These islanders retain the fervour instilled in them by the early missionaries and while fear is certainly a component of their faith, their prayers to the Christian God seem to retain a plea to their old god Tangaroa, who protected them from the ravages of storms and the sea and aided them in procreation, fishing and crops. Like natives of many of the islands, they accepted this new faith and melded it into their own, just as they, in their innate inability to be anything other than amicable, accept all visitors as friends.

We took only one of our carry-on bags to Atiu, the tiny island forty minutes from Rarotonga by Beachcomber aircraft. At the Rarotongan air terminal, we and the bag were weighed as was everything that went on board. There were eight other passengers plus the pilot who made a perfect landing on the little unpaved airstrip fashioned out of materials at hand by volunteer workers of the island. Out of the crowd of smiling faces strode a tall, lean young man, quite evidently not a native, for he was fair complexioned. He was Roger Malcolm who had the only tourist accommodation on the island—three beautiful bungalows built by himself entirely from wood of the coconut palms. He had married an Atiuan girl who owned the land and who had borne him two lovely children, a boy and a girl. Roger, a New Zealander, could never own the land since Cook Island law forbids foreigners from acquiring property, but his children, born of a Cook Island mother, could inherit it.

Roger approached us knowing we were the couple who booked one of his bungalows when we bought our tickets at Air Rarotonga. We accompanied him to his beat-up old Datsun truck which was one of the very few four-wheeled vehicles on the island. I got in beside him while Annette chose to ride in the back with a young New Zealander who hoped to marry a girl from the islands someday. Roger drove halfway down the airstrip and turned sharply into the jungle. I voiced my amazement of driving between the great cones of lava and over the lush green vegetation. There were no tracks, but he assured me this was a road. I asked to be let out so I could take a picture and it must have been at that time that I lost the hat I bought in Tahiti. I had taken it off in the cab of the little truck for my head was shaded from the warm sun. When we got out of the truck again it couldn't be found, so off we went to a store to get another. The store, much like the country general stores of rural North America in pre-World War II times, had a great variety of hats, but I couldn't find one that was big enough. I settled for a white cap with an extra long visor which, being too small, provided a source of amusement for Annette. The cap cost considerably less than the Tahiti hat, although it didn't fit as well!

The bungalow was stocked with groceries and drinks. The rental was $30 ($21 Canadian) per day, and at the end of your stay you paid for the foodstuffs you used. The cost of each item was only slightly higher than the prices in the food markets on the main island of Rarotonga. Roger also had three 50 c.c. motorcycles for hire at $12 ($8.40 Canadian) per day. Since they were the only rental vehicles on the island, we decided to try one. Neither of us had ever attempted to ride a motorcycle before, but we both rode bicycles so it seemed plausible to try. With very basic instructions from Roger, I found I was able to drive the machine but felt I wouldn't be capable having a passenger on the back, so Annette tried one. We drove around the yard and, feeling confident, we took off towards the beach which brought us to the five villages clustered in the centre of the island. Before the coming of Captain Cook and missionaries of the London Missionary Society, the villages had been scattered around the perimeter of the island and had suffered considerable damage and loss of life when hurricanes lashed the land. It was the missionary, John Williams, who encouraged the natives to move their villages to the high ground in the centre of the island.

It was at the centre of the island where we encountered the only hostile person we came in contact with on the Cook Islands. I went around an "island" in the middle of the roadway on the right instead of the left, forgetting that this was the same as New Zealand where traffic drives on the left. A pick-up truck forced me to stop by driving in front of me and a stern face came out the window and a stern voice berated me for driving improperly. There was not another vehicle of any description in sight! The man asked for my licence and upon showing him my Cook Islands driver's licence, I noticed it was valid for cars only. Either he didn't notice the restriction or he chose to ignore it, but when he handed the licence back to me, he told me that I should be ashamed of myself. He told me in a voice that was somewhat slurry that he was the Chief of Police. He then accepted my apology and heeded his wife's suggestion to go. She smiled at me in a way as if to say she was sorry her husband was such a grouch. Roger told us later that the slurry voice indicated the Chief had been drinking too much of the liquor illegally made by the natives. Roger also told us that the Chief was Atiu's only police officer.

On we went undaunted on our mini motorcycles. As we commenced the descent from the high ground to the beach I realized I should apply the brake to the rear wheel only, and on the next level stretch thought of stopping to advise Annette to do likewise. How I wished later that I had done so, but thinking I might have a second reprimand that day, I continued on in front of her. The next downgrade was steeper and longer, so much so that I felt nervous about turning around to see how Annette was faring. When I got to the bottom of the hill, I glanced back to see Annette getting up from a fall. I raced back up the hill to find she had terrible gashes in her right leg from the crushed lava roadway, and she couldn't lift her right arm. She was in great pain. The island's baker came along on his little Yamaha and rushed to get Roger. Roger and his wife Kura came in the Datsun. Kura drove Annette to the little hospital while Roger and I followed on the motorcycles. It took some time to find the island's only doctor, but a sweet and kindly nurse was on duty and she cleaned and bandaged Annette's leg wounds. When the doctor arrived, he gave the opinion that the arm was not broken or dislocated. It was badly bruised as was evident from the ugly black and blue colour it was rapidly becoming. This was Friday and the next plane would not be coming until Monday, so we would have to wait for a further diagnosis back in Rarotonga.

That evening we talked with Roger and Kura, and Bill the Englishman who was renting one of the other bungalows. Bill had worked in the South Pacific for an oil company since the end of World War II. He went back to England when he retired, but he missed the islands so much he returned and vowed he would live out his life there. We talked for a long time about the pros and cons of the whole South Pacific area as we gazed at the stars and the moon directly overhead while the gentle trade winds cooled the air sufficiently to allow us to sleep.

Sleep was a fleeting thing for Annette that night, for her arm bothered her a great deal. Her knee and her ankle had sizeable holes in them as a result of the gouging by the crushed lava, but it didn't seem to affect her walking. Perhaps the pain of her arm was so intense, the pain of her leg seemed insignificant by comparison. But it was her leg that received all the attention by the nurse who applied new dressings every day.

On the Saturday, I had planned a "can" dinner since Annette was not able to manage in the kitchen. I was saved by Roger and Kura who invited us to a big barbecued dinner which was attended by Bill the Englishman, the Catholic priest who was of Dutch ancestry, and a German couple who came originally as tourists and stayed to grow coffee on leased land.

On Sunday, we awoke early in the morning to the sound of beating drums which continued for an hour. Roger dismissed our queries with a noncommittal answer and by his demeanour I sensed he didn't want to talk further, so I didn't press the subject just then, thinking I would bring up the matter later. I forgot in the excitement of Annette's outcry at that moment. I rushed in to see a huge orange and black centipede in the washbasin. She breathlessly explained she had been washing her face with her left hand, had reached across with the same hand for the towel when she felt a furry object. She dropped the towel in the basin and when she picked it up again the centipede was there. I went to call Roger. Roger came in with a little stick, calling for Annette not to touch the centipede as it was very poisonous. When he saw it, he turned the water on so it couldn't crawl out and went outside again to get a bigger stick explaining that it was the biggest centipede he had ever seen. He killed it and said, "I must get some chickens." When I asked him why, he replied, "Chickens eat little centipedes, so that big ones like this are rarely seen".

Later that morning, Akai the baker came in his truck to take us on a tour of the island. Annette sat in the car this time with her arm in a sling which eased the pain. I sat in the back with Roger's two children who came along for the ride and to play on the beach. Annette, the shell collector, sat on the beach while I searched for and found some of the prettiest shells of our collection.

We left Atiu the next day with a large bag of pineapples given to us by our host. We learned later that Atiu pineapples are superior to any in the world and sell for higher prices in New Zealand where most of the produce of the Cook Islands finds a market. The nurse came down to wish Annette well and the Catholic priest came but he had not come to see us off. He was going to Rarotonga too. It is quite evident who was held in highest esteem of those leaving Atiu that day. A picture taken with my camera of several of us departing shows the Catholic priest with at least a dozen flower leis around his neck. Annette had two very beautiful ones made of hibiscus, frangipani and the starlike tiare maori which brought a lovely smile to her face. The young chap had three so I guessed how many girls he had talked to. I rated only one rather small lei with small white flowers. When we were in the air I made a comment to the effect I felt secure with two pilots up front. The Catholic priest in the seat beside the pilot didn't respond at all.

Back on Rarotonga, we met a sweet little Chinese lady who was married to a man from Tahiti. Her husband's father was French and his mother was Chinese. They were a handsome couple and Sui was an expert in massage. She worked on Annette's arm which gave her great relief, and the nurses at the clinic dressed her wounds everyday. Such a precaution is necessary in the tropics to guard against infection.

We also met Canadian couples visiting from Vancouver, British Columbia, all of them terrific people. One of the men, Ron Park, was said to have been taken for my brother and it was because of this he looked me up. I thought he looked like my father—not that he was older than me, but that he looked like my father as I remember him at that age. Ron had written some articles about the beauty of the Cook Islands, and these were published in a Vancouver newspaper. He confided that he was sorry they were published since the place is now so crowded with people from British Columbia that he had found it difficult to obtain reasonably priced accommodation for the six months he and his lovely wife spend there every year.

The Cook Islands are very special to us and we knew we would be tempted to return at some time in the future, but the lure of other islands beckoned. On our next trip to the South Pacific, in 1988-89, we chose to go west from Fiji to Vanuatu, that group of islands in Melanesia that was formerly called the New Hebrides.

We had spent some time on the islands of Molokai and Kuwai in Hawaii before taking a dreadful middle-of-the-night flight from Honolulu to Nadi, Fiji. Since we had been in Fiji on other occasions, we stayed only long enough to pick up Air Fiji's weekly flight to Port Vila, Vanuatu's capital city on the island of Efate. The security people at Nadi Airport took everything out of Annette's purse much to her dismay. They finally found the suspicious article...her folding fan! As they replaced the fan, they smiled and voiced their apologies.

The fan was a much-used piece of equipment since Annette found the heat oppressive in Vanuatu. My prime purpose in coming to these islands was not to see Port Vila but to visit Tanna, an island 160 kilometres south. I had read of its luxuriant growth, its active volcano, its primitive peoples and its balmy climate. To leave Port Vila's steamy heat was foremost in Annette's mind and so we arranged with Air Melanesie to go to Tanna the next day. The fan found continuous use as we sat in the fourteen seat Trislander awaiting takeoff. It was a plane of questionable vintage with noisy engines which made conversation extremely difficult for the fifty-five minute flight. On the bright side, the air was cooler and the fan was folded. As we were about to land on a rough, grassy strip cut out of the jungle, the fan came into use again. If I had had a fan, I might have waved it around too, for it seemed that the pilot had trouble keeping the plane on an even keel as we raced down a hill and slowed only when we started to ascend another hill. The landing strip was like a deep saucer although, apparently, it was the least hilly section of the island!

Chief Tom Numake, a handsome, powerful looking man came to meet us. We got in his four-wheel-drive vehicle which took us ten kilometres over a muddy trail to his "White Grass Bungalows". As we drove, we passed native people carrying foodstuffs harvested from their little gardens or garnered from the jungle. Some carried, in an upright position, large bamboo containers of water. All were barefoot and wore only sarongs. As they gracefully ambled along their faces reflected a serenity that comes from peace of mind and lack of tension. Chief Tom told us that his people had little money and little need of any since they lived a subsistence lifestyle, one in which the land provided most of their needs.

We were shown to our "bungalow", a little grass hut built on a slab of concrete. It had one room with two beds, a table, hooks on the walls and two windows. Attached to the back was a bathroom constructed of beach stones and mortar. Hot water was procured by

Our voyage through the Suez Canal.

The docks at Yanbu, Saudi Arabia.

Old Paul aboard the Hellenic Challenger.

Dubai, United Arab Emirates.

Market at Dubai, United Arab Emirates.

Building a teak boat in Bahrain, the island nation in the Persian Gulf.

Sun reflecting a cross on the dome of an Islamic temple.

Baking bread at the Northwestern Hotel in Karachi, Pakistan. (Not a standard hotel kitchen!)

Transportation with camel power in Karachi, Pakistan.

A leper in Bombay.

At prayer, the Koran.

Washeteria in Bombay.

Carved elephants at a temple in Sri Lanka.

Scarecrow to ward off wild elephants, Sri Lanka.

Travel by stilts in Sri Lanka.

Tea factory in Sri Lanka.

In the beautiful Royal Botanical Gardens at Kandy, Sri Lanka.

Outrigger boat in Sri Lanka.

Paradise! French Polynesia.

Moon on the South Pacific.

A Sunday morning at church on the island of Moorea.

Ayers Rock at dawn, Northern Territories, Australia.

Giant anthill on the Atherton Tablelands, Queensland.

Worn steps at Convict's Separate Prison (solitary confinement), Port Arthur, Tasmania.

Devil's Kitchen, Tasmania.

Kiwi fruit in Tasmania.

Boat building on the Greek isle of Patmos.

View of loaded donkey, taken from our balcony on Patmos.

Custom Dance, Tanna.

Yasur Volcano in action, Tanna.

Annette with village chief and others. Note chief's "penis purse"!

A family dwelling, Tanna.

solar energy, but I used it solely for shaving. On the front of the hut was a pleasant little verandah which faced the sea. As we sat there in the cooling trade winds we felt at peace. Tanna has a tranquility all its own.

Tanna was not always calm and bloodless. There were cannibals in this paradise, some say as recently as thirty years ago, but Chief Tom scoffs at that assertion and told us a story about a trading ship coming to the island over a hundred years ago to replenish its fresh water supply. He said, "As the sunburned, swarthy men disembarked from their longboat, Tannese warriors attacked them with stones. The traders fired their guns and the warriors retreated into the jungle but came back in such great numbers that the traders fled, leaving behind one of the crew who had fallen in the water after being struck on the head with a stone. As the longboat pulled away, more shots were fired and the Tannese again retreated into the jungle. They came out to claim their prize only when they saw the ship disappear beyond the horizon. They picked the body out of the water and took off the strange clothes. When they saw the white skin, so different from their own, they felt revulsion and decided that he wouldn't be fit to eat. However, the strange 'skin' covering the feet was a better colour so they took it off, cooked it and attempted to eat it. Not only was it exceedingly difficult to bite but it didn't taste good. Disgusted, they threw the canvas shoes in the water and vowed never to eat a white man again. They were too tough!"

Chief Tom laughed heartily and so did we, after which we went on to the restaurant, a larger grass hut with a nice screened verandah on which we ate our evening meal. Some of the food is grown locally and some is brought in from Port Vila by boat or plane, so that there is almost as much choice on that primitive island as there is in Vanuatu's capital city and the prices were equally reasonable.

The following day, Chief Tom escorted us to a large clearing in the Middle Bush district circled by great banyan trees. He told us that this was the meeting place for several villages. A minor chief, or elder, stood below each banyan with the men and boys of his village and was engaged in what appeared to be an animated discussion. Chief Tom said they were preparing for a "custom" dance and that we would be able to witness it. Without any visible sign, all the males moved from the banyan trees to the centre of the clearing and stood facing each other. They wore only some grass wrapped around their penises which Chief Tom referred to as "penis purses". After the men did one or two routines, girls came into the clearing dressed only in short grass skirts. They encircled the men doing a sort of snake dance as they changed directions but always forming an outer circle around the men. Then they all dispersed, returning to their respective villages.

These types of dances and the drinking of kava, a beverage associated with ritualistic and social significance, were suppressed by Christian missionaries after the Europeans "discovered" these islands. The Tannese had inhabited their land possibly some three thousand years before the arrival of the white man, and this excessive repression resulted in a rebellion of sorts. Thus, the Jon Frum movement began.

The Jon Frum movement is predominant on the island of Tanna. It was born in an attempt to revive the way of life before the coming of the white man. The origin of the name is obscure, but there are several theories including one of a black man who brought many gifts during the years of the World War II. His name was John and he was from (Frum) America.

There are two branches of the movement: the red cross and the black cross. Although they use what might be considered a Christian symbol, the cross, it seems they do not attach the same Christian significance to it. However, it appears to be revered by all members, men and women alike. Women, though, are not allowed to view their most sacred site, and while I was escorted to the place, Annette was asked to remain behind. It was a circle about five metres in diameter and divided by stones into five sections. In one of the sections was a larger stone with red colouring on it which symbolized the beginning of life. The next two sections represented early periods of time "when men were bad and committed crimes". The fourth section represented the present day when all men were supposed to be good and honourable, but since men today are just as bad as they were in the first two eras, another segment had to be added. My escort told me that they still call this place "The Four Corners" even though there is a fifth section because it is only then when peace and goodwill will be practised by all men. I asked if I could take a picture, thinking that my request would be denied, but I was assured it would be alright. My escort told me, and Chief Tom later confirmed, that I could show it to Annette; it was just that neither she nor any woman could stand on that sacred ground.

In the afternoon before our scheduled departure from Tanna, Sam, Chief Tom's son, drove us to Yasur, a continuously active volcano near the southeast coast of the island. This entailed a journey of some thirty-five kilometres through the mountainous interior where one part of the road replaced New Zealand's Skipper's Canyon as the most terrifying of all roads we had travelled. In addition, the road or trail leading up the side of the volcano can be extremely treacherous since the ash surface constantly changes. Even the four-wheel-drive vehicle can become hopelessly stuck, making a long climb on foot the hapless fate of those still wanting to reach the crater. Fortunately, we were able to get within five hundred metres before we were forced to leave the vehicle and walk. Sam led the way, Annette followed and I took up the rear. Even as we started out, the explosions could be heard and felt as the ground trembled beneath our feet. With feelings of trepidation, we continued our climb and were rewarded with the sight of sparks and lava shooting skyward. The rumblings and belchings continued unabated with occasional spectacular explosions which sent streaks of fear up the spines of all three of us. Even Sam, who had been there many times, recoiled and turned away from the sight at one point.

Sam had brought a large flashlight to find our way back to the vehicle, anticipating that we would want to stay after nightfall to experience the true majesty of the eruptions. But Annette was adamant in her decision to leave that awesome place before dark. She was thinking not only of the dangerous descent from the volcano but also of the road over the mountain interior, the part that had so terrified us on the way to the volcano. The road had only recently been washed away and then been poorly repaired.

Sam had said it would be safe if it didn't rain, but that is exactly what it did as we approached the mountain. As we started the climb, the sky opened up to release a torrent of water. In the complete blackness of night and the driving rain, the headlights penetrated no more than a few metres. It was only through this young man's eyes and knowledge of the road that we were able to avoid going into a washout that may have had disastrous results. We were stopped by a huge hole a scant metre from the left-front wheel. Sam told us that we could either wait while he filled in the hole or we could try walking, keeping in the right hand rut away from the precipice. Taking his flashlight, we elected to walk, thinking that there could be other washouts ahead and that we wouldn't want to ride in that vehicle over a muddy repair job. We tried to persuade Sam to leave his vehicle where it was and to walk with us, but he wanted to try.

Hand in hand, Annette and I slogged through the mud to where the road seemed to be more solid and where there were a few shrubs and trees on the down side of the mountain. We stood there in the absolute darkness of that primitive island with no light save our own in sight and no sound except that of the pouring rain. We felt very much alone. In quiet voices, we talked about our predicament; this was probably the worst situation we had experienced. We were at least twenty kilometres from the White Grass Bungalows over a trail completely unknown to us, with similar trails leading off to native villages in the mountains. We had sloshed our way up the mountainside possibly seven hundred metres. It would be more hazardous to go back to Sam and, in any case, what good would that do? We waited and let the warm rain pelt down on us.

Perhaps we waited no more than half an hour, but it seemed much longer. Annette heard the first sounds of a motor and soon headlights shone around the bend. Sam seemed as relieved to see us as we were to see him. There were no more washouts, and the rain subsided shortly after we started down the other side of the mountain. Chief Tom was waiting to greet us. He had become concerned when he had seen the black cloud in the distance and knew we would be caught in a downpour. We felt somewhat relieved, knowing now that he would have come in search of us.

After a refreshing shower, we sat out on the verandah and watched the moon and the beam of light it created on the calm sea. A dark shadow passed the verandah. It was Chief Tom who asked, "Are you happy to be back?" We told him how much we loved this little bit of paradise and he replied, "Stay with us. Build your own house any place you like. You pay nothing." We were quite overwhelmed at this display of generosity and thanked him profusely but explained why we couldn't accept. We just couldn't bring ourselves to give up our roots and move so far from our loved ones.

The return flight to Port Vila was not lacking in the dramatic element either. Just as we were about to take off, a battered pick-up truck drove onto the runway and came directly towards the plane. It was not a highjacking. It was an errand of mercy. Lying on a stretcher in the box of the truck was a boy with bandages on his head, arms and legs. An attendant held the intravenous bottle over the boy. The man seated directly behind me said, "That's the boy who fell from a coconut tree this morning". Apparently he was injured too severely for the local medical people to handle him. "He must get to Port Vila", shouted the attendant. The pilot cut his engines, disembarked and supervised the transfer of baggage from the rear of the plane to the passenger's laps and to the floor under our feet. The stretcher and the boy were then placed in the small baggage compartment. The attendant followed and must have remained in a crouched position for the full hour's flight. Because of the added weight we had difficulty in getting sufficient speed for takeoff. We were nearing the end of the runway and were still bumping along on the rough turf. As we left the ground I felt I could have reached out and touched the tops of the palms.

Although we didn't have much of a headwind, we barely made it to Port Vila. The re-starting of the engines and the added weight resulted in a greater fuel usage. According to the instrument panel which I could see from my seat, there were only forty-four litres of fuel left when we touched the ground. I had wanted to confirm this with the pilot, but he was so busy with the patient and the medical attendant that I didn't have the heart to take up his time.

Our next destination was New Caledonia, farther west in Melanesia. Noumea, its capital city, is the antithesis of Tanna, for it is a virtual paragon of a suave French community. While walking along the beach promenade, taking in the sights of the topless tanners, a couple in our age group stopped and spoke to us in French. From my poor attempt at a reply in their language they knew we were not locals and told us in English that they were from Australia, had lived there for thirty years, that they had been born in France and came to Noumea every two years to satisfy their nostalgic yearnings for things French. Where did we come from, America? Did we like Noumea? All these words gushed forth so rapidly that we just wagged our heads sideways or nodded without any verbal replies until at last they laughed so merrily after realizing their exuberance had monopolized the conversation. Their laughter was infectious and their personalities matched their lightheartedness. We ended up having lunch with them at the Club Med where we sat at a table with four other people, a young couple from New Zealand and the resident doctor and his wife. It was a happy group with our newly found friends engaged in an animated discussion with the French-speaking doctor while we chatted with the quiet New Zealanders...about New Zealand, of course, for that was our next destination.

In the dining room of the Club Med, beer and wine were available from taps in the wall, but we saw no one over-indulging. I over-indulged in dessert, however. There was such an array that I couldn't make up my mind so came back to the table with a plate loaded with four sweets: grasshopper pie, chocolate pudding, cherry cheesecake, and a compote of fresh tropical fruits topped with great mounds of whipped cream. The doctor suggested that I write down his phone number; after eating all that I might need him! To ensure that I wouldn't need him, I shared all the desserts with Annette, and we both survived very nicely.

While we thoroughly enjoyed the European elitism of Noumea, our thoughts returned to Tanna, its primitive way of life and the harrowing experiences we had there. It is not the smooth-running trips that stand out in your memory. The near disasters or the unusual happenings, which can occur when travellers take the unconventional routes of the vagabonder, become cherished memories which never fade away.

Part II

Preparing for the Vagabonding Experience

In order to fully appreciate "vagabonding", it is assumed that you possess the spirit of adventure, the desire to explore and, above all, the imagination to dream of far-off lands where balmy breezes blow over soft, silvery sands while harsh, wicked winds whip sleet and snow around the cottage at home. Or, perhaps you wonder about places where peoples's lifestyle is different from your own, and you want to satisfy your curiosity by actually going there. Perhaps once you do, then you will be content to stay home. But let us warn you, once you get hooked into this style of travel, you can never go back to the humdrum existence of living in one place all year long. It gets in your blood. You may be tempted at times to "settle down" in a country which seems to fulfill your every need, but after a few months you find you still have 'itchy feet' and want to move on.

Often friends of ours, seniors like ourselves, have expressed concern when they contemplate a journey, even one of rather short duration. People have told us how "brave" we are to travel as we do and this, as much as anything else, prompted me to write of our experiences to show these friends and other senior citizens that there is very little necessity for apprehension if ordinary care is taken. Here, I'll deal with the practical aspects of travel which might cause concern to seniors. By following some simple words of advice and using common sense, any one can feel confident leaving home to see the world in the same manner as we have.

This section is a guide in the sense that it will hopefully relieve causes of concern to seniors travelling on their own and offer helpful hints in preparing for the vagabonding experience. It is not a guide in the manner of the standard "How To" travel book which gives detailed information on obtaining passports or what goods may be purchased abroad and brought back through Customs. Nor does it contain a wide choice of accommodation and fare prices. I leave all such specifics to those "How To" books. If I were to include them, the book would lose its main theme - vagabonding.

Having said all that, I do not censure the standard travel publications. On the contrary, I use them, often referring to them for information on accommodation. For example, if we are going to Greece, I will go to the library to study a travel book on that country and look at the prices of accommodations. I will take notes, but will use them only as a measure of costs, bearing in mind that experience has shown places which charge less are not generally listed in these books. I use them, too, for hints on places to see and things to do while I am visiting a particular area. In general, I make use of any data I can get. No one book can possibly be all-informative so it is prudent to read several.

While you may want to purchase some of these books, libraries are a source of information second to none and they are pleasant, peaceful places in which to spend time planning your trip. While I love to roam, to vagabond about a country until I absorb some of its atmosphere and its philosophical outlook, it is gratifying to be aware of the geographical, historical and political significance of the country you are visiting. The world is full of interesting people and places and it is within the reach of many North American retirees. All it takes is a measure of planning and a mildly adventuresome spirit.

So many seniors believe travel requires a great deal of money. The happy fact is that it doesn't. Because you are not bound to travel in peak times, you can obtain cheaper fares. As seniors, you can get many other reductions and discounts. In particular, costs of accommodation, which can be the most expensive part of your travel expenses, do not have to be so high as to take the joy out of your adventure.

Do you really want the poshest accommodation, or are you satisfied with staying in accommodation similar to that you have at home or, occasionally, in places that are inferior? If your answer to the last part of this question is "yes", you qualify for vagabonding and can see the world on a budget. I have never fully understood why people of modest means feel they must have five-star hotels when they travel. You will not always meet interesting people in these hotels for they will be tourists on organized tours or out-of-country business people who are not anxious to talk with strangers or North Americans travelling on their own.

Contrast this with a stay in more modest types of accommodation where business people, government officials and others from within the country find reasonably priced rooms. Here, too, you will meet people from many foreign lands who are more interested in coming into contact with others like themselves, people with whom they can converse about the everyday life of the country they are visiting, rather than the purely touristic sights and shows put together by tour operators. Some of our most delightful periods of foreign travel have been spent in the company of local people or vagabonds from other countries. For people who are still in the work force, a holiday in an expensive hotel at a seaside resort or on an organized tour or cruise is an acceptable means of travel, but unless you have unlimited funds, retired folks away from home for extended periods of time simply cannot afford these highly priced lodgings and tours.

Occasionally we like to splurge, to leave the hoi polloi and mix with the upper crust or at least with the upper middle classes. Then we will take a cruise, stay a night or two in a posh hotel or opt for the best compartment on an overnight train. Still, as a general rule, we have found the most observant, intelligent and stimulating people on the beaches of New Zealand, in the coffee houses of the Mediterranean, in the small communities of Scandinavia or in the outback of Australia. In all such places and, indeed, in all corners of the world, there is a considerable amount of goodwill and sincerity among the informed people everywhere. Meeting people of cultures different from our own and staying in their communities long enough to observe their everyday activities furthers our understanding of their feelings and aspirations. You come to realize there is little cause for concern in travelling to foreign lands.

On the Home Front

During the summer months, Annette and I decide where we would like to go during the winter. We make full use of the public library by reading about the countries we propose to visit. Then, we go to a travel agent and determine the cheapest and most interesting ways of getting there.

An example of our preparations for a winter away from home is the chronology of events leading to a recent trip to Italy and the Greek Islands. We had read a considerable amount of material on both countries and since, during previous trips to Europe, we had missed Italy completely and had been only in the Athens area of Greece, we resolved to start our winter's sojourn in that area of the world.

In July, I went to a travel agent to ask for the cheapest airfares from Montreal to Rome and from Athens to Montreal. KLM and CP Air were advertising special rates in the travel section of the newspaper. These were rates for return fares to each place. Since we would be flying to Rome but not returning from there, I asked if we could have the special return fare at half-price. I asked for the same consideration on the flight from Athens to Montreal. Both requests were readily granted. The airlines never advertise this 'mix and match' type of travel. Invariably, the specials refer only to return fares.

The price quotations from KLM and CP Air were the same, but we chose KLM because their flights were more conveniently timed for us to take the bus to and from Ottawa. Incidently, the bus fares for seniors are greatly reduced, but you do have to ask for the senior rate when purchasing your ticket.

How would we get from Rome to Athens? Flights within Europe are very expensive for the comparatively short distances involved. So an element of adventure enters the picture. We decided we would make our way from Rome to Athens by surface means.

I had hoped to travel by ship from Sicily to Santorini or Crete and, accordingly, I borrowed "The Worldwide Cruise and Shipline Guide" from our travel agent. This contains not only the routes of the expensive cruise ships but also worldwide information about local and district ferries. While it is not complete, it did reveal that there were ferries crossing the Adriatic Sea on a fairly regular basis. Nowhere, however, could I find any ships plying the route that we really wanted to take—from someplace in the south of Italy to somewhere in the Greek Islands. I did not know, in advance, how we would get to Athens from Rome and realized that I would have to wait until we were in Italy to make a final decision. I did use the "Guide", however, to prepare a list of possible routes so that we would be better prepared when making enquiries over there. It is often this sort of spontaneous move that makes our trips the adventures that they are.

Leaving Home

Leaving home for a long period of time involves only slightly more planning than a short vacation. We have had a summer cottage for thirty years so we were well acquainted with the regimen. On retirement, we sold our house in the city and moved "lock, stock and barrel" to the cottage. We now keep a detailed checklist of the steps required to turn off our water system in the fall and another to turn it on again in the spring. In addition, we keep a list of miscellaneous things to do, such as storing the boat and the car, putting the shutters on, storing foodstuffs and other items which could freeze, emptying the electric kettle, locking all buildings and turning the electric main switch to "OFF".

Fortunately, we have neighbours who watch our cottage daily and we have had no break-ins, so we feel confident in leaving our only permanent abode for months at a time. We can return in the spring fairly well-assured that everything will be as we left it in the fall.

Those of you who live in an apartment will have considerably less preparation in respect to leaving home. However, if you have a paper delivered you should remember to cancel it and, of course, you will want to arrange for your mail to be picked up. We have a neighbor get our mail at the same time they get their own, but that is at our local post office. In the city, where mail is delivered, it would be necessary to arrange for a neighbor to collect it for you or ask the post office to hold or forward your mail. In the latter cases, a fee is normally charged.

If you live in a house in the city, your problems increase somewhat since very few houses have plumbing designed for draining all the water from the pipes. Also, shutters on the windows or an unplowed driveway are sure signs of vacancy which can invite thieves and vandals. Often the best solution is to rent your house to responsible people for the period of your absence. We have friends who do this and the rental money they receive comes close to paying the expenses of their trips. One spring they returned to find a hefty bill for repairs to their furnace, but another year they were delightfully surprised to find all their bedrooms had been repainted in delicate pastel shades. They had been intending to redecorate those rooms for several years, but just couldn't seem to find the time! They reckoned they were well ahead financially since the furnace would have required repairs whether they or someone else were living in the house, and to have all that painting done at no cost to them was a bonus indeed.

In most cases, we continue with our usual cottage life until mid-October when we commence preparations for our departure. Annette gets a haircut and a permanent wave. We wrap Christmas presents for our children and grandchildren. We ship a large parcel of Christmas presents to our daughter and her family in Edmonton, even though we may occasionally visit there during the Christmas season.

Before we leave, I buy ten rolls of film for our camera, both because that number of rolls is usually sufficient for the duration of our trip and because I get a discount for buying ten or more. We go to our doctors to obtain prescriptions which will allow us sufficient medication to last the winter months.

As usual, there are lists: "Things to do before we leave", "Things to take" and one year, because we intended to make three decidedly different trips during the winter season, we added further lists: "Things to take to Edmonton" and "Things to take to Myrtle Beach". This might seem like a lot of unnecessary organization, but such lists provide assurance that you won't forget anything at the last moment.

Then there is the business of banking. I usually charge a lot of our expenses, such as accommodation and travel costs, to our Visa credit card. However, caution dictates that I take enough cash and travellers' cheques to tide us over in case we have difficulty using the credit card. This can prove to be a wise decision since, in many countries, only the more expensive hotels accept credit cards.

Of course, there are the usual duties of closing up the cottage and storing the car in the garage until our return. The storing of the car is a simple matter. I drive it on to pieces of chipboard so that the tires are in contact with wood instead of concrete, and I take the battery out. Our son takes the batteries from the car, the lawn tractor and the boat, along with our paints, glues and foodstuffs that would deteriorate by freezing, to his home in Ottawa. At the same time, he will take his parents to the airport or bus terminal where we will commence our adventure.

Finances

Senior citizens can arrange to have their pension cheques sent directly to a bank for deposit thus eliminating the worry of cheques being misplaced. Also, this way interest is being compounded on your money. If you have any other income, such as bond interest or rental income, you can also arrange to have it deposited to your account. Your bank manager will be pleased to help you with such arrangements. Further, if you plan to use a credit card while you are away for a long period of time, you might consider having the monthly statements sent to your bank and have the bank charge your account. The bank may charge a small fee for this service, but it is worth this expense to save paying interest to the credit card company.

Just before we leave for the winter, we pay our hydro and telephone companies a sum of money calculated to cover the bills for the duration of our absence. Other bills, such as car and fire insurance, come due in the summer months since we made such arrangements years ago after commencing our vagabonding to other parts of the world. If you are renting an apartment, you can leave post-dated cheques with the landlord or have a good friend or neighbor look after them.

If you are going to travel in a true vagabonding manner, it is wise not to take along costly jewelry. Rings and brooches that are precious because of their monetary or sentimental value are best left in a safety deposit box along with your important documents. Seniors can rent a box at most banks for around $20 per year. And if you have some very valuable pieces of furniture, china or silverware and are apprehensive about the possibility of them being stolen while you are away, perhaps you could leave them with your children or a responsible friend. We solved such problems by bestowing family treasures upon our children in advance of our wills being read!

Protecting valuables and looking after finances at home is a fairly simple matter, but you may wonder how we protect our money, travellers' cheques, passports and other documents we carry with us. It is wise not to carry any of these items in your carry-on bag. Each of our bags do, however, contain photostats of pages 2 and 3 of our passports, our certificates of citizenship and birth, and the addresses and telephone numbers of our children. The latter, while being in our heads, are also in my diary, but having this information readily available could relieve anxiety should a stressful situation arise. We have never had occasion to require these sheets, but we always take them along.

The passports themselves are always carried on our person. Of course, if we are renting a house or an apartment which we look after ourselves, we treat it like a home and select a place to keep our passports and money, but when we travel we ensure they are with us. Annette prefers to be unencumbered by documents so I carry both passports, our transportation tickets and the bulk of our money and travellers' cheques.

I have four places on my person which are fairly secure. I buy trousers which have the opening of the side pockets parallel with the belt rather than a slit beside the seam. My favourite trousers are the 'Hopsack Jeans' made by G.W.G. (Great Western Garments). I don't like blue jeans, but the Hopsack, a dressy jean with a gentleman's fit, available in several colours, suits my taste. It is rugged, durable, washable and never needs pressing so it is the perfect pant to wear for travel purposes. When purchasing these I ensure that they are longer than necessary. When Annette hems the legs she has sufficient material left to make flaps for the side pockets. She makes button holes on these so that the flaps can be buttoned shut. She also extends the pockets to accommodate my long wallets. In addition, I have a terry cloth "pocket" with a strap of the same material that I can hang over my neck. I have felt the need to use this only occasionally when walking in crowded areas such as the marketplaces of Bombay or Tangier. Tilley Endurables of Toronto, a company specializing in travel clothing, have some excellent products which would appeal to many seniors. Their hats have a small compartment for hiding money and are especially good for protection from the tropical sun.

What I always use is a money belt—not the type that goes inside your clothing, although they are good—but a leather belt which looks ordinary but has a zipper on the inside. I have made it a practice while travelling to carry some bills in Canadian and American currency in this belt.

I carry a third wallet, a regular sized one, where I place the local currency so that there is no need to open my big wallets when purchasing items in foreign countries. Even so, I do not carry this wallet in a back pocket which would be the easiest target for a pickpocket. We have been fortunate since we have never lost anything, but being prepared relieves your mind of uncertainty and allows you to go where others might feel apprehensive.

Spotting potential danger, too, helps considerably. When we were on our way to the railway station in Rome, Italy, two young boys ran up to us with eyes darting all over our clothing. They ran off and returned with a horde of children. Some of these children had newspapers with which to distract us while others were to dip in our pockets for wallets. I did not allow them to get close since I had heard of these bands of children, all gypsies, who are to be found in some of the large cities of the Mediterranean countries.

In some countries, where we have spent an extended period of time, we have opened bank accounts. This helps considerably when transferring moneys from your account at home. In New Zealand, for example, we have written a cheque on our account at home and deposited it to our account in New Zealand. The bank there issues a passbook that you can take to any branch throughout the country in order to make a withdrawal. Not all countries are as accommodating as that, but if you have an account you will have no trouble cashing a draft or cashier's cheque from your bank at home.

These types of transactions allow you to carry less money and fewer travellers' cheques and to leave your money in the bank at home earning interest for a longer period. Of course, if you are on the move constantly, arrangements such as these are difficult to make. When we took our first around-the-world trip we had a Letter of Credit with us, but banks no longer issue these to ordinary travellers.

So many seniors, as well as other people, think that it takes a lot of money to travel, so they stay home and endure the cold winters and some even convince themselves that they like it! We have done a comparison of costs between staying the winter at our cottage in Rideau Ferry and renting a house in New Zealand, based on the exchange rates in 1985-86.

Monthly Costs at Rideau Ferry		Monthly Costs in New Zealand	
Heating...oil and wood	$150	House rental	$350
Electricity	50	Car	
Snow clearance	25	-insurance	9
Extra telephone calls	25	-pro-rated loss in	
Car insurance(not		buying & selling	34
required when car stored)	30	-pro-rated transfer cost	7
Canadian	$280	New Zealand	$400
		Canadian	$300

Not taken into account are the many vegetables and fruits we used from the garden of the house in New Zealand which the owners urged us to use. Considering that we saved at least $20 per month in our produce food bill, our costs were the same. Of course, the cost of getting to New Zealand is a very significant factor, but our actual living expenses were comparable.

On our latest visit to New Zealand, in 1989, we were not as lucky in buying a used car since we had to pay $500 (N.Z.) for repairs. Even so, for the ninety days we owned the car, our net cost worked out to only $10 (N.Z.) per day. At the current rate of exchange, that was $7 Canadian, which is very reasonable compared to a rental car.

Discounts (or getting your money's worth)

Most senior citizens are cautious in how they spend their money, having worked during their early years at low-paying jobs and being now on fixed incomes. So it is natural to seek bargain fares and ask for discounts.

When we go to a travel agent we make it known that we want the cheapest fare available, that we will travel on weekdays or on weekends, in the daytime or at night and by any carrier. Some airlines have special rates on weekends while others have cheaper rates during the week. Night flights are often cheaper than daytime flights. Not having to meet deadlines or to schedule all our sightseeing into a few hours or a few days means we can arrive at our destination at any hour or any day of the week. We can rest and relax at our own pace. In addition, we stress to the travel agent that any discounts available to senior citizens be applied. Often, we have paid less than the original quoted price simply by asking, "What reduction is there for senior citizens?" We have asked for discounts at many hotels around the world and seldom have we failed to be obliged.

Travelling by bus, train or ferry is often considerably cheaper than by air and infinitely more interesting. This is certainly the case when you are vagabonding around countries like New Zealand or Greece. In Fiji you can travel across three hundred kilometres of the main island by bus for one-fifth the price of the airfare. Air travel is cheaper than surface transportation when crossing great distances over the oceans. Even travel by freighter, once thought of as being the least expensive means of going overseas, is more costly than travelling the same route by air. Occasionally, it is cheaper to rent a car than to take other means of transportation. Then, too, you may decide to go to a place accessible by taxi or rental car only.

Often, a comparison of travel costs is required on an as-you-go basis, particularly when you are vagabonding in the true sense with no planned itinerary. Strangely, making these inquiries and decisions can become an integral part of the enjoyment of the whole experience. It takes a relatively short time but gives great satisfaction and certainly saves a considerable amount of money.

Many foreign countries, particularly in Europe, offer discounts such as Switzerland's Senior Half-Fare Travel Card. These are not only for trains; they can be used on lake boats and some buses. In France and Germany, similar cards can be purchased for a small fee and it is not necessary to prepare for these before leaving home. They can be purchased at the depots shortly before boarding. In all cases, though, presentation of your passport is a must.

There are discounts which can be obtained on train or bus travel in Australia, if tickets for specific periods of one, two or three weeks validity are purchased before leaving home. Some people may find this advantageous, but pre-planning to this extent takes away from the spontaneity of vagabonding. Seldom are we positive of the date we will arrive in any one spot, so we have discarded this manner of purchasing fares. Similarly, discounts can be obtained on car rentals, not only in Australia but in other countries as well. Considerable savings can be realized if you have definite ideas of where you are going and for what period of time.

Leasing or purchasing a car are other alternatives to be considered. Our experience of buying a car in Nelson, New Zealand had a happy result, but it may be wiser in some instances to purchase a car through a dealer. Except for short trips to Europe where I know we will want a car for two or three weeks as soon as we land, I prefer to wait until we reach our destination, assess the situation and then bargain for the cheapest rate possible. In many cases I have got more for less than people who pre-arranged their deal.

In many countries of the world you can bargain for lower prices on a great variety of goods and services. In some places, in fact, it is expected. During our first around-the-world trip, Annette initially declared a dislike of the practice, but she became so proficient at bargaining that I realized that this was her domain and so I seldom interfered in any of the intricacies of this practice. In markets, for example, Annette would offer less than half the quoted price and when the vendor would counter with a price higher than hers but well below the original price she was confident of purchasing the item for only slightly above her first offer. Annette became so accustomed to bargaining that when we returned home she instinctively resorted to the procedure, even in stores where prices were definitely fixed. At a market in Tbilisi, Georgia, U.S.S.R., she couldn't resist bargaining for a straw broom. Imagine arriving home with an ordinary straw broom as a souvenir! Out of curiosity she had asked the price of the broom and when the merchant, a hefty, ruddy-faced woman from the countryside, put up three fingers, Annette put up two fingers. I happened to be taking a picture of the scene and have the proof on film. I still tease Annette about trying to fly out of the Soviet Union on a broom!

Clothing

Most people take far too much clothing when they travel. We have had friends come to visit for a week at our cottage bringing along several huge suitcases filled with more clothing than they could use in a month if they changed their wardrobe every day. While there can be variations in the weather, it is almost certain that three sweaters will not be needed in July. Nor is it likely that a business suit would be appropriate wear at any time in such an informal setting. These people invariably take home their elaborate luggage with the majority of the contents untouched.

No matter where we travel, we restrict our luggage to one carry-on bag each. It is so much better to take less than is considered necessary. I have had to buy extra clothing in Tasmania, Australia when unexpectedly cold weather forced me to buy a sweater, but this was a rare occurrence. Of course, if you travel to places where you will be attending ceremonial rites with dignitaries present, then formal attire will be required, but vagabonds are seldom invited to such functions.

Yet, the vagabonding writer and his wife did dine with royalty one evening in Karachi, Pakistan and were dining companions, for two days in the beautiful dining car of the India-Pacific train across Australia, with an educator known worldwide for his lectures at medical universities. Despite our informal attire, we were graciously accepted on both occasions which is sufficient evidence that great stocks of garments are completely unnecessary. It is true that we get a little tired of seeing each other in the same two sets of clothing which we label our "uniforms", but the people we meet and converse with don't know that we are restricted to this degree.

Footwear is an item of great importance insofar as safety is concerned and one that often receives insufficient attention. Since vagabonding travel generally involves considerable walking, comfortable and sturdy walking shoes are of immense importance for both men and women. They not only provide better support, but also provide surer traction so that you are much less apt to fall. A friend whom we met at the airport in Auckland one year had nurtured the dream of seeing New Zealand for many years. She had to see it from the seat of a car while trying to navigate with crutches and a broken ankle, all because she wasn't wearing sturdy walking shoes. We regard our walking shoes in the same light as our clothing...while they may not be as attractive as other shoes, they are most practical and are a part of our "uniform".

If our plans include a long period of time in one place, such as a three month stay in New Zealand, we make special arrangements before leaving home. Since we have relatives in New Zealand, we sent a parcel of clothing and other things to them by surface mail about two months before our departure. In this way we had plenty of dressier things to wear when necessary during our extended stay. We could have sent this parcel of clothing to the people from whom we were renting the house, for we had pre-arranged that part of our sojourn. When we left New Zealand we took a larger parcel to the post office to mail home. This parcel contained the dressier clothes we had originally sent, as well as some that we had bought and the souvenirs we had collected along the way. We were back to our "uniforms" again.

Naturally, if you are going to a country where it is cold, you have to take some warm clothing. If you are going on a ship, not only will a warm, wool sweater be advisable, but a light-weight, windproof coat is necessary. If you are going to spend most of your time in the tropics, you will want to have light-weight cottons, including cotton undergarments. The World Climate Charts issued by IAMAT (International Association for Medical Assistance To Travellers) [see section on Health and Diet] include recommended clothing and temperature variations for all seasons of the year in all parts of the world.

Baggage

The bane of travellers of all ages is baggage, and it can be especially irksome for seniors if it is heavy or in great quantity. The trick is to travel with as little as possible. It took us a few years to learn to restrict our travel requirements to the barest necessities, but it has paid off in the ease with which we travel from place to place with only a carry-on bag each. We don't have a knapsack like many young people carry, but we use the largest size of carry-on bag available, complete with a handle and a shoulder strap. Naturally, it is made of very light-weight material.

Finally, there is the packing of our luggage. Take, for example, our trip to the Mediterranean. Although we knew from temperature charts obtained from IAMAT that we could expect cool days and cooler nights in Italy and Greece in November and December, we were determined to maintain of practice of travelling with only a carry-on bag each. We would get our warmth not by changing clothes but by adding an extra piece of underwear, an extra sweater or jacket, all lightweight and crushable things which would not add too much weight or bulk to our bags. We had the smallest toothbrushes and tubes of toothpaste available, disposable razors and, instead of a can of shaving lather, I took a small tube of shaving cream that doesn't require a brush.

I never take an electric razor for they are weighty and in many parts of the world the amperage is such that a converter is necessary. Annette takes only a few curlers for her hair and keeps away from glass or bulky containers for her cosmetics. When we have packed everything on our "Things to take" list, we go over every item again and ask ourselves the question, "Do we really need this?" Invariably, we can lighten our load by taking something out. I ensure that we have our wallets, tickets, passports, money, travellers' cheques and our credit card, most of which is carried on my person deep in the extra long pockets of my pants or the inside pockets of my jacket. Annette carries some cash and cheques, too.

We can leave feeling confident that we have everything in order. We can get off airplanes, buses, ships or trains without having to wait for our baggage and without assistance from anyone. We are independent!

When preparing to pack, estimate the number of films you will require for the whole trip and buy them here in North America for, comparatively speaking, they are very expensive in foreign countries. Too, the type of film you use may not be available. On our first big trip, I found that my favourite film could not be found in some out-of-the-way place where I ran out. The result? Pictures of varying hues, not the proudest of my photographic achievements.

Documentation

Passports

Canadian passports are valid for five years. Applications are available at post offices and the completed forms may be sent or taken to any regional office of the Passport Office. For complete information write to Passport Office, Department of External Affairs, Ottawa, Ontario K1A 0G3. Application forms indicate the cities where passports may be obtained. It is preferable to go in person since, in most cases, the passport can be obtained in a shorter length of time. Further, if you have completed the form incorrectly or you are missing a necessary document, the clerk will be able to advise you immediately.

U.S. passports are valid for ten years. Applications are available at post offices and the completed forms may be sent or taken to any office of the U.S. Passport Agency. For complete information write to Bureau of

Consular Affairs, Passport Services, Room 386, Department of State, 425 K Street, Washington, D.C. 20524.

Visas

A visa is an endorsement stamped on your passport by representatives of the country you are visiting. This stamp shows that the passport has been examined and that you have been granted entry into that country. Not all countries require visitors to have a visa, and reliable travel agents should be conversant with such requirements.

Health and Diet

Before you leave on any trip, make an appointment with your doctor and tell your doctor at that time where you plan to go and what you plan to do. He will advise you on your physical limitations, such as avoiding extremely high altitudes or areas of volcanic gases if you have a heart or respiratory problem. He will be able to advise you on any need for vaccinations or preventative medicines you should take for the areas of the world you intend to visit. He may refer you to the District Health Unit of the county in which you live, but the need for many immunizations has been reduced considerably in recent years. Your doctor can prescribe any regular medication for the full period of your absence and he can also prescribe something for motion sickness and stomach disorders. It is possible to have a stomach upset while travelling in your own country yet alone on trips abroad, so it is reassuring to have such medication with you. And while you are at your doctor's, obtain a note outlining your physical condition and your prescriptions. It may be helpful to a foreign doctor or at a border crossing. While we have never had occasion to use such a note, we have always carried one as a precaution.

The World Immunization and World Malaria Risk charts supplied by the International Association for Medical Assistance to Travellers (IAMAT) provide particularly helpful information with respect to prevention of illness. These charts give the latest status of every country of the world and are excellent guidelines for travellers of varying ages. IAMAT will also supply World Climate charts which indicate information on sanitary conditions of water, milk and foods, as well as clothing recommended for every season of the year in every area of the world. IAMAT publishes a little directory showing institute clinics and doctors in many countries of the world where medical assistance can be obtained, and where the staff or the medical practitioner has a command of the English language. These establishments have also agreed to a stated and standard list of medical fees for their services. The IAMAT membership and the directory are free, but since it exists solely on voluntary funding, it's a good practice to send a small donation each year. The charts are invaluable in planning a trip and the presence of the directory in your pocket or bag is another assurance for seniors in case of illness while abroad. IAMAT can be contacted in Canada at 1287 St. Clair Avenue West, Toronto, Ontario M6E 1B8 and in the U.S. at 736 Centre Street, Lewiston, N.Y. 14092.

To avoid illnesses associated with eating and drinking, it is only sensible to take precautions. In tropical countries and in the Near East and the Far East, as well as in the Mediterranean area of Europe, it is generally wise to avoid drinking water, drinks with ice cubes, and milk. It is far better to drink tea, coffee, soft drinks, beer and wine. Sometimes bottled water and shelf milk are available. Avoid eating melons or salads and peel all fruits before eating them raw.

We did not follow our own advice in the dining room of a hotel in Tangier, Morocco. The salad looked so appetizingly crisp and fresh that we succumbed to temptation, thinking that surely anything that looked so good and tasted so good couldn't be anything but good. The next morning, however, we found out how fast we could move in the direction of the bathroom when nature rebels against food washed in tainted water.

We have not repeated that mistake; but some years previously in Taipei, Taiwan, hungry for something other than Chinese food, I ordered spaghetti and meat sauce. Annette warned me against such a dish, in such a place, but I insisted I had a 'cast iron' stomach. I found out otherwise. Of course, change of water or a tainted dish, even here in North America, can result in an uncomfortable episode, but you can do much to avoid these incidents if you are careful of what you eat and drink. Again, though, taking along a prescription of Lomotil or some other such remedy is an additional assurance of a pleasant trip.

The best way to follow a diet is to eat as little as possible in restaurants and to buy and prepare your own food. Following this regimen while vagabonding around the world is not as difficult as it might seem. The main objective is to find reasonably priced accommodation with cooking facilities, in an area which takes your fancy and in a location where you can walk to shops and a marketplace to buy foods compatible with your diet. Not only do you eat correctly, but you absorb some of the local atmosphere while saving a great deal of money.

In Monte Gordo, Portugal, we had an apartment right on the beach of beautiful Algarve province. Connected to the hotel was a supermarket where food was in abundance at reasonable prices and only a block behind the hotel was a farmer's market. We had no trouble keeping to the dictates of our diets there, nor on the island of Madeira, New Zealand or Australia, not even on the exotic island of Bali in Indonesia. Admittedly, there are times when you cannot adhere strictly to your diet. But since this is not likely to cause any direct consequences in our cases, we can revel in some of the food specialties of other lands.

Safety

Naturally, there is always the remote possibility of a plane crash, a ferry sinking, or a train or car accident. However, if such fears stop you from travelling, you probably qualify for a good 'armchair vagabond'. We have a relative who, through extensive reading, knows as much or more about many features of places we have visited as we do. She would dearly love to experience actually being there, but she has a dreadful fear of flying or of being on the water.

While my wife, Annette, had flown many times to her home state of Virginia, I had flown very little before our first around-the-world trip. As we started to travel, I was apprehensive for the first few take-offs and landings, but I have come to feel exhilarated by air travel and now enjoy most of our many flights. We are both fortunate, too, in being good sailors, although Annette occasionally has felt the need for Dramamine or some other remedy to combat a slight feeling of motion sickness.

A fear of air travel is a common one and can strike anyone at any age. Our own daughter dreads every flight she takes and has to boost her courage with determination before boarding. A good friend, one of the people who look upon us as being brave, used to be fearful of planes, boats and even cars. She somehow trusted bus drivers for she rode city buses almost daily, yet her husband who is a good driver had to use extraordinary measures of persuasion to get her in a car. Fortunately, in her later years, she has become more resigned and has flown to Europe twice. However, on both occasions her method of travel while there was exclusively by bus!

As far as personal safety is concerned, a lot depends on attitude and common sense. You would not poke your finger into a shredding machine or a beehive, nor would you get in a rowboat half-full of water or walk into a line of fire between army troops and terrorists. If strangers attempt to involve you in a deal which arouses your suspicions, even remotely, decline. This doesn't mean that you don't talk to strangers, just that you can be selective.

If you plan to visit foreign lands where you might feel some degree of apprehension, you might feel safer carrying the addresses and telephone numbers of your home embassy in those countries. These are generally obtainable from passport offices in major cities across the country. The embassies will not help you with things that travel agents normally do, but they can advise and help you with any serious troubles which might occur. We have often taken along a list of embassy addresses, but luckily have never had occasion to use it.

Communication with Family and Friends

Being out of touch with children, grandchildren and friends is sometimes a concern to seniors away from home for long periods of time. It is often a worry for the senior's family as well. To alleviate the concern of others, simply send cards or letters whether you are in Europe, New Zealand, Indonesia or some idyllic South Sea island.

In some places, it is best to ensure the stamps are put on your cards or letters. We wrote fourteen cards shortly after our arrival in Karachi, Pakistan and went to the sub-post office near the hotel to mail them. Since the cards were addressed to several different countries around the world, we couldn't ask for fourteen stamps of the same denomination, so we handed the cards to the postal clerk to determine what stamps were required. He dutifully chose the different stamps and said that he would put them on the cards. I paid him the money. Not one of those fourteen cards were ever received by the addressees!

You can telephone home from most countries, but it is often expensive unless set rates are clearly established. It is especially so if you call from a pay telephone. If you cannot dial direct, it is best to go to a post office. When we are abroad, we seldom telephone home or write lengthy letters, but we do send an abundance of cards which seem to be greatly appreciated. I have made it a practice to send a card to my sister from every country we have visited. She saves them for me and I am missing only one...the card from Karachi, Pakistan!

If you take a cruise on a freighter, the shipping company will supply you with a list of their shipping agents in the ports to be visited, as well as the approximate dates of arrival. You can pass these on to relatives and friends so that letters can be waiting for you when you arrive in each port. Some international agents, such as Thomas Cook, provide a similar service. While it is not encouraged, embassies will forward mail also, particularly in emergency situations.

Conclusion

While this part of the book has been written to inform seniors and persons approaching that classification, I hope that younger people find it and the narrative helpful and of interest. So many of the 'vagabonds' we have talked with in the coffee houses of the Mediterranean, on otherwise deserted beaches in New Zealand, and in out-of-the-way places around the world have been recent university graduates, the middle-aged taking a few months away from the stresses of demanding jobs, and occasionally people who choose to live the simple life unfettered by the demands of a structured society. Whatever their status, or from what country they came, or to what doctrine they adhere...almost all have been interesting and stimulating. In all cases—young, middle-aged or old—when I told them of my writing, they asked to be advised at the time of publication. So, while I write of senior vagabonds for seniors, I anticipate that vagabonds of all ages will be encouraged to venture into lands with cultures and outlooks different from their own.

For those who still prefer to be armchair vagabonds, take off in your imaginary vehicle and 'see' the canals of Thailand with their colourful boats laden with tropical fruits or draperies, 'see' the even more colourful temples of that fascinating country, or stroll through the marketplaces in the back streets of Hong Kong, Bombay or Hobart. Take the "sugar train" across the cane fields of Fiji, walk the clean, secluded beaches of New Zealand, 'taste' the nutty flavour of the witchety grub in Australia's outback. 'Feel' your armchair tremble as it climbs the slopes of Tanna's active volcano, or turn your conveyance into a camel as you lope along the shoreline in Karachi. Or would you rather dine with a Nawab in Pakistan, eat with a Vanuatu Chief whose ancestors were cannibals, or have tea with a former Prime Minister of New Zealand? All these things are possible in your imagination...or in reality if you choose to turn your dreams to action.

Either way, happy vagabonding!

Epilogue

The latest population statistics show the U.S.A. with 241,489,000 people of which 28,530,000 are aged 65 and over, and 44,922,000 are between the ages of 45 and 64. This means that over 30% are mature people, retired or on the verge of retirement. The Canadian statistics, showing 2,698,000 aged 65 and over, with 4,874,000 between the ages of 45 and 64 out of a total population of 25,309,000 substantiates the proportion. The ever-increasing numbers of seniors are becoming a significant factor in the travelling population and they tend to travel more often and for much longer periods of time than the two or three week holiday packages taken by people still in the work force. This publication is, therefore, timely and apt.

Although the book bears some resemblance to a travel guide for senior citizens, it was not intended to be so designated nor to have such restrictions. From reading the narrative, seniors and adults of all ages may very well glean some helpful hints on what to do and what not to do, and that was intended. Indeed, a young lady not yet twenty years of age, who did some typing for me, declared a profound interest in visiting the country about which she was typing. She added she hoped to do so, after she finished her education, in the vagabonding style! Although the prime purpose is to entertain, I sincerely hope that seniors will be inspired to travel as my young typist was.

Keeping active through work, voluntary or otherwise, helps seniors maintain a healthy body and a healthy mind. If you refuse to let your body and mind slip into a routine of inactivity and apathy, your general health-physical and mental-will bloom with renewed vigour. Travel, in the manner chosen by Annette and me, has not only resulted in a renewal of physical well-being, but has helped to free us from bigotry and prejudice.

Vagabonding, as my wife and I have experienced it, has not turned us into hobos or tramps since we have vagabonded in a form quite unlike that of the homeless people of the world. We have often roamed about without a specific route which authenticates the vagabonding appellation I have given our style of travel, but we have always had an ultimate destination in mind and have always returned to our home in Canada. It is at home where we reminisce about the trips we have had, about the friends we have made, and about the new, strange and unplanned events we experienced on the latest of our journeys. It is at home where we formulate ideas for new excursions. And when our bodies are no longer capable of such activity, home is where we will dream of past adventures and, with the aid of many pictures, relive the happiest and most fulfilling years of our lives.